The
Gates of
Hell

(Matt Drake #3)

David Leadbeater

Books by David Leadbeater:

The Bones of Odin (Matt Drake #1)

The Blood King Conspiracy (Matt Drake #2)

The Gates of Hell (Matt Drake #3)

The Tomb of the Gods (Matt Drake #4)

Chosen

Walking with Ghosts (a short story)

Connect with the author on Twitter:

@dleadbeater2011

Visit the author's website:

www.davidleadbeaternovels.com

Follow the author's Blog

www.davidleadbeaternovels.blogspot.co.uk/

All helpful, genuine comments are welcome. I would love to hear from you.
davidleadbeater2011@hotmail.co.uk

.

DEDICATION AND AUTHOR'S NOTE

First of all, I would like to say a huge thank you by dedicating this book to all the wonderful readers who have stayed with me to this point, and to everyone who has emailed me and contacted me on Twitter and Facebook expressing your fantastic support. It is hugely appreciated and is the major reason I carry on writing.

At this stage in proceedings, I thought a few lines of explanation might be helpful.

The Matt Drake series has always been planned as a four-book arc—what I have come to think of as 'the Odin Cycle.' That isn't to say there won't be more in the series—there definitely will be—just that the continuing mysteries unearthed in Books 1, 2 and 3 will all be solved by the time we reach the extremely explosive end of book 4! Thanks for bearing with me. It certainly has been a rollercoaster ride and I am going to try to make sure book 4—*The Tomb of the Gods*—finishes it in style. Release planned for January 2013.

Oh, and as you know by now, I just can't guarantee everyone will survive...

.

ONE

The hate in his heart burned brighter than molten steel.

Matt Drake went up and over the wall and landed in silence. He crouched among the swaying shrubbery, listening, but sensed no change in the stillness around him. He paused for a moment and re-checked the Glock 'subcompact.'

All was ready. The Blood King's henchmen would go down hard tonight.

The house before him stood semi-dark. The downstairs kitchen and lounge was ablaze. The rest of the place was in darkness. He paused a second longer, carefully going over the layout he'd obtained from the previous now-dead henchman, before moving soundlessly forward.

His old training served him well and ran hot again in his veins, now he had a highly personal reason and requirement for it. Three of the Blood King's henchmen had died horribly in three weeks.

Regardless of what he told him, Rodriguez would be number four.

Drake reached the rear entrance and checked the lock. Within minutes he had turned the handle and slipped inside. He heard a blast from the television and a muffled cheer. Rodriguez, bless the old mass-murderer, was watching the game.

He paced across the kitchen, not needing the light of his compact torch because of the glow emanating from the main room ahead. He paused at the hallway to listen intently.

Was there more than one guy? Hard to tell above the noise of the damn TV. No matter. He would kill them all.

The despair he'd suffered during the last three weeks since Kennedy's death had come close to overwhelming him. He'd left his friends behind, making only two concessions. First, he'd called Torsten Dahl to warn the Swede about the Blood King's vendetta and caution him to get his family to safety. And second, he'd enlisted the help of his old pals in the SAS. He'd entrusted them to look after Ben Blake's family because he couldn't.

Now, Drake fought alone.

He rarely spoke. He drank. Violence and darkness were his only friends. There was neither hope nor mercy left in his heart

He moved noiselessly up the passage. The place stank of dampness, sweat and fried food. The beer fumes were almost visible. Drake made a hard face.

Easier for me.

His intel said one man lived here, a man who had helped kidnap at least three of the Blood King's infamous 'captives.' Since the sinking of his ship and the man's clearly well-planned escape, at least a dozen high-profile figures had tentatively and covertly come forward to explain that a member of their families was being held by the underworld figure. The Blood King was manipulating the decisions and actions of the United States by preying on its figurehead's love and compassion.

His plan had been truly superb. No single man knew that any other man's loved ones were in jeopardy, and the Blood King had influenced them all with a rod of iron and blood. Whatever was necessary. Whatever worked.

Drake figured they hadn't even scratched the surface of who had been kidnapped yet. They couldn't understand just how far the Blood King's depraved control actually went.

A door opened to his left and an unshaven, fat man walked

out. Drake acted instantly and with deadly force. He charged the man, drawing his knife and burying it deep into his gut, then forcing him with sheer momentum through the open door and into the lounge.

The fat man's eyes bulged with disbelief and shock. Drake held him tight, a wide, screaming shield, burying the blade hard before letting it go and drawing the Glock.

Rodriguez was quick, despite the shock of Drake's appearance. He had already rolled off the sagging couch to the floor and was fumbling at his belt. But it was the third man in the room who captured Drake's attention.

A thick-set, long-haired man was grooving in the corner, a set of big black headphones clamped to his ears. But even as he grooved, even as he tapped out the beats of an anthem with his dirt-caked fingers, he was reaching for a sawn-off shotgun.

Drake made himself small. The deadly shot ripped into the fat man. Drake pushed the convulsing body aside and came up firing. Three shots took most of the music-man's head off and sent his body crashing into the wall. The headphones flew away independently, arcing through the air and coming to rest on the enormous TV, perched nicely over the edge.

Blood trickled down the flat screen.

Rodriguez was still scrambling across the floor. Discarded chips and beer bounced and sprayed all around him. Drake was beside him in a heartbeat and shoved the Glock hard against the roof of his mouth.

"Taste good?"

Rodriguez gagged, but still scrabbled at his belt for a small knife. Drake watched with contempt, and when the Blood King's lackey brought it around in a vicious slash, the ex-SAS man caught it and buried it hard into his assailant's bicep.

"Don't be a fool."

Rodriguez sounded like a pig being slaughtered. Drake spun him around and leaned him back against the couch. He met the man's pain-masked eyes.

"Tell me all you know," Drake whispered, "about the Blood King." He withdrew the Glock but kept it highly visible.

"The... the what?" Rodriguez's accent was thick, hard to decipher due to his race and the pain.

Drake smashed the Glock hard into Rodriguez's mouth. At least one tooth snapped off.

"Do not fuck with me." The venom in his voice disclosed more than just hate and despair. It let the Blood King's man know hard death was truly imminent.

"Alright, alright. I know about Boudreau. You want me to tell you about Boudreau? That I can do."

Drake tapped the Glock lightly against the man's forehead. "We can start there if you like."

"Alright. Be cool." Rodriguez rambled on through obvious pain. Blood coursed down his chin from his shattered teeth. "Boudreau's a fuckin' freak, man. You know the only reason the Blood King let him live?"

Drake ground the pistol into the man's eye. "Do I look like a man who answers questions?" His voice grated like steel on steel. "Do I?"

"Aggh. Alright, alright. There's a lot of death to come. That's what the Blood King said, man. *A lot of death to come, and Boudreau will be happy to be in the meat of it.*"

"So he's using Boudreau to clean up. No surprise. He's probably destroying all the ranches."

Rodriguez blinked. "You know about the ranches?"

"Where is he?" Drake felt the hate grab him. "Where?" In another second he was going to lose it and start beating Rodriguez to a pulp.

No loss. Piece of crap doesn't know anything anyway. Just like the rest of them. If one thing could be said for the Blood King, it was how well he concealed his tracks.

At that moment there was a flicker in Rodriguez's eye. Drake rolled as something heavy passed where his head had been.

A fourth man, probably passed out in a nearby room and roused by the noise, had attacked.

Drake whipped around, flicking out a foot and nearly taking his new assailant's head off. When the man crashed to the ground, Drake appraised him quickly—the heavy eyes, the tram-lines down both arms, the filthy T-shirt—and shot him twice in the head.

Rodriguez's eyes bulged. "No!"

Drake shot him in the arm. "You haven't been helpful to me."

Another shot. His knee exploded.

"You know nothing."

A third bullet. Rodriguez doubled-over, holding his gut.

"Like all the rest of them."

A final shot. Right between the eyes.

Drake surveyed the death around him, taking it in, letting his soul drink the nectar of vengeance for just a moment.

He left the house behind, escaping through the garden, letting the deep darkness take him.

TWO

Drake woke deep in the night, bathed in sweat. Eyes caked together with partly shed tears. The dream was always the same.

He had been the man who always saved them. The man always first to utter the words *'trust me.'* But then he failed.

Failed them both.

Twice now. First Alyson. Now Kennedy.

He slipped out of bed, reaching for the bottle he kept beside the gun on the nightstand. He swigged from the open top. Cheap whisky burned a path down his throat and into his gut. The medicine of the weak and the damned.

When guilt threatened to bring him yet again to his knees, he made three quick calls. The first to Iceland. He spoke briefly to Torsten Dahl and heard the sympathy in the big Swede's voice, even as the man told him to stop ringing every night, that his wife and kids were safe and well and that no harm would come to them.

The second was to Jo Shepherd, a man he had fought many battles alongside during his days in the old regiment. Shepherd politely painted the same scenario as Dahl, but didn't comment on Drake's slurred words or the raw croak in his voice. He assured Drake that Ben Blake's family was well guarded and that he and a few of his friends sat in the shadows, proficiently guarding the guards.

Drake closed his eyes as he made the last call. His head spun and his gut burned like the lowest level of hell. It was all welcome. Anything to draw his attention away from Kennedy Moore.

You even missed her damn funeral. . .

"Hello?" Alicia's voice was calm and assured. She too had lost someone close to her recently, though she showed no outward sign.

"It's me. How're they doing?"

"All fine. Hayden's healing well. Another few weeks and she'll be back to her saintly CIA self. Blake's okay, but pining for you. His sister just turned up. Quite the family reunion. Mai's AWOL, thank God. I'm watching them, Drake. Where the hell are you?"

Drake coughed and wiped his eyes. "Thank you," he managed before he broke the connection. Funny she should mention hell.

He felt he was camped outside those very gates.

THREE

Hayden Jaye watched the sun rise over the Atlantic Ocean. It was her favorite part of the day and one she liked to spend in solitude. She slipped gingerly out of bed, wincing at the pain in her thigh, and padded carefully over to the window.

A relative peace settled over her. Creeping fire touched the waves and for a few minutes all her pain and worries melted away. Time stood still and she was immortal, and then the door opened behind her.

Ben's voice. "Nice view."

She nodded at the sunrise and then turned to see he was looking at her. "You don't need to get fresh, Ben Blake. Coffee and a buttered bagel is enough."

Her boyfriend brandished a drink carrier and paper bag like a weapon. "Meet me on the bed."

Hayden took a last look at the new dawn and then took a slow walk over to the bed. Ben placed the coffee and bagels within easy reach and gave her puppy-dog eyes.

"How—"

"Same as last night," Hayden said quickly. "Eight hours ain't gonna make a limp go away." Then she softened a little. "Anything from Drake?"

Ben settled back on the bed and shook his head. "No. I spoke to Dad though, and they're all doing well. No sign of—" He faltered. "Of. . ."

"Our families are safe." Hayden laid a hand on his knee. "The Blood King failed there. Now all we have to do is find him and get the vendetta lifted."

"Failed?" Ben echoed. "How can you say that?"

Hayden took a deep breath. "You know what I meant."

"Kennedy *died.* And Drake . . . he didn't even go to her funeral.*"*

"I know."

"He's gone, you know." Ben stared at his bagel as if it were a hissing snake. "He won't come back."

"Give him time."

"He's had three weeks."

"Then give him three more."

"What do you suppose he's doing?"

Hayden gave a half-smile. "From what I know of Drake... Covering *our* backs first. Then he'll be trying to find Dmitry Kovalenko."

"The Blood King might never turn up again." Ben's mood was so depressing, it leached away even the bright promise of the new morning.

"He will." Hayden shot the young man a glance. "He has an agenda, remember? He won't go to ground like previously. The time displacement devices were just the beginning. Kovalenko has a much bigger game planned."

"The Gates of Hell?" Ben mused. "You believe that shit?"

"Doesn't matter. He believes it. All the CIA has to do is figure it out."

Ben took a long swallow of coffee. "That's all, eh?"

"Well..." Hayden slipped him a sly smile. "Our geek forces are doubled now."

"Karin *is* the brains," Ben admitted. "But Drake would break Boudreau in a minute."

"Don't be too sure. Kinimaka didn't. And he's not exactly a poodle."

Ben paused as there was a knock at the door. His eyes betrayed terror.

Hayden took a moment to reassure him. "We're inside a secure CIA hospital facility, Ben. The layers of security

9

surrounding this place would put the President's inauguration parade to shame. Chill."

A doctor popped his head around the door. "All good?" He entered the room and proceeded to check Hayden's charts and vitals.

When he closed the door on the way out, Ben spoke again. "You think the Blood King will try for the devices again?"

Hayden shrugged. "You're assuming he didn't get the first one I lost. He probably did. As for the second one we recovered from his boat?" She smiled. "Nailed on."

"Don't be complacent."

"The CIA aren't complacent, Ben," Hayden said immediately. "Not anymore. We're ready for him."

"What about the kidnapping victims?"

"What about them?"

"They're certainly high profile. Harrison's sister. The others you mentioned. He'll use them."

"Of course he will. And we're ready for him."

Ben finished his bagel and gave his fingers a lick. "I still can't believe the entire *band* had to go into hiding," he said wistfully. "Just as we were beginning to get famous."

Hayden made a diplomatic grunt. "Yeah. Tragic."

"Well, maybe it will make us more notorious."

There was another quiet knock and Karin and Kinimaka came into the room. The Hawaiian looked despondent.

"That bastard ain't gonna squeal. No matter what we do, he won't even whistle for us."

Ben rested his chin on his knees and pulled a gloomy face. "Damn, I wish Matt was here."

FOUR

The man from Hereford watched carefully. From his vantage point atop a grassy knoll to the right of a dense thicket of trees, he could use the telescopic scope mounted on his rifle to accurately pinpoint the members of Ben Blake's family. The military-grade scope included *reticle illumination* — an option that allowed for extensive use under adverse light conditions and included BDC — Bullet Drop Compensation.

Truth be told, the rifle was equipped to the hilt with every high-tech sniper aid imaginable, but the man behind the sights certainly didn't need them. He was trained to the highest level. He watched now as Ben Blake's father stepped up to the television and turned it on. With the slightest adjustment he saw Ben Blake's mother gesticulate at the father with a small remote. The crosshairs of his sights wavered not a millimeter.

With a practiced motion, he swept the scope across the grounds surrounding the house. It was set back from the road, hidden by trees and a high wall, and the man from Hereford proceeded to silently count the guards hiding amongst the shrubbery.

One-two-three. All accounted for. He knew there was another four inside the house and two more completely hidden. For all their sins, the CIA were doing a bang up job of protecting the Blakes.

The man's brow furrowed. He detected movement. A darkness blacker than night was creeping along the base of the high wall. Too big to be an animal. Too stealthy to be an innocent.

Had the Blood King's men found the Blakes? And, if so, how good were they?

A slight breeze blew in from the left, straight off the English Channel, carrying with it the salty tang of the sea. The man from Hereford compensated mentally for the revised bullet trajectory and zoomed in a bit closer.

The man wore all black, but the gear was clearly homemade. This guy was no professional, just a mercenary.

Bullet fodder.

The man's finger tightened briefly and then released. Of course, the real question was—how many had he brought with him?

Without releasing the target from his crosshairs, he quickly appraised the house and its environs. A second later he was sure. The vicinity was clear. This black-clad man was acting alone, the man from Hereford was confident.

A mercenary for hire, killing for pay.

Hardly worth a bullet.

He squeezed the trigger gently and absorbed the kick-back. The sound of the bullet leaving the barrel barely registered. He saw the mercenary go down without any fuss, collapsing among the overgrown bushes.

The Blake family guards never noticed. In a few minutes, he would make a surreptitious call to the CIA, informing them their new safe house had been compromised.

The man from Hereford, Matt Drake's old SAS pal, continued to guard the guards.

FIVE

Matt Drake twisted off the top of a fresh bottle of Morgan's Spiced and tapped a speed-dial number on his cell-phone.

Mai sounded flustered when she answered. "Drake? What do you want?"

Drake swigged from the bottle as he frowned. For Mai, betraying emotions was about as uncharacteristic as a politician honoring his election vows. "You okay?"

"Of course I'm okay. Why wouldn't I be? What is it?"

He took another heavy swig and ploughed on. "The device I gave you. Is it safe?"

There was a moment's hesitation. "I don't have it. But it is safe, my friend." Mai's soothing tones were back. "It's as safe as it could possibly be." Drake took another mouthful. Mai said, "Is that it?"

"No. I believe I've almost exhausted my leads at this end. But I have another idea. One closer to. . . home."

The silence clicked and crackled as she waited. This was not the normal Mai. Maybe she was with someone.

"I need you to use your Japanese contacts. And the Chinese. And especially the Russians. I want to know if Kovalenko has any family."

There was a sharp intake of breath. "You're serious?"

"Of course I'm fucking serious." He said it more harshly than he had intended, but offered no apology. "And I want to know about Boudreau too. And his family."

Mai took an entire minute to answer. "Alright, Drake. I'll do what I can."

Drake breathed deeply, as the connection went dead. After a minute, he stared at the bottle of spiced rum. Somehow it was half empty. He glanced up to the window and tried to see the city of Miami, but the glass was so dirty he could barely see the pane.

His heart ached.

He upended the bottle again. Without further thought he took action and hit another speed dial number. In action, he had found a way of putting the grief aside. In action, he had found a way of moving forward.

The cell phone rang and rang. Eventually a voice answered. *"Fucksake, Drake!* What?"

"Smooth talking, bitch," he drawled, then paused. "How... how's the team?"

"Team? Christ. Okay, you want the bloody football analogy? The only person you can reasonably use as your striker at this point is Kinimaka. Hayden, Blake and his sister wouldn't even make the sub's bench." She paused. "No focus. Your fault."

He paused. "Me? You're saying if an attempt was made on them it would succeed?" His head, slightly fogged, began to pound. "Because an attempt will be made."

"The hospital is well secured. The guards are reasonably competent. But it's good you asked me to stay. And good I said yes."

"And Boudreau? What about that bastard?"

"About as chirpy as a fried egg. He won't break. But remember, Drake, the whole U.S. government's working on this now. Not just us."

"Don't remind me." Drake shuddered. "A government that's badly compromised. Information travels up and down lines of contact within the government, Alicia. It only takes one bad blockage to cram it all up."

Alicia remained silent.

Drake sat and thought about it. Until the Blood King was

physically located, any intel they had should be considered undependable. That included the Gates of Hell information, the Hawaii connection and any tidbits he had gleaned from the four dead henchmen.

Maybe one more would do the trick.

"I have one more lead. And Mai's looking into Kovalenko's and Boudreau's family connections. Maybe you could ask Hayden to do the same?"

"I'm here as a favor, Drake. I'm not your bloody sheepdog."

This time Drake remained silent.

Alicia sighed. "Look, I'll mention it. And as for Mai, don't trust that crazy sprite as far as you can throw her."

Drake smiled at the video game reference. "I'll agree to that when you tell me which one of you crazy bitches killed Wells. And why."

He expected a long silence and got it. He took the opportunity to swig down a few more gulps of the amber medicine.

"I'll talk to Hayden," Alicia finally whispered. "If Boudreau or Kovalenko have family, we'll find them."

The connection went dead. Drake's head throbbed like a jackhammer in the sudden silence. One day, they would tell him the truth. But for now, it was enough he had lost Kennedy.

It was enough he had once believed in something that was now as distant as the moon, a bright future turned to ashes. The hopelessness inside him twisted his heart. The bottle fell from nerveless fingers, not smashing, but spilling its fiery contents across the dirty floor.

For a moment Drake contemplated scooping it up into a glass. The spilled liquid reminded him of the promises he had made, vows and assurances that had evaporated in a split-second, leaving lives wasted and ruined like so much water scattered on the floor.

How could he ever do that again? Promise to keep his friends safe. All he could do now was kill as many enemies as he could.

Vanquish the world of evil, and let the good live on.

He sat on the edge of the bed. Broken. There was nothing left. Everything except death had died inside him, and the broken shell that remained wanted nothing more from this world.

SIX

Hayden waited until Ben and Karin had retreated to one of the facilities IT rooms. The brother and sister team were researching Hawaii, Diamond Head, the Gates of Hell, and other legends involving the Blood King, hoping to string together some kind of theory.

When the coast was clear, Hayden slipped on some fresh clothes and walked to a small office where Mano Kinimaka had set up a small workstation. The big Hawaiian was tapping away at the keys, looking a bit frustrated.

"Still catching two keys at once with those sausage fingers?" Hayden asked lightly and Kinimaka turned with a smile.

"*Aloha nani wahine,*" he said and then almost blushed when she showed knowledge of the words' meaning.

"You think I'm beautiful? Is that because I got stabbed by a madman?"

"Because I'm glad. So very glad, that you're still with us."

Hayden laid a hand on Kinimaka's shoulder. "Thank you, Mano." She allowed a few moments to pass, then said, "But now with Boudreau, we have both an opportunity and a dilemma. We have to know what he knows. But how do we break him?"

"You think that crazy bastard knows where the Blood King is hiding? Would a man as careful as Kovalenko really tell him?"

"Boudreau's the worse kind of crazy. A clever one. My guess is he knows something."

A sardonic voice came from behind Hayden. "Drakey thinks we should torture his family." Hayden spun. Alicia gave her a cynical smile. "That okay with you, CIA?"

"You spoke to Matt again?" Hayden said. "How is he?"

"Like his old self," Alicia said with an irony she clearly didn't mean. "The way I used to like him."

"Hopeless? Drunk? Alone?" Hayden couldn't keep the contempt from her voice.

Alicia shrugged. "Edgy. Hard. Deadly." She locked eyes with the CIA agent. "Believe me, sweetie, this is how he has to be. It's the only way he'll come out of this thing alive. And..." She paused as if considering whether to go on. "And. . . it might just be the only way you all come out of it alive and with your families intact."

"I'll see if Boudreau has any family." Hayden turned back to Kinimaka. "But the CIA sure as hell won't be torturing anyone."

"Is your facility pass current?" Kinimaka was eyeing the ex-British army soldier.

"Give or take, big boy." Alicia flashed a mischievous smile and squeezed deliberately past Hayden into the small room, taken up mostly by Kinimaka's bulk. "Watcha doin'?"

"Work." Kinimaka flicked the screen off and crushed himself into a corner, as far from Alicia as he could.

Hayden came to his rescue. "You used to be a soldier back when you were human, Alicia. Do you have any suggestions that might help us break Boudreau?"

Alicia turned to Hayden with a challenge in her eyes. "Why don't we go talk to him?"

Hayden smiled. "I was just about to."

*****

Hayden led the way down to the holding area. The five minute walk and elevator journey didn't cause her any pain, though she took it steady, and her spirits rose. She had come to realize being stabbed was relatively like any other illness that made you take time off work. Sooner or later, you just got friggin' bored and wanted to get the hell back into the fray.

The holding area consisted of two rows of cells. They walked on a highly polished floor until they reached the only one with an occupant, the last cell on the left. The front of the cell was wide open, its occupant contained by rows of bars reaching from floor to ceiling.

The smell of chlorine stung the air. Hayden nodded at the armed guards stationed outside Boudreau's cell as she came to meet the man who had tried several times to kill her three weeks earlier.

Ed Boudreau was lounging on his bunk. He smirked when he saw her. "How's the thigh, blondie?"

"What?" Hayden knew she shouldn't bait him, but couldn't help it. "Your voice sounds a bit husky. Been strangled lately?" Three weeks with a limp and the trauma of a knife wound made her reckless.

Kinimaka came up behind her, grinning. Boudreau met his eyes with a furious hunger. "Sometimes," he whispered. "Table's get turned."

Kinimaka flexed his big shoulders, making no reply. Alicia then came around the big man's bulk and stepped right up to the bars. "This scrawny fuck's got your tiny panties in a twist?" She aimed the jibe at Hayden but didn't take her eyes off Boudreau. "Wouldn't take more'n a minute."

Boudreau unfolded himself from the bunk and approached the bars. "Pretty eyes," he said. "Dirty mouth. Ain't you the one who was banging that fat guy with the beard? The one my men killed?"

"That's me."

Boudreau gripped the bars. "How you feel 'bout that?"

Hayden sensed the guards starting to get antsy. This kind of confrontational weighing up was getting them nowhere.

David Leadbeater

Kinimaka had already tried to make the mercenary talk a dozen different ways, so Hayden asked something simple. "What do you want, Boudreau? What will persuade you to tell us what you know about Kovalenko?"

"Who?" Boudreau didn't take his eyes away from Alicia. They were separated by the width of the bars between them.

"You know who I mean. The Blood King."

"Oh, him. He's just a myth. Thought the CIA would know that."

"Name your price."

Boudreau finally broke eye contact with Alicia. "'Desperation is the English way.' In the words of Pink Floyd."

"We're getting nowhere—" Hayden was disturbingly reminded of Drake's and Ben's *Dinorock* ribbing contests and hoped Boudreau was just firing off aimless remarks. "We're—"

"I'll take *her*," Boudreau suddenly hissed. Hayden turned to see him facing Alicia again. "One on one. If she beats me, I talk."

"Done." Alicia was practically squeezing through the bars. The guards rushed forward. Hayden felt her blood rise.

"*Stop!*" She reached out and pulled Alicia back. "Are you crazy? This asshole's never going to talk. It's not worth the risk."

"No risk," Alicia whispered. "No risk at all."

"We're going," Hayden said. "But—" She thought about what Drake had asked. "We'll be back soon."

*****

Ben Blake leaned back and watched his sister work the modified CIA computer with ease. It hadn't taken her long to get used to the special operating system required by the government agency, but then she was the brains of the family.

Karin was a sassy, black-belt-owning, strip-bar-working layabout, who'd been knocked for six by life in her late teens and had taken her brains and degrees and set about to do absolutely nothing. It was her aim to hurt and hate life for what it had done to her. Squandering her gifts was one way of showing she no longer cared.

She turned to look at him now. "Behold and worship the power of the female Blake. Everything you ever wanted to know about Diamond Head in one quick read."

Ben flipped through the information. They had been doing this for a few days now — researching Hawaii and Diamond Head — Oahu's famous volcano — and reading up on the journeys of Captain Cook — the legendary discoverer of the Hawaiian Islands back in 1778. It was important they both scanned and retained as much information as they could because when the breakthrough came the authorities expected events to move very fast indeed.

The Blood King's reference to the Gates of Hell remained an enigma though, especially when applied to Hawaii. It seemed that most Hawaiians don't even believe in the traditional version of hell.

Diamond Head itself was part of a complex series of cones and vents known as the Honolulu Volcanic Series, a chain of events that formed most of the infamous Oahu landmarks. Diamond Head itself, probably the most famous landmark, erupted only once about 150,000 years ago, but with such a one-time explosive force that it managed to retain its incredibly symmetrical cone.

Ben smirked a little at the next comment. *It is thought Diamond Head will never erupt again.* Hmm...

"Did you clock the bit about Diamond Head being a series of cones and vents?" Karin's accent was broad Yorkshire to the point of obscurity. She'd already had a lot of fun with the CIA Miami locals with it, and had no doubt upset more than a few.

Not that Karin cared. "You deaf, mate?"

"Don't call me *mate*," he whined. "It's what men call other men. Girls shouldn't say it. Especially my sister."

"OK, broth. Truce, for now. But you know what *vents* means? In your world, at least?"

Ben felt as though he was at school again. "Lava tubes?"

"Got it. Hey, you're not dumb as a doorknob, like Dad used to say."

"Dad never said—"

"Chill, bitch. To put it simply, lava tubes mean *tunnels*. All over Oahu."

Ben shook his head at her. "I know that. Are you saying the Blood King's hiding down one of them?"

"Who knows? But we're here to do research, right?" She tapped the keys of Ben's own CIA computer. "Get to it."

Ben took a breath and turned away from her. Like the rest of his family, he missed them whilst they were apart, but after an hour of catching up, the old niggles came rushing back. Still, she had come a long way to help.

He opened a search for '*Captain Cook legends*' and sat back to see what came up, his thoughts very much with Matt Drake and his best friend's state of mind.

SEVEN

The Blood King surveyed his territory through a plate glass, floor-length window built for a single purpose—to frame the panoramic view it offered over a lush, rolling valley, a paradise where no human feet ever trod, except for his own.

His mind, usually firm and focused, flitted today over numerous topics. The loss of his ship—his home for decades—though expected, aggravated him. Perhaps it was the sudden nature of the ship's demise. He'd had no time to say good-bye. But then good-byes had never before been important or sentimental to him.

He was a hard, emotionless man, raised during some of Russia's most arduous times and in many of the country's toughest areas. Despite this, he'd flourished with relative ease, built an empire made up of blood and death and vodka, and made billions.

He knew very well why the loss of the *Stormbringer* maddened him. He considered himself untouchable, a king among men. To be affronted and frustrated in such a way by the paltry U.S. government was no more than a fly in his eye. But it still stung.

The ex-soldier, Drake, had proven to be a particular thorn in his side. Kovalenko felt as if the Englishman had personally set about trying to derail his well-laid plans, plans that had been set in motion over a number of years, and took the man's involvement as a personal affront.

Hence, the Blood Vendetta. His own personal touch had been to dispatch Drake's girlfriend first; the rest of the maggots he would leave to his global mercenary links. He was already anticipating the first phone call. Another would die soon.

Beyond the edge of the valley, nestling over the far green rise, stood one of his three ranches. He could just make out the camouflaged rooftops, visible to him only because he knew exactly where to look. The ranch on this island was the largest. The other two were on different islands, smaller and well defensible, established purely to divide an enemy attack three ways, if it ever came.

The value of placing hostages in separate locations was that an enemy would have to split his forces in order to rescue every one of them alive.

The Blood King had a dozen different ways to escape this island unnoticed but, if all went according to plan, he wouldn't be going anywhere. He would find what Cook found, beyond the Gates of Hell, and the revelations would surely turn a king into a god.

The gates alone were enough to do that, he mused.

But any thoughts of the gates inevitably led to memories that burned deep—the loss of both displacement devices, an effrontery that would be avenged. His network had quickly learned the whereabouts of one device—the one in CIA custody. He already knew the location of the other one.

It was time to get both of them back.

He drank in the view for a final minute. Dense foliage stirred to the beat of a tropical breeze. The deep peace of tranquility held his attention for a moment, but didn't move him. What he'd never had, he'd never miss.

Right on cue there was a discreet tap on his office door. The Blood King turned and said, "Come." His voice reverberated like the sound of a tank running over a gravel pit.

The door opened. Two guards entered, dragging with them a terrified-looking, but well-treated girl of Japanese origin. "Chika Kitano," the Blood King grated. "I trust you have been looked after?"

The girl stared hard at the ground, not daring to raise her eyes. The Blood King approved. "Are you awaiting my permission?" He didn't acquiesce. "I'm told your sister is a most dangerous adversary, Chika," he went on. "And now she is just another resource for me, like Mother Earth. Tell me. . . does she love you, Chika, your sister, Mai?"

The girl didn't even breathe. One of the guards sent the Blood King a questioning glance, but he ignored the man. "No talk necessary. I understand that more than you will ever know. It is just business for me, trading you. And I know very well the value of keeping carefully silent during a business deal."

He brandished a sat-phone. "Your sister—Mai—she contacted me. Very cleverly, and in the way of unspoken threat. She is dangerous, your sister." He said it for the second time, almost relishing the prospect of a face-to-face.

But it just couldn't happen. Not now when he was so close to his lifelong goal.

"She offered a trade for your life. You see, she has a treasure of mine. A very special device, which she will swop for you. That is good. It shows your value in a world that rewards ruthless men like me."

The Japanese girl timidly raised her eyes. The Blood King twitched his mouth into the approximation of a smile. "Now we see what she is willing to give up for you."

He tapped out a number. The phone rang once and was answered by a cool female voice.

"Yes?"

"Mai Kitano. You know who this is. You know there is no chance of tracing this call, yes?"

"I do not intend to try."

"Very good." He sighed. "Ah, if only we had more time, you and I. But never mind. Your lovely sister, Chika, is here." The Blood King motioned the guards to bring her forward. "Say hello to your sister, Chika."

Mai's voice echoed down the handset. "Chika? How are

you?" Reserved. Betraying none of the fear and fury the Blood King knew must be boiling under the surface.

It took a moment, but Chika finally said, *"Konnichiwa, shimai."*

The Blood King laughed. "It is surprising to me that the Japanese ever created such a fierce fighting machine as yourself, Mai Kitano. Your race does not know adversity in the same way as my own. You're all so fucking *reserved.*"

"Our fury and passion rises from that which makes us feel," Mai said quietly. "And from the things that are done to us."

"Do not think to preach to me. Or are you threatening me?"

"I need do neither. It will be as it will be."

"Then let me tell you how it's going to *be.* You meet my men tomorrow night in Coconut Grove, at the CocoWalk. Eight p.m. They will be inside the restaurant, in the crowd. You will hand over the device and leave."

"How will they know me?"

"They will know you, Mai Kitano, as I do. That is all you need to know. Eight p.m. It would be wise for you not to be late."

There was a sudden quickening in Mai's voice, which made the Blood King smile. "My sister. What about her?"

"When they have the device, my men will give you the directions." The Blood King ended the call and basked for a moment in his victory. All his plans were fitting together.

"Get the girl ready for her journey," he told his men in a detached voice. "And make the stakes high for Kitano. I want entertainment. I want to see how good this legendary fighter really is."

EIGHT

Mai Kitano stared at the dead phone in her hands and knew her objective was a long way from being achieved. Dmitry Kovalenko was not a man who would let go of a possession easily.

Her sister, Chika, had been abducted from a Tokyo flat weeks before Matt Drake had first contacted her with his wild theories about the Bermuda Triangle and a mythical underworld figure called the Blood King. By then, Mai had already learned enough to know the man was very real and very, very deadly.

But she had had to play her true intentions down and keep her secrets close. In truth, not a difficult task for a Japanese woman, but made more difficult by Matt Drake's obvious loyalty and unyielding conviction to protect his friends.

Many times she had almost told him.

But Chika was her priority. Even her own government didn't know where Mai was.

She exited the Miami side street where she'd taken the call and headed across the busy road toward her current favorite Starbucks. A homely little branch where they took the time to write your name on the cups and always remembered your favorite drink. She sat for a while. She knew the CocoWalk well, but still intended to grab a cab over there shortly.

Why CocoWalk?

The sheer volume of people, both locals and tourists, would work both for her and against her. But the more she thought about it, the more she believed the Blood King had made a very shrewd decision. In the end, it was all about who held the upper hand.

Kovalenko did, because he was holding Mai's sister.

So, amidst the throng, it would not seem out of place for her to be handing off a bag to some guys. But if she then challenged those guys and forced the issue about her sister—that would attract attention.

And one other thing—she felt she knew Kovalenko a little better now. Knew which way his mind worked.

He would be watching.

*****

Later that afternoon, Hayden Jaye placed a private phone call to her boss, Jonathan Gates. Immediately, she could tell he was on edge.

"Yes. What's wrong, Hayden?"

"Sir?" Their professional relationship was so good she could sometimes turn it personal. "Is everything okay?"

There was hesitation at the other end of the phone, something else out of character for Gates. "It's as good as can be expected," the Secretary of Defence muttered at length. "How's your leg?"

"Good, sir. Healing well." Hayden stopped herself from asking the question she wanted to ask. Feeling suddenly nervous, she skirted the issue. "And Harrison, sir? What's his status?"

"Harrison's going to prison, as are all of Kovalenko's informants. Manipulated, or otherwise. Is that all, Miss Jaye?"

Stung by the cold tones, Hayden collapsed into a chair and squeezed her eyes shut. "No, sir. I have to ask you something. It may have already been covered by the CIA, or another agency, but I really need to know…"She paused.

"Please, Hayden, just ask."

"Does Boudreau have any family, sir?"

"What the hell does that mean?"

Hayden sighed. "It means exactly what you think it means, Mr. Secretary. We're getting nowhere down here and times running out. Boudreau knows something."

"Goddamn it, Jaye, we're the American Government, and you're CIA, not Mossad. You should know better than to talk openly that way."

Hayden had known better. But desperation had beaten her down. "Matt Drake could do it," she said quietly.

"Agent. That will not do." The secretary was quiet for a time and then spoke. "Agent Jaye, you're under a verbal reprimand. My advice—keep a low profile for a while."

The connection died.

Hayden stared at the wall, but it was like seeking inspiration from a blank canvas. After a while she turned and watched the sunset fall across Miami.

*****

The long delay ate away at Mai's soul. A woman of decision and action, any single period of inactivity grated on her, but when her sister's life was in the balance, it practically tore her spirit apart.

But now the waiting was over. Mai Kitano approached the CocoWalk at Coconut Grove and moved quickly to the vantage point she had scoped out a day earlier. With hours still to go before the exchange, Mai settled in at the dimly lit bar of the Cheesecake Factory and placed the device-filled rucksack on the counter before her.

A chattering bank of TV screens perched just above her head, playing various sports channels. The bar area was loud and hectic but nothing compared to the pandemonium filling the restaurant's entrance and check-in desk. She had never seen a restaurant so crazily popular.

The bartender came over and placed a napkin on the counter. "Hello again," he said, a twinkle in his eye. "Another round?"

Same guy as last night. Mai didn't need the distraction. "Save it. I'll take a bottled water and tea. You wouldn't last three minutes with me, friend."

Ignoring the bartender's stare she continued to survey the entrance. Scrutinizing dozens of people at the same time was never hard for her. Humans are a creature of habit. They tend to stay within their circle. It was the new arrivals she had to constantly review.

Mai sipped tea and observed. There was a happy atmosphere in here and the delicious smell of mouth-watering foods. Every time a waiter passed with an enormous oval-shaped tray, loaded to breaking point with huge plates and drinks, she found it hard to keep her attention on the doors. Laughter filled the place.

An hour passed. Near the end of the bar, an old man sat alone, head down, nursing a pint. Loneliness surrounded him like a coat of bristles, warning everyone off. He was the single blight in the whole place. Directly behind him, as if to distinguish his peculiarity, a British couple asked a passing waiter to take a photo of them sitting together, arms around each other. Mai listened to the man's excited voice *"We just found out we're pregnant."*

Her eyes never stopped roving. Her bartender approached several times but didn't get fresh again. Some football match played out on the TV screens.

Mai kept tight hold of the rucksack. When the readout on her phone said eight o'clock, she saw three men in dark suits enter the restaurant. They stood out like Marines in a church. Big, broad shoulders. Neck tattoos. Heads shaved. Hard, unsmiling faces.

Kovalenko's men were here.

Mai watched them move, assessing their prowess. All were

competent, but several leagues behind her. She took a last sip of her tea, fixed Chika's face firmly in her mind, and slipped off the barstool. With consummate ease she stole up behind them, holding the rucksack against her legs.

She waited.

Seconds later one of them noticed her. The shock on his face was gratifying. They knew her reputation.

"Where is my sister?"

It took them a moment to recover their tough demeanor. One said, "Do you have the device?"

They had to speak loudly to hear one another above the din of people arriving, leaving, and being called to go to their tables.

"Yes, I have it. Show me my sister."

Now one of the hard-cases managed a smile. "Now that" — he smirked — "I can do."

Careful to stay amongst the milling crowd one of Kovalenko's goons fished out a new-looking iPhone and tapped out a number. Mai sensed the other two staring at her as she watched, most likely assessing what form her reaction might take.

If they had hurt Chika, she wouldn't care about the crowd.

Tense moments passed. Mai saw a pretty young girl race happily toward a big display of cheesecakes, followed quickly and just as happily by her parents. How close they were to death and mayhem they just couldn't know, and Mai had no wish to show them.

The iPhone crackled into life. She strained to see the small screen. It was out of focus. After a few seconds the blurred image came together to show a close-up of her sister's face. Chika was alive and breathing, but looking scared out of her mind.

"If any of you bastards have hurt her. . ."

"Just keep watching."

The picture kept panning away. Chika's whole body came

into view, tied so tightly to a solid oak chair she could barely move. Mai grated her teeth. The camera continued to retreat. Its user was walking away from Chika, across a big, well-lit warehouse. At one point, they paused near a window and showed her the view outside. She immediately recognized one of Miami's most iconic buildings—the Miami Tower—a three-tier skyscraper renowned for its ever-changing color display. After a few more seconds, the phone returned to her sister and the owner began retreating once again until, eventually he stopped.

"He is against the door," the more chatty of Kovalenko's men told her. "When you give us the device, he will walk outside. Then you will be able to see exactly where she is."

Mai studied the iPhone. The call had to be current. She didn't think it was a recording. Besides, she had watched him dial. And her sister was definitely in Miami.

Of course, they could kill her and escape even before Mai managed to get away from the CocoWalk.

"The device, Miss Kitano." The thug's voice, though harsh, held a great deal of respect.

As it should.

Mai Kitano was a shrewd operative, one of the best Japanese intelligence had to offer. She had to wonder how badly Kovalenko wanted the device. Was it as badly as she wanted her sister back?

You don't play roulette with your family. You get them back and get even later.

Mai raised the rucksack. "I'll let you have this when he steps out the door."

If it was anyone else, they might have tried to snatch it away. They might have bullied her a bit more. But they valued their lives, these goons, and they nodded as one.

The one with the iPhone spoke into the microphone. "Do it. Walk outside."

Mai watched carefully as the picture jumped around,

taking the focus away from her sister until a battered, metal door-frame came into view. Then, the outside of a tired-looking warehouse, somewhere badly in need of a paint job and a sheet metal worker.

The camera retreated further. Street parking spaces came into view, and a large white sign that read *Parking Garage*. The red blur of a car flashed by. Mai felt her impatience begin to boil, and then the camera suddenly refocused back on the building and specifically to the right of the door, to reveal a battered, old plaque.

A building number, and then the words: *Southeast 1st Street.* She had her address.

Mai dropped the rucksack and took off like a starving cheetah. The crowd melted away before her. Once outside, she ran to the nearest escalator, vaulted the railings, and landed sure footed about half-way down. She yelled and people jumped aside. She hit ground level at a sprint and reached the car she had carefully parked on Grand Ave.

Turned the ignition. Slammed the stick shift into gear and floored the accelerator. Burned rubber out into the traffic flow of Tigertail Avenue and didn't hesitate to take chances. As she wrenched at the wheel, she turned three-quarters of her attention to the Sat-Nav, punching the address in, heart hammering.

The nav guided her onto SW 27th. With a straight road pointing north ahead of her, she literally jammed the pedal into the carpet. She was so focused she didn't even think about what she would do when she reached the warehouse. A car ahead didn't like her antics. It pulled out in front of her, tail-lights flashing. Mai slammed its rear fender, making the driver lose control and send his car slewing into a row of parked motorcycles. Bikes and helmets and shards of metal scattered in all directions.

Mai narrowed her focus. Shop fronts and cars zipped past as blurry walls of tunnel vision. Pedestrians screamed at her.

A biker was so shocked at her high-speed maneuvers he wobbled and fell off at a set of lights.

The nav took her east on Flagler. The readout told her she'd be there in five minutes. A fish market was a haze of color to the left. A quick dogleg and she saw a sign that read SW1st Street.

Fifty seconds later and the nav's Irish accent declared: *you have reached your destination.*

*****

Even now, Mai took no major precautions. She remembered to lock the car and leave the keys behind the front, passenger side wheel. She sprinted over the road and found the plaque she'd seen a little while ago on the shaky camera.

Now she took a breath to steel herself against *what* she might find. She closed her eyes, centered her balance, and calmed her fear and her fury.

The handle turned freely. She walked through the threshold and quickly slipped to the left. Nothing had changed. The space was about fifty feet from the door to the back wall and about thirty feet wide. There were no furnishings. No pictures on the walls. No drapes on the windows. There were several glaring, hot banks of lights above her.

Chika still sat tied to the chair at the back of the room, eyes bulging now as she fought to move. And fought, it was clear, to tell Mai something.

But the Japanese Intelligence agent knew what to look for. She spotted half-a-dozen CCTV cameras positioned around the place and knew immediately who was watching.

Kovalenko.

What she didn't know was why? Was he expecting some kind of show? Whatever it was, she knew the Blood King's reputation. It wouldn't be quick or easy, which discounted a hidden bomb or gas canister.

The dog-leg at the end of the room, just before her sister's chair, no doubt concealed a surprise or two.

Mai inched forward, elated to find Chika still alive but under no illusions as to how long Kovalenko intended that to last.

As if in reply, a voice boomed out over hidden speakers. "Mai Kitano! Your reputation is unprecedented." It was Kovalenko. "Let us see if it is well deserved."

Four figures slipped out from behind the blind dogleg. Mai stared for a second, hardly able to believe her eyes, but then had to choose a stance as the first of the killers raced toward her.

Running fast, shaping himself for a flying kick, until Mai easily slipped aside and executed a perfect spin kick. The first fighter crashed to the ground, shaken. The Blood King's laughter resounded through the speakers.

The second fighter came at her now, giving her no chance to finish the first one off. The man was twirling a *chakram*—a steel ring with a razor sharp outer edge—on the end of a finger and smiling as he advanced.

Mai paused. This man was an adept. Deadly. To be able to wield such a dangerous weapon with confident ease spoke of years of hard practice. He would be able to throw the *chakram* with a mere flick of the wrist. She quickly evened the odds.

She ran toward him, cutting down his range. When she saw his wrist jerk she dived into a slide, slipping underneath the arc of the weapon, straining her head as far back as she could as the evil blades sliced the air above her.

A lock of her hair fell to the floor.

Mai crashed feet first into the adept, kicking at his knees with all her might. This was no time to take prisoners. With a crunch, she both heard and felt, the man's knees gave way. His scream preceded his fall to the ground.

So many years of training lost in an instant.

The man's eyes betrayed much more than personal anguish. Mai briefly wondered what Kovalenko might have over him, but then a third fighter entered the fray and she sensed the first was already up on his feet.

The third was a big man. He pounded the floor toward her like a big bear stalking its prey, bare fleet slapping the concrete. The Blood King urged him on with a series of grunts and then burst out laughing, a maniac in his element.

Mai looked him straight in the eyes. "You don't have to do this. We are close to catching Kovalenko. And freeing the hostages."

The man wavered for a moment. Kovalenko was snorting high overhead. "You make me quiver, Mai Kitano, quiver with fear. Twenty years I have been but a myth and now I break my silence on my own terms. How could you..." He paused. "Or anyone like you, ever measure up to me?"

Mai continued to stare into the big fighter's eyes. She sensed the one behind her also pausing, as if awaiting the outcome of a mental struggle.

"Fight!" the Blood King suddenly screamed. *"Fight, or I will have your loved ones flayed alive and fed to the sharks!"*

The threat was real. Even Mai could see that. The big man exploded into action, running at her with arms outstretched. Mai reviewed the strategy. Hit and run, strike swift and devastatingly hard, then get out of harm's way. If possible, use his size against him. Mai let him come, knowing he would expect her to use some kind of evasive move. When he got to her and grabbed at her body, she stepped inside his reach and swept his legs.

The sound of him hitting the floor drowned out even the demented cackling of the Blood King.

The first fighter now struck her hard, aiming for her lower back and landing a painful blow before Mai twisted and rolled, coming up behind the downed man and giving herself a bit of space.

Now the Blood King let out a shriek. *"Chop her sister's fucking head off!"*

A fourth man now emerged, wielding a samurai sword. He headed straight for Chika, six steps away from ending her life.

And Mai Kitano knew now was the time to execute the best play of her life. All her training, all her experience, came together in a life or death, last-ditch attempt to save her sister.

Ten seconds of lethal grace and beauty or a lifetime of burning regret.

Mai leapt onto the heaving back of the big man, using him as a springboard to launch a flying kick against the first fighter. His shock barely registered as Mai's leading foot cracked several bones in his face, but he went down like dead weight. Mai immediately tucked her head in and rolled, landing hard on her spine, but the momentum of her leap carried her far across the concrete floor in minimal time.

She landed farther away from her sister and the man with the sword.

But right next to the *chakran*.

In a millisecond of pause she centered her being, steadied her soul, and turned, letting loose the deadly weapon. It skimmed through the air, its deadly blade flashing, glinting, already streaked red with Mai's own blood.

The *chakran* sliced into the swordsman's neck, quivering. The man collapsed without sound, without registering anything at all. He never knew what hit him. The sword clattered to the floor.

The big man was the only fighter capable of standing against her now, but his leg kept on giving way as he tried to stand up. She had probably taken out a tendon or two. Tears of agony and helplessness coursed down his face, not for himself but for his loved ones. Mai locked her gaze on Chika and forced herself to run over to her sister's side.

She used the sword to cut the ropes, gritting her teeth on seeing the purple wrists and the bloody chaffs caused by constant struggle. Finally, she pulled out her sister's gag.

"Go limp. I will carry you."

The Blood King had stopped laughing. "Stop her!" He was bellowing at the big fighter. "Do it. Or I will end your wife by my own hands!"

The big man screamed as he tried to crawl toward her, arms outstretched. Mai paused near him. "Come with us," she said. "Join us. Help us destroy this monster."

For a moment, hope lit the man's face. He blinked and looked as if the world's weight had been lifted from his shoulders.

"You go with them and she dies," the Blood King grated.

Mai shook her head. "She's dead anyway, friend. The only vengeance you will get is by following me."

The man's eyes were imploring. For a moment Mai thought he would actually drag himself out along with her, but then the clouds of doubt returned and his gaze turned downcast.

"I can't. So long as she still lives. I just can't."

Mai turned away, leaving him lying there. She had her own wars to fight.

The Blood King sent her a parting shot. "Run far away, Mai Kitano. My war is about to be declared. And the gates await me."

NINE

The Blood King's hands flew to his knife. The weapon had been stuck point-first into the table before him. He brought it close to his eyes, studied the blood engrained blade. How many lives had he ended with this knife?

One, every other day, for twenty-five years. At least.

If only to keep the legend, the respect, and the fear fresh.

"Such a worthy adversary," he said to himself. "A shame I have no time to test her again." He rose to his feet, twirling the knife slowly, its edge catching the light as he walked.

"But my time for action is almost here."

He stopped at the opposite end of the table where a woman with dark hair had been tied to a chair. She had already lost her composure. It sickened him to have to observe her red eyes, heaving body and quivering lips.

The Blood King shrugged. "Worry not. I now have the first device, though I missed Kitano. Your husband should be delivering the second device about now. If he comes through, you will go free."

"How—how can we trust you?"

"I'm a man of honor. It's how I survived through my youth. And if honor was questioned..." He showed her the stained blade. "There was always more blood."

There was a subdued ping from his computer screen. He walked over and clicked a few buttons. The face of his commander over in Washington DC appeared.

"We're in position, sir. Target due in ten minutes."

"The device is the priority. Above anything else. Remember that."

"Sir." The face moved away, revealing a view from an elevated position. They were looking down into a parking lot, rubbish strewn and practically abandoned. The grainy picture showed a tramp moving around at the top of the screen and a blue Nissan departing through a pair of automatic gates.

"Get rid of that down-and-out. He could be *Politsiya.*"

"We've checked him out, sir. He's just a bum."

The Blood King felt a slow rage start to burn. "Get rid of him. Question me again and I will bury your family alive."

The man simply worked for him. But the man knew what Dmitry Kovalenko was capable of. Without another word he took aim and dropped the bum with a head shot. The Blood King smiled when he saw a dark stain begin to spread across the roughly concreted lot.

"Five minutes to mark."

The Blood King spared a glance for the woman. She had been his guest for some months now. The wife of the Secretary of Defense was no little prize. Jonathan Gates was about to pay a dear price for her safety.

"Sir, Gates has passed the deadline."

In any other situation, the Blood King would use the knife now. Without pause. But the second device was important to his plans, though not imperative. He picked up the sat-phone that lay next to the computer and dialed a number.

Listened to it ring and ring. "It would seem your husband does not care for your safety, Mrs. Gates." The Blood King twitched his lips in the approximation of a smile. "Or perhaps he has already replaced you, hmm? These American politicians. . ."

A click, and a scared voice finally answered. "Yes?"

"I hope you are close and that you have the device, my friend. Otherwise. . ."

The voice of the Secretary of Defense was strained to the point of breaking. "The United States does not bow down to tyrants," he said, the words clearly costing him the greater part of his heart and soul. "Your demands will not be met."

The Blood King thought about the Gates of Hell and what lay beyond. "Then listen to your wife die in agony, Gates. I do not need the second device for where I'm going."

Making sure the channel stayed open, the Blood King raised the knife and set about fulfilling his every murderous fantasy.

TEN

Hayden Jaye stepped away from the computer when her cell phone began to ring. Ben and Karin were busy resurrecting the sea voyages of Captain Cook, and in particular those concerned with the Hawaiian Islands. Cook, although widely known as a famous explorer, was a man if many talents, it seemed. He was also a renowned navigator and an expert cartographer. A man who mapped everything, he recorded the lands from New Zealand to Hawaii and, as was more widely known, made first landfall on Hawaii—a place he named the Sandwich Islands. A statue still stands in the town of Waimea, on Kauai, as a testament to the place he made first contact in 1778.

Hayden backed away when she saw the caller was her boss, Jonathan Gates.

"Yes, sir?"

Only ragged breathing came from the other end. She walked over to the window. "Can you hear me? Sir?"

They hadn't spoken since he gave her the verbal reprimand. Hayden felt a bit unnerved.

Gates's voice finally came through. "They killed her. Those bastards killed her."

Hayden stared out the window without seeing anything. "They did what?"

Behind her both Ben and Karin, alerted by her tone, turned around.

"They took my wife, Hayden. Months ago. And last night they killed her. Because I wouldn't do their bidding."

"No. It couldn't—"

"Yes." Gates's voice cracked as his whisky-fuelled charge of adrenalin clearly began to dissipate. "It's not your concern, Jaye, my wife. I- I have always been a patriot, so the president knew within hours of her abduction. I remain..." He stammered. "A patriot."

Hayden hardly knew what to say. "Why tell me now?"

"To explain my next actions."

"No!" Hayden shouted, banging the window in sudden terror. "You can't do it! Please!"

"Relax. I have no intentions of killing myself. I will help avenge Sarah first. Ironic isn't it?"

"What?"

"That now I know how Matt Drake feels."

Hayden closed her eyes, but the tears rolled down her face anyway. Kennedy's memory was already fading from the world, a heart once so full of fire now diminished to eternal night.

"Why tell me now?" Hayden finally repeated.

"To explain this." Gates paused, then said, "Ed Boudreau has a baby sister. I'm sending you the details. Do—"

Hayden was so shocked she interrupted the secretary before he could continue. "Are you sure?"

"Do whatever you have to do to take this fucker down."

The line went dead. Hayden heard the email report chime out on her phone. Without checking she turned smartly and walked out of the room, ignoring the worried stares of Ben Blake and his sister. She walked over to Kinimaka's little closet and found him working on a chicken and chorizo sub.

"Where's Alicia?"

"Got her pass revoked yesterday." The big Hawaiian's words were distorted.

Hayden bent in close. "Don't be a fucking idiot. We both know she doesn't need a pass. Now where is Alicia?"

Kinimaka's eyes widened into dinner plates. "Umm, one minute. I'll trace her. No, she's too sharp for that. I'll—"

"Just ring her." Hayden's stomach sank even as she said the words and blackness blighted her soul. "Tell her to get hold of Drake. He's got what he asked for. We're going to hurt an innocent person to get information."

"Boudreau's sister?" Kinimaka seemed sharper than usual. "He's actually got one? And Gates signed off on it?"

"You would too"—Hayden wiped her eyes dry—"if someone just tortured and killed your wife."

Kinimaka absorbed that in silence. "And that makes it okay for the CIA to do the same to an American citizen?"

"It does for now," Hayden said. "We're at war."

ELEVEN

Matt Drake had started on the expensive stuff. A bottle of Johnnie Walker Black was beckoning and looking none too shabby.

Would the better stuff stifle the memory of her face faster? This time, in his dream, would he actually save her like he'd always promised to?

The search continued.

The whisky burned. He emptied the glass immediately. He refilled. He struggled to center himself. He was a man who helped others, who gained their trust, who stood up to be counted and never let anyone down.

But he had failed Kennedy Moore. And, before that, he had failed Alyson. And he had failed their unborn child, a baby dead before it even had chance to start living.

The Johnnie Walker, like every other bottle he had tried before, was making the desperation run deeper. He had known it would. He wanted it to hurt. He wanted it to carve a slice of agony out of his soul.

The pain was his penance.

He stared at the window. It stared back, blank, unseeing and unfeeling— dirtied to the point of blackness, just like him. The updates from Mai and Alicia were becoming less frequent. The calls from his friends in the SAS were still very much on time.

The Blood King had made an attempt on Ben's parents a few days ago. They were safe. They never knew the danger and Ben would never know how close they came to being victims in the Blood King's vendetta.

And neither would the CIA agents who were guarding the Blakes. The SAS did not need recognition or pats on the back. They simply did the job and moved on to the next.

A haunting tune started to play. The song was as moving as it was beautiful—'My Immortal' by Evanescence—and it reminded him of everything he had ever lost.

It was his ringtone. He scrabbled around the bed sheets a little blearily, but eventually got a hold on the phone.

"Yes?"

"It's Hayden, Matt."

He sat up a little straighter. Hayden had known about his recent exploits, but had chosen to ignore them. Alicia had been their go between. "What's happened? Is Ben—?" He couldn't even bring himself to speak the words.

"He's fine. We're all fine. But something has come up."

"You found Kovalenko?" Eagerness cut through the alcohol haze like a blazing searchlight.

"No, not yet. But Ed Boudreau does have a sister. And we've been sanctioned to bring her in."

Drake sat up, the whisky forgotten. Hate and hellfire burned twin tracks through his heart. "I know exactly what to do."

TWELVE

Hayden steeled herself for what was to come. Her entire career in the CIA had not prepared her for this situation. The Secretary of Defense's wife murdered. An international terrorist holding unknown numbers of powerful people's relatives hostage.

Did the government know the identities of all of those involved? No way. But you could be damn sure they knew a lot more than they would ever let on.

It had seemed so much simpler back when she first enrolled. Maybe it had been simpler back then, before September 11th. Maybe in the day of her father, James Jaye, the legendary agent she strived to emulate, it *had* been black and white.

And ruthless.

This was the sharp edge. The war against the Blood King was being fought on many levels, but hers may yet prove to be the most terrible and successful.

The diverse personalities of the people she had on her side gave her an edge. Gates had spotted it first. That was why he had let them conduct their own investigation into the mystery surrounding the Bermuda Triangle. Gates was cleverer than she had ever given him credit for. He had seen straight away the advantage provided by such contrasting personalities as Matt Drake, Ben Blake, Mai Kitano and Alicia Myles. He had seen the potential of her team. And he had thrown them all together.

Genius.

A team of the future?

Now a man who had lost everything wanted justice to be brought against the man who had so brutally murdered his wife.

Hayden walked up to Boudreau's cell. The laconic mercenary gave her lazy eyes from over the top of his steepled hands.

"Can I help you, agent Jaye?"

Hayden would never forgive herself if she didn't try one more time. "Give us Kovalenko's location, Boudreau. Just give him up and this is over." She spread her hands. "I mean, it's not like he seems to give a shit about you."

"Maybe he does." Boudreau unfolded his body and slipped off the bunk. "Maybe he doesn't. Maybe it's too early to tell yet, huh?"

"What is his agenda? What is this Gates of Hell?"

"If I knew. . ." Boudreau's face portrayed the smile of a feasting shark.

"You do know." Hayden remained very matter of fact. "I'm giving you this last chance."

"Last chance? Are you going to shoot me? Has the CIA finally recognized the dark sins they must commit to stay in the game?"

Hayden shrugged. "There's a time and a place."

"Sure. I could name a few places." Boudreau sneered at her, the crazy showing through as spittle flew. "There is nothing you can do to me, Agent Jaye, that would make me betray a man as powerful as the Blood King."

"Well..." Hayden forced a smile. "That's what got us thinking, Ed." She fixed the joviality in her voice. "You got nothing here, man. Nothing. Yet you won't spill. You sit there, wasting away, happy to accept imprisonment. Like a washed up motherfucker. Like a loser. Like a piece of Southern shit." Hayden laid it on thick.

Boudreau's mouth tightened into a tense white line.

"You're a man who's given up. A quitter. A sacrifice. Impotent."

Boudreau moved toward her.

Hayden pushed her face up against the bars, taunting him. "A fucking limp dick."

Boudreau struck out, but Hayden backed away faster, still forcing the grin on her face. The sound of his fist striking steel was like a wet slap.

"So we wondered. What makes a man like you, a soldier, become a limp dick?"

Boudreau now stared at her with slowly comprehending eyes.

"That's it." Hayden mocked him. "You got there, didn't you? Her name is Maria, yes?"

Boudreau slammed the bars in an unspeakable rage.

It was Hayden's turn to sneer. "As I said. Impotent."

She turned away. The seeds were sown. It was about speed and severity. Ed Boudreau would never crack under normal conditions. But now. . .

Kinimaka wheeled the TV they had strapped to a chair to where the mercenary could see it. The trepidation in the man's voice was obvious even though he tried to hide it.

"What the hell are you people trying to pull?"

"Keep watching, motherfucker." Hayden made her voice sound as if she just didn't care anymore. Kinimaka turned the TV on.

Boudreau stared. "No" he mouthed quietly. "Oh, no."

Hayden met his eyes with a totally believable sneer. ""We're at war, Boudreau. You still don't wanna talk? Choose a fuckin' appendage."

*****

Matt Drake made sure the camera was firmly fixed in position before he stepped into the picture. The black balaclava was pulled down over his features more for effect than disguise, but the body armor he was dressed in and the weapons he carried made the seriousness of the girl's position stand out, starkly accurate.

The girl's eyes were pools of desperation, of fear. She had no idea what she had done. No idea what they wanted her for. She didn't know what her brother did for a living.

Maria Fedak was an innocent, Drake thought, if anyone was these days. Caught by chance, snared by misfortune in a globally cast net that fizzled and crackled with death, heartlessness and hate.

Drake stopped next to her, brandishing the knife in his right hand, the other resting lightly on his gun. It didn't matter to him anymore that she was innocent. It was retribution, nothing less. A life for a life.

He waited patiently.

*****

"Maria Fedak," Hayden said. "She is your sister, married, Mr. Boudreau. Your sister, oblivious, Mr. Mercenary. Your sister, terrified, Mr. Murderer. She doesn't know what her brother is, or what he does on a regular basis. But she *does* know you. She knows the doting brother, who visits once or twice a year with the fake stories and the thoughtful gifts for her kids. Tell me, Ed, do you want them to grow up without a mother?"

Boudreau's eyes were bulging. His naked fear was so intense Hayden actually felt pity for him. But this wasn't the time. His sister's life was truly in the balance. That was why they had chosen Matt Drake, alone, as the point man.

"Maria." The word spilled out of him, wretched and despairing.

*****

Drake barely saw the terrified girl. He saw Kennedy, dead in his arms. He saw Ben's blood-soaked hands. He saw Harrison's guilty face.

But most of all he saw Kovalenko. The Blood King, the mastermind, a man so hollow and void of feeling he might be nothing but an animated corpse. A zombie. He saw the man's face and wanted to throttle the life out of everything around him.

His hands moved toward the girl and locked around her throat.

*****

Hayden blinked as she watched the monitor. Drake was rushing things. Boudreau had hardly had time to soften up yet. Kinimaka stepped toward her, always the kind mediator, but Alicia Myles yanked him back.

"Not a chance, big guy. Let these fuckers sweat. They have nothing but death on their hands."

Hayden made herself sneer at Boudreau the way she remembered him sneering when he ordered the murder of her men.

"You gonna squeal, Ed, or you wanna find out how they make *sushi* in the UK?"

Boudreau glared at her with murder in his eyes. A thin drool slid from the corner of his mouth. His emotions were getting the better of him, just as they did when he smelled a close kill. Hayden didn't want him shutting down on her.

Alicia was already close to the bars. "You ordered the execution of my boyfriend. You should be glad it's Drake doing the dicing and not me. I'd make the bitch suffer twice as long."

Boudreau stared between both of them. "You had both better make sure I never get out of here. I swear I will cut you both to pieces."

"Save it." Hayden was watching Drake squeezing Maria Fedak's neck. "She doesn't have much time."

Boudreau was a hard man, and his face shut down. "The CIA won't hurt my sister. She's a United States citizen."

Now Hayden truly believed the madman truly didn't get it. "Listen to me, you crazy bastard," she hissed. "We're at war. The Blood King has murdered Americans on American soil. He has kidnapped dozens. *Dozens.* He wants to hold this country to ransom. He doesn't give a shit about you or your stinking sister!"

Alicia muttered something into her earpiece. Hayden heard the instruction. So did Kinimaka.

So did Drake.

He let go of the woman's neck and unholstered the gun.

Hayden ground her teeth together so hard, the nerves around her skull screamed. Gut instinct almost made her cry out and order him to stop. Her focus blurred for a second, but then her training kicked in and told her this was the best chance they had of tracking down Kovalenko.

One life to save hundreds, or more.

Boudreau had noticed the play of emotions across her face and suddenly he was at the bars, convinced, reaching out and snarling.

"Don't do it. Don't you fucking do it to my baby sister!"

Hayden's face was a mask of stone. "Last chance, killer."

"The Blood King's a ghost. Whatever I know, it might be a distraction. He loves that sort of thing."

"Understood. Try us."

But Boudreau had been a mercenary too long, a killer too long. And his hate for authority figures had blinded his judgment. "Go to hell, bitch."

Hayden's heart sank, but she tapped the monitor on her wrist mic. "Shoot her."

Drake raised the gun and put it to her temple. His finger squeezed the trigger.

Boudreau bellowed in horror. "No! The Blood King's in—"

Drake let the horrible sound of gunfire mask all other sounds. He watched as blood exploded from the side of Maria Fedak's head.

"North Oahu!" Boudreau finished. "His biggest ranch is there. . ." His words tailed off as he sank to the floor, watching his dead sister slump in the chair and looking at the blood-spattered wall behind her. He stared in shock as the balaclava-clad figure came up to the screen until he filled it. Then he removed the mask.

Matt Drake's face was cold, detached, the face of an executioner who loved his job.

Hayden shuddered.

THIRTEEN

Matt Drake stepped out of a taxi and shielded his eyes to study the tall building that rose before him. Grey and nondescript, it was the perfect frontage for a secret CIA operation. The local agents would enter via an underground parking garage after running the gamut of multiple security levels. Anyone else, be it agents or civilians, entered through the front door, purposely presented as sitting ducks.

He took a deep breath, almost sober for the first time in as long as he could remember, and pushed through the one-man revolving door. At least this setup seemed serious about its security. A plain desk faced him, manned by half a dozen stern-looking men. No doubt many more were watching.

He walked across the polished tile floor. "Hayden Jaye is waiting to see me."

"The name?"

"Drake."

"Matt Drake?" The guard's stoic exterior slipped a little.

"Sure."

The man gave him the kind of look a person might use upon seeing a celebrity or a convict. Then he made a call. Seconds later, he was showing Drake to a discreet elevator. He inserted a key and pressed a button.

Drake felt the lift shoot up as if on a cushion of air. He chose not to think too hard about what was about to happen, he would let events take care of themselves. When the door slid open, he was facing a hallway.

At the end of the hallway stood his welcoming committee.

54

Ben Blake and his sister, Karin. Hayden. Kinimaka. Somewhere at the back stood Alicia Myles. He didn't see Mai, but then he didn't really expect too.

The scene was wrong though. It should have included Kennedy. The whole thing looked odd without her. He exited the elevator and tried to remember they were probably feeling the same way. But did they lie in bed every night, seeing through her eyes, wondering why Drake hadn't been there to save her?

Then Ben was in front of him and Drake said nothing and enfolded the young lad in his arms. Karin was smiling uneasily over her brother's shoulder, and Hayden came forward to lay a hand on his arm.

"We missed you."

Desperately, he held on. "Thanks."

"You don't have to be alone," Ben said.

Drake took step back. "Look," he said, "it's important to get one thing straight. I'm a changed man. You can't rely on me anymore, especially you, Ben. If you understand that, all of you, then there's a chance we can work together."

"It wasn't your—" Ben started in on the problem straight away, as Drake had known he would. Karin, surprisingly, was the hand of reason. She grabbed him and pulled him aside, leaving Drake a clear route through to the office behind them.

He strode through, giving Kinimaka a nod on the way. Alicia Myles regarded him with solemn eyes. She had also suffered the loss of someone dear to her.

Drake stopped. "It's not over, Alicia, not by a long shot. This bastard needs to be eliminated. If not, he might burn down the world."

"Kovalenko will die screaming."

"Hallelujah."

Drake continued past her into the room. Two big computers stood to his right, hard-drives whirring and clicking as they searched and fed off data. A pair of floor-length, bulletproof windows faced him, looking out over Miami Beach. He was suddenly struck by an image of Wells, pretending to be a pervert and asking for a sniper scope to pick out the tanned bodies down there.

The thought gave him pause. It was the first time he'd thought of Wells coherently since Kennedy had been murdered. Wells had died badly at the hands of Alicia or Mai. He didn't know which one and he didn't know why.

He heard the others filing in behind him. "So…" He concentrated on the view. "When do we go to Hawaii?"

"In the morning," Hayden said. "Many of our assets are now focused on Oahu. We are also checking the other islands because it's known Kovalenko has more than one ranch. Of course, it's now also known that he is a master of deception, so we are continuing to follow up other leads in different areas of the world."

"Good. I remember a reference to Captain Cook, Diamond Head, and the Gates of Hell. Have you pursued that?"

Ben took that one. "Extensively, yes. But Cook landed at Kauai, not Oahu. His—" The monologue abruptly broke off. "Umm, in a nutshell. We've found nothing unusual. Yet."

"No direct links between Cook and Diamond Head?"

"We're working on it." Karin spoke up a bit defensively.

"But he *was* born in Yorkshire," Ben added, testing Drake's new barrier. "You know, God's Land."

It seemed as though Drake hadn't even heard his friend speak. "How long did he spend in Hawaii?"

"Months," Karin said. "He returned there at least twice."

"He may have visited every island then. What you should do is check out his logs, not his history or his achievements. It's the things he *isn't* famous for that we need to know about."

"That…" Karin paused. "That actually makes sense."

Ben said nothing. Karin hadn't finished. "What we do know is this: the Hawaiian god of fire, lightning and volcanoes is a woman called Pele. She is a popular figure in many ancient tales of Hawaii. Her home is said to be at the summit of one of the world's most active volcanoes, but that's on the Big Island, not Oahu."

"Is that it?" Drake asked shortly.

"No. Although most of the tales are about her sisters and siblings, some of the legends tell of the Gates of Pele. The gates lead into fire and the heart of a volcano—does that sound like Hell to you?"

"Could be a metaphor," Kinimaka said without thinking, then blushed. "Well, it could be. You know. . ."

Alicia was the first to laugh. "Thank God someone's still got a sense of humor." She chortled, then added "No offence" in a voice that showed she didn't really care which way people took her.

"Gates of Pele might be useful," Drake said. "Keep at it. I'll see you in the morning."

"Aren't you staying?" Ben blurted, obviously hoping he'd get a chance to talk to his friend.

"No." Drake stared out the window as the sun began to set over the ocean. "Tonight, I have somewhere to be."

FOURTEEN

Drake walked out of the room without looking back. As expected, Hayden caught him up just as he was about to step on the elevator.

"Drake, slow down. Is she alright?"

"You know she's alright. You saw her on the video feed."

Hayden grabbed his arm. "You know what I mean."

"She'll recover. It had to look good, you know that. Boudreau had to think it was for real."

"Yes."

"I wish I could have seen him snap."

"Well, I was the one he stabbed, so I got that pleasure, thanks to you."

Drake pressed the button for the ground floor. "Your agents should have his sister by now. They'll take her to the hospital, and get her cleaned up. Fake blood's a devil to get outta the hair, you know."

"Boudreau's turned even crazier if that's possible. When his sister stood up, alive—" Hayden shook her head. "Ultimate meltdown."

"The plan worked. The idea was sound," Drake told her. "We got the information. It was worth it."

Hayden nodded. "I know. I'm just glad the maniac's behind bars."

Drake stepped into the elevator and waited for the doors to close. "If it were up to me," he said as Hayden vanished from sight. "I'd shoot the bastard in his cell."

*****

Drake took a cab to Biscayne Boulevard and headed for the Bayside Marketplace. The person who had called him, sounding subdued and shaky and completely out of character, had wanted to meet outside the Bubba Gump. Drake had experienced a moment of humor and suggested Hooters, a place probably more fitting for them, but Mai had acted as though she hadn't even heard him.

Drake joined the throng, listened to the rowdy merriment all around him, and felt completely out of place. How could these people be so happy when he had lost something so dear? How could they not care?

His throat was dry, his lips cracked. The bar at Bubba Gump beckoned. Maybe he could sink a few before she arrived. He was under no illusions, though; this had to stop. If he was going to Hawaii to hunt the murderer of the woman he loved, if he was going to extract vengeance and not become a victim— this had to be the last time.

Had to be.

He was about to push through the door when Mai shouted at him. She was right there, leaning against a pillar not six feet away. If she had been an enemy, he'd be dead right now.

His resolve for savagery and retribution was worthless without focus and expertise.

Mai headed for the restaurant and Drake followed. They took seats at the bar and ordered Lava Flows in honor of the forthcoming Hawaiian trip.

Drake remained silent. He had never seen Mai Kitano nervous before. He had never seen her scared before. He couldn't imagine the scenario that would faze her.

And then his world collapsed again.

"Kovalenko abducted my sister, Chika, from Tokyo. Many months ago now. He has been holding her ever since as captive." Mai took a deep breath.

"I see. I understand what you did," Drake said in a whisper. It was obvious. Family always came first.

"He has the device."

"Yes."

"I came to the US to find her. To find Kovalenko. But I failed until you and your friends contacted me. I owe you."

"We didn't save her. You did."

"You gave me hope, made me part of the team."

"You're still part of the team. And don't forget the government has the other device. They're not about to give it up."

"Unless one of them has had a loved one in captivity."

Drake knew what had happened to Gates's wife but said nothing. "We will need you in Hawaii, Mai. If we're to beat this man, we will need the best. The government knows it. That's why you and Alicia and the others have been cleared to go."

"And you?"

"And me."

"What of your loved ones, Drake? Has the Blood King tried to make good on his vendetta?"

Drake shrugged. "He failed."

"And yet he will keep trying."

"Is your sister safe? Does she need extra protection? I know some people—"

"It is taken care of, thank you."

Drake studied the untouched drink. "Then it will all end in Hawaii," he said. "And now that we have almost found him, it will be soon."

Mai took a long sip of her drink. "He will be prepared, Drake. He has been planning this for a decade."

"It's a land of fire," he said. "Add Kovalenko and all of us to the equation and the whole place might just explode."

*****

60

He watched Mai walk away toward the parking lot and headed over to where he thought a cab might be. The Miami nightlife was in full swing. Alcohol wasn't the only intoxication available and the mix of endless, balmy nights, the fine men and women, and the up-tempo tunes were working hard to boost even his shattered morale.

He rounded a corner and the marina was laid out before him—yachts bristling to take pride of place, crowds thronging the walkways, an open-air restaurant studded with beautiful people without a care in the world.

Due for most part to people like Matt Drake.

He turned back. His cellphone began to ring that haunting, melodic tune.

A quick jab of the button. "Yes?"

"Matt? Good day. Hello." The fine Oxford educated tones surprised him.

"Dahl?" he said. "Torsten Dahl?"

"Of course. Who else sounds this good?"

Panic struck Drake. "Is everything okay?"

"Do not worry, mate. All is well at this side of the world. Iceland is great. The kids are fantastic. The wife is. . . the wife. How goes it with Kovalenko?"

"We found him," Drake said with a smile. "Almost. We know where to look. There's some mobilization taking place right now and we should be in Hawaii tomorrow."

"Excellent. Well, the reason I am ringing may or may not be of some use to you. You can decide yourself. As you know the exploration of the Tomb of the Gods continues cautiously. You remember back at Frey's chateau when I stood on the edge of Odin's tomb with my tongue hanging out? You remember what we found?"

Drake remembered his immediate awe. "Sure."

"Believe me when I say we are discovering treasures equal to or surpassing even that almost every day. But something more mundane caught my eye this morning, mainly because it reminded me of you."

Drake stepped into a narrow alleyway to better hear the Swede. "Reminds you of me? Did you find Hercules?"

"No. But we did find markings on the walls of every niche of the tomb. They were hidden behind the treasures so weren't apparent at first."

Drake coughed. "Markings?"

"They matched the picture you sent me."

It took Drake a moment and then a bolt of lightning struck his heart. "Wait. You mean exactly like the picture I sent? The picture of the whorls we found on the time-displacement devices?"

"Thought that would get you biting, my friend. Yes, those markings- or whorls, as you say."

Drake was momentarily at a loss for words. If the markings in the Tomb of the Gods matched the markings they had found on the ancient displacement devices, then that meant they were from the same era.

Drake spoke through a bone-dry mouth. "That means—"

But Torsten Dahl had already thought it through. "That the gods made the devices for the purpose of travelling through time. If you think it through, it makes perfect sense. We know from what we found in Odin's tomb that they existed. Now we know how they manipulated the course of time."

FIFTEEN

The Blood King stood at the edge of his small preserve, watching a few of his Bengal tigers stalk a small deer that had been loosed for them. His emotions were torn. On the one hand, it felt good to own and observe at leisure one of the greatest killing machines the planet had ever produced. On the other—it was a crying shame they should be held captive. They deserved more.

Not like his human captives. They deserved what they were about to get.

Boudreau.

The Blood King turned as he heard a number of people trudging through the grass. "Mr. Boudreau," he grated. "How was CIA detention?"

The man came to a stop several yards away, affording him the respect he demanded but facing him without fear. "Tougher than I had imagined," he admitted. "Thank you for the quiet extraction."

The Blood King paused. He sensed the tigers at his back, stalking the terrified deer. The deer would squeal and run, overwhelmed by terror, unable to stare its own death in the eye. Boudreau wasn't like that. The Blood King gave him a measure of respect.

"Did Matt Drake best you?"

"The CIA was more resourceful than I gave them credit for. That's all."

"You do know that if it were me holding the gun, your sister's death would not have been faked."

David Leadbeater

Boudreau's silence showed he understood.

"The time has come for action," the Blood King said. "I need someone to destroy the other ranches. The ones on Kauai and the Big Island. Can you do that for me?"

The man he had ordered to be saved from lifelong detention suddenly looked hopeful. "That I can do."

"You must kill every hostage. Every man, woman and child. Can you do that?"

"Yes, sir."

The Blood King leaned forward. "Are you sure?"

"I'll do whatever you ask of me."

The Blood King betrayed no outward emotion, but was pleased. Boudreau was his most competent fighter and commander. It was good he remained so loyal.

"Go prepare yourself then. Await your instructions."

His men led the American away and the Blood King motioned for one man to wait behind. It was Claude, the overseer of his Oahu ranch.

"As I said, Claude, the time has come. You are ready, yes?"

"All is prepared. How long should we hold out?"

"You will hold out until you are dead," the Blood King rasped. "Then your debt to me will be paid. You are part of the distraction. Only a small part, granted, but your sacrifice will be worth it."

His Oahu overseer stayed silent.

"Does this bother you?"

"No. No, sir."

"That's good. And once we have their focus on the ranches, you will unleash the local island cells. It is I who will be going through the Gates of Hell, but Hawaii will burn."

SIXTEEN

The private CIA jet cruised along at thirty-nine thousand feet. Matt Drake rattled the ice in his empty glass and cracked the seal to another miniature whisky. He had positioned himself alone at the back of the plane in the hope they might respect his solitude. But the constant sideways glances and furious whispers told him the 'welcome back' wagon would stop alongside him soon.

And the whisky hadn't even started to take the edge off yet.

Hayden sat across the aisle from him, Kinimaka at her side. Despite the nature of his mission, the Hawaiian seemed quite cheerful about the return to his homeland. His family was being carefully guarded, but the ever-optimistic giant seemed quite certain he would still get chance to see them.

Hayden was talking to Jonathan Gates by sat-phone. "Three more? That makes twenty-one captives, sir. Well, yes, I'm sure there are more than that. And no location yet. Thank you."

Hayden broke the connection and hung her head. "I can't talk to him anymore. How do you talk to a man whose wife was just murdered? What do you say?"

Drake watched her. It took a moment but then she turned a haunted look toward him. "I'm sorry, Matt. I didn't think. So much going on."

Drake nodded and drained the glass. "Shouldn't Gates be taking a leave of absence?"

"The situation's too volatile." Hayden clicked the phone against her knee. "In a war no one gets to take a back seat."

Drake smiled at the irony. "I didn't think Hawaii was that big."

"You mean why haven't they found at least one of his ranches yet? Well, it isn't *big*. But there's an awful lot of tough forest, hillsides and valleys out there. The ranches are probably camouflaged too. And the Blood King's prepared for us. Washington seems to think the locals will help us more than outright manpower."

Drake raised an eyebrow. "Surprisingly, they're probably right. Which is where our friendly giant comes in."

Mano gave him a big unselfconscious grin. "I do know a large portion of the population of Honolulu."

There was a blur and Ben Blake was suddenly at his side. Drake stared at the young man. It was the first time they'd seen each other properly since Kennedy had died. A wealth of emotion rose inside him, which he quickly squashed and covered up by taking another drink.

"It all happened so quick, mate. There was nothing I could do. She saved me but. . . but I couldn't save her."

"I don't blame you. It wasn't your fault."

"But you left."

Drake was looking at Karin, Ben's sister, who was staring at her brother with angry eyes. They'd obviously discussed Ben's rash move and he'd gone against the grain. Drake cracked another whisky and sat back, his gaze fixed. "About a thousand years ago I joined the SAS. The world's best fighting force. There's a reason they're the best, Ben. Among other things, it's because they're hard men. Ruthless. Killers. They are not like the Matt Drake you know. Or even like the Matt Drake who looked for the bones of Odin. That Matt Drake wasn't SAS. He was a civilian."

"And now?"

"Whilst the Blood King is alive and the Vendetta still exists, I can't be the civilian. No matter how much I want to be."

Ben looked away. "I get that."

Drake was surprised. He half-turned as Ben stood up and walked back to his seat. Maybe the young lad was starting to grow up.

If the last three months hadn't accelerated that process, nothing ever would.

Hayden was watching him. "He was with her, you know. When she died. It's been hard on him too."

Drake swallowed and said nothing. His throat closed and it was all he could do not to start blubbering. Some SAS man. The whisky burned a hot trail down to the pit of his stomach. After a moment he said, "How's the leg?"

"Sore. I can walk and even run. Wouldn't want to fight Boudreau for a few more weeks though."

"So long as he's in jail you won't have to."

A commotion caught his attention. Mai and Alicia were seated a few rows in front and across the aisle from each other. Relations between the two women had never been more than frosty, but something was getting the two of them riled up.

"*You* compromised us!" Alicia started to shout. "To save your own damn sister. How else could they have found the hotel?"

Drake slipped out of his seat and started down the aisle. The last thing needed on the flight was a fight between the two deadliest women he had ever known.

"Hudson died in that hotel," Alicia snarled. "They shot him whilst. . . whilst—" She shook her head. "Was that your intel, Kitano? I dare you to tell the truth."

Alicia stepped into the aisle. Mai rose to face her. The two women were almost nose-to-nose. Mai backed up to give herself room. An unskilled observer might think that was a sign of weakness on the Japanese girl's part.

Drake knew it to be a deadly indicator.

He raced forward. "Stop!"

"My sister is worth ten Hudson's."

Alicia snarled. "Now I get me some Mai-time!"

Drake had known Mai would not back down. It would be easier to tell Alicia what she already knew—that Hudson had given himself away—but Mai Kitano's pride would not allow her to yield. Alicia jabbed. Mai parried. Alicia shuffled sideways to give herself more space. Mai came at her.

Drake darted toward them.

Alicia fake-kicked, stepped in and drove an elbow toward Mai's face. The Japanese warrior didn't move, but turned her head ever so slightly, allowing the blow to whistle a millimeter past her.

Mai struck hard at Alicia's ribs. There was a high whistle of escaping breath and Alicia staggered back against the bulkhead. Mai advanced.

Hayden was on her feet, shouting. Ben and Karin were up too, both curious about who would win the fight. Drake stormed in hard, shoving Mai against a nearby seat and slamming an arm across Alicia's throat.

"Stop." His voice was quiet as the grave but loaded with menace. "Your dead fucking boyfriend is not the issue here. And neither is your sister." He threw a glare toward Mai. "Kovalenko is the enemy. Once that bastard is FUBAR, you can fight all you want, but until then, save it."

Alicia twisted her arm away. "The bitch should die for what she did."

Mai didn't bat an eyelash. "You have done much worse, Alicia."

Drake saw the fire rekindled in Alicia's eyes. He blurted out the only thing he could think of. "Instead of arguing, maybe you could explain to me which one of you really killed Wells. And why."

The fight went out of them.

Hayden was right behind him "Hudson was tracked through a hi-tech tracer, Myles. You know that. No one here is happy about the way Mai gave away the device." Her voice was steel. "Let alone the way she obtained it. But even I understand why she did it. Some top government officials are currently going through the same thing. Kovalenko is already playing his end game and we're barely at second base. And if the leaks aren't plugged—"

Alicia snarled and returned to her seat. Drake found another stash of miniatures and headed back up the aisle toward his own. He kept his eyes fixed straight ahead, unwilling to make any kind of conversation with his best friend yet.

But on the way, Ben leaned toward him. "FUBAR?"

"Fucked Up Beyond All Recognition."

SEVENTEEN

Before they landed, Hayden received a call to tell them Ed Boudreau had been broken out of the CIA prison. The Blood King used an insider and, against his own inclinations, extracted Boudreau in a low-key, no-fuss operation.

"You people never learn," Drake said to her and wasn't surprised when she had nothing to say in return.

Honolulu airport flashed by in a blur, as did the swift car ride into the city. The last time they had been in Hawaii, they had attacked Davor Babic's mansion and been placed on a hit list by his son, Blanka. At the time, that had appeared serious.

Then Dmitry Kovalenko came along.

Honolulu was a busy city, not unlike most American or European cities. But somehow, the mere thought of Waikiki Beach being not more than a twenty minute drive away tempered even Drake's murky thoughts.

It was early evening and they were all weary. But Ben and Karin insisted they head straight for the CIA facility and get themselves set up on the local network. They were both anxious to start delving into the whereabouts of Captain Cook's logs. Drake almost smiled at that one. Ben always loved a mystery.

Hayden speeded up the paperwork, and before long, they were secured into another tiny office, similar to the one they had left back in Miami. The only difference was from the window they could see the high-rise hotels of Waikiki, the famous Top of Waikiki revolving restaurant and, in the far distance, Oahu's biggest feature, the long-extinct volcano known as Diamond Head.

"God, I want to live here," Karin said with a sigh.

"I do," Kinimaka murmured. "Though I'm sure most vacationers spend more time here than me."

"Hey, you got to visit the Everglades not so long ago," Hayden wisecracked as she logged both Ben's and Karin's computers onto the privileged system. "And got to meet one of the locals."

Kinimaka looked blank for a moment, then grunted. "You mean the gator? That was a lot of fun, yeah."

Hayden finished what she was doing and looked around. "How about a quick meal and an early night? We get to work at sunup."

There were nods and mutterings of agreement. When Mai acquiesced, Alicia walked out. Drake watched her go before turning to his colleagues. "You should all know something I learned today. I have a feeling it could be one of the most important bits of information we will ever uncover." He paused. "Dahl contacted me yesterday."

"Torsten?" Ben blurted. "How is the mad Swede? The last time I saw him he was staring at the bones of Odin."

Drake pretended there had been no interruption. "During their exploration of the Tomb of the Gods, they have found markings consistent with the whorls we found on the displacement devices."

"Consistent?" Hayden echoed. "How consistent?"

"They're exactly the same."

Ben's brain slammed into gear. "That means the same people who built the Tomb also built the devices. That's crazy. The theory is the gods built their own tombs and literally lay down to die whilst creating extended life through a mass extinction event. Now you're saying that they also built the time-travel devices?" Ben paused. "Actually that makes perfect sense—"

Karin shook her head at him. "Dummy. Of course it makes

sense. It's how they travelled through time, manipulated events and created people's fates."

Matt Drake turned away without a sound. "I'll see you in the morning."

*****

The night air was balmy, tropically warm and laced with a hint of the Pacific. Drake walked the streets until he found an open bar. *The clientele should be poles apart from other bars in other countries, shouldn't it?* he thought. This was paradise after all. Then why were the lifers still playing pool, looking like they owned the joint? Why was there a drunk at the end of the bar, head lolling? Why were the perpetual couple sat apart, lost in their own little worlds, out together but alone?

Well, one thing was different. Alicia Myles was at the bar, downing a double-shot. Drake thought about leaving. There were other bars to avoid his sorrows in, and if most of them looked like this, he'd feel right at home.

But maybe the call to action had altered his view a little. He walked over to her and sat down. She didn't even look up.

"Fucksake, Drake." She slid her empty glass toward him. "Buy me a drink."

"Leave the bottle," Drake instructed the barman and poured himself half a glass of Bacardi Oakheart. He lifted his glass in a toast. "Alicia Myles. A ten year relationship that went nowhere, eh? And here we find ourselves, in paradise, getting drunk in a bar."

"Life has a way of fucking you up."

"No. The SRT did that."

"It sure didn't help."

Drake glanced sidelong at her. "Is that a sentence of honesty? From you? How many of those have you sunk?"

"Enough to take the edge off. Not as many as I need."

"And yet you did nothing to help those people. In that

village. Do you even remember? You allowed our own soldiers to interrogate them."

"I was a soldier, like them. I had my orders."

"And then you threw down to the highest bidder."

"I served my dues, Drake." Alicia topped her rum off and banged the bottle down hard. "It was time to reap the rewards."

"And look where that got you."

"You mean *look where it got us*, don't you?"

Drake remained silent. It could be said that he'd taken the high road. It could also be said that she'd taken the low road. It didn't matter. They had ended up in the same place with the same losses and the same future.

"We deal with the Blood Vendetta first. And Kovalenko. Then we see where we're at." Alicia sat gazing into the distance. Drake wondered if her thoughts centered around Tim Hudson.

"We still have to talk about Wells. He was my friend."

Alicia laughed, sounding like her old self. "That old perv? No way was he your friend, Drake, and you fucking know it. We *will* talk about Wells. But at the end. That's when it'll happen."

"Why?"

A soft voice floated over his shoulder. "Because that's when it has to happen, Matt." It was Mai's feathery tones. She had sidled up to them with soundless ease. "Because we need each other to get through this first."

Drake tried to hide his surprise at seeing her. "Is the truth about Wells so terrible?"

Their silence said that it was.

Mai moved between them. "I'm here because I have a lead."

"A lead? From who? I thought the Japs had subbed you."

"Officially, they have." Mai's voice carried an amused lilt. "Unofficially, they're talking to the Americans. They know the importance of capturing Kovalenko. Do not think my government are without eyes to see."

"Wouldn't dream of it." Alicia snorted. "I just wanna know how you found us." She shook her jacket as if to throw off a tracker.

"I'm better than you," Mai said, and now laughing. "And this is the only bar for three blocks."

"It is?" Drake blinked. "How ironic."

"I have a lead," Mai repeated. "Do you want to come with me now and check it out or are you both too drunk to care?"

Drake was off his stool in a second and Alicia swung around. "Lead the way, little sprite."

*****

A short cab ride later, they were huddled around a busy street corner, listening as Mai updated them.

"It comes directly from a man I trust at the Intelligence Office. Kovalenko's ranches are managed by a few individuals he trusts. This has always been the case, though it aids him now more than ever when he needs time to. . . well, do whatever it is he plans to do. In any case, his Oahu ranch is managed by a man called Claude."

Mai drew their attention ahead to the line of young people filing through the arched and gaudily lit entrance to an upscale club. "Claude owns this club," she said. Flashing lights advertised 'Live DJ's, Friday night bottle specials and special guests.' Drake scanned the crowd with a sinking feeling. It consisted of about a thousand of Hawaii's most beautiful young people in various states of undress.

"We might stand out a bit," he said.

"Now I know you're all washed up." Alicia smirked at him. "The Drake of a year ago would've stood by the two hot women he's with, grabbed a cheek in each hand, and goosed us over there."

Drake rubbed his eyes, knowing she was uncannily correct. "The mid-thirties changes a man," he managed, suddenly feeling the weight of Alyson's loss, of Kennedy's murder, of constant intoxication. He did manage to fix a steely eye on both of them.

"The search for Claude starts here."

They smiled their way past the doormen to find themselves in a narrow tunnel filled with flashing light and fake smoke. Drake was momentarily disoriented and put it down to the weeks of inebriation. His thought processes were fuzzy, his reactions more so. He needed to sharpen up fast.

Beyond the tunnel, a wide balcony gave a birds-eye view of the dance floor. Bodies moved in unison to the deep-bass beats. The wall to their right held thousands of bottles of liquor and reflected light in sparkling prisms. A dozen bar staff worked the punters, reading lips, giving short-change and serving the wrong drinks to the club's uncaring patrons.

Same as any bar anywhere. Drake laughed with some irony. "At the back." He pointed, not needing to be covert in the crowd. "The roped-off area. And beyond that, curtains."

"Private parties," Alicia said. "I know what goes on back there."

"Of course you do." Mai was busy scanning as much of the place as she could. "Is there a back room you've never been in, Myles?"

"Don't even go there, bitch. I know about your exploits in Thailand. Even I wouldn't try some of that stuff out."

"What you heard was hugely understated." Mai started down the wide staircase without looking back. "Believe me."

Drake frowned at Alicia and nodded toward the dance-floor. Alicia looked surprised but then realized he meant to cut right across and head for the private area. The Englishwoman shrugged. "You lead, Drake. I'll follow."

Drake experienced a sudden, irrational rush of blood. Here was a chance to get closer to the man who might know the whereabouts of Dmitry Kovalenko. The blood he had shed so far was but a drop in the ocean compared to what he was prepared to spill.

As they threaded through the laughing, sweaty bodies out on the dance-floor, one of the guys managed to spin Alicia around. "Hey," he shouted to his friend, voice barely audible above the pumping beat. "I just got lucky."

Alicia struck stiffened fingers into his solar plexus. "You were never lucky, son. Just look at your face."

They moved on swiftly, focusing beyond the pounding music, the swaying bodies, the bar-staff threading in and out of the crowd with trays balanced precariously above their heads. A couple was arguing loudly, the man pressed against a pillar with the woman screaming into his ear. A group of middle-aged women were sweating and puffing in a circle with a round of vodka-Jell-O's and little blue spoons held in their hands. Low tables dotted the floor everywhere, most loaded with gaudy umbrella-drinks. No one was alone. Many of the men did double takes when Mai and Alicia passed, to the great annoyance of their girlfriends. Mai sensibly ignored the attention. Alicia provoked it.

They approached the roped-off area, which consisted of a thick, gold braid stretched between two heavy-duty, brass rope stands. It seemed the establishment assumed no one would actually challenge the two bruisers situated at either end.

One of them came forward now, palm out, and politely asked Mai to retreat.

The Japanese girl smiled quickly. "Claude sent us to see. . ." She paused as if pondering.

"Pilipo?" The other bruiser quickly filled in. "I can see why, but who's the guy?"

"Bodyguard."

The two big men eyed Drake like cats that had cornered the mouse. Drake gave them a big smile. He didn't speak, just in case his English accent aroused suspicion. Alicia held no such misgivings.

"So, this Pilipo. What's he like? We in for a good time, or what?"

"Oh, he's the best," the first bouncer said with a wry smile. "The perfect gentleman."

The second bouncer was eyeing their clothing. "You're not exactly—dressed—for the occasion. You sure Claude sent you?"

Mai's voice carried no trace of derision when she said, "Quite sure."

Drake was using the exchange to assess the hidden alcoves. A short flight of stairs led to a raised dais where a large table took precedence. Around the table sat about a dozen people, most of whom looked rapturous enough to have recently snorted some serious powder. The others just looked scared and sad, young women and a couple of guys, clearly not members of the party group.

"Hey, Pilipo!" the second bouncer shouted. "Fresh meat for you!"

Drake followed the girls up the short stairway. It was much quieter up here. So far he'd counted twelve unmistakable bad guys, all of who were probably carrying arms. But when he weighed the twelve local enforcers against Mai, Alicia and himself he wasn't worried.

He stayed behind them, keeping as low a profile as possible. Pilipo was the target, and now they were within a few feet of him. This nightclub was about to really start rocking.

Pilipo stared at the girls. The sound of his throat clicking drily registered his interest. Drake vaguely saw his hand lunge toward a drink and tip it back.

"Claude sent you?"

Pilipo was a short, thin man. His wide, expressive eyes betrayed to Drake immediately that this man wasn't a friend of Claude's. Wasn't even an acquaintance. He was more a puppet, a figurehead for the club. An expendable asset.

"Not really." Mai had figured it out too and switched from passive female to kick-ass killer in the blink of an eye. Stiffened fingers jabbed into two of the nearest men's throats and a deep front-kick sent a third falling off his chair into oblivion. Alicia leapt onto the table at her side, landed on her ass, feet up high and slapped a man with flowing neck-tattoos hard across the face with her heel. He crashed into the bruiser next to him, taking them both down. Alicia leapt onto a third.

Drake was slow by comparison, but much more devastating. An oriental with long hair stood up to him first and drove forward with a jab, front-kick combination. Drake sidestepped, caught the leg and twisted with immense, sudden power until the man screamed and dropped into a blubbering ball.

The next man drew a knife. Drake grinned. The blade shot forward. Drake caught the wrist, snapped it and buried the weapon deep into its owner's stomach.

Drake moved on.

The unfortunate hangers-on were fleeing from the table. It didn't matter. They wouldn't know anything about Claude. The one man who might was predictably huddled as far into his plush leather chair as humanly possible, eyes wide with fear, lips working soundlessly.

"Pilipo." Mai sidled in next to him and put a hand on his thigh. "First you want our company. Now you don't. It's rude. What's it take to be my friend?"

"I... I have men." Pilipo was gesturing wildly, his fingers shaking like a man on the verge of alcohol addiction. "Everywhere."

Drake faced the two bouncers who had almost made it to the top of the stairs. Alicia was mopping up the stragglers to his right. The heavy dance music blasted from below. Bodies threw themselves in various stages of intoxication all around the dance floor. The DJ mixed and grunted to a captive audience.

"Claude *didn't* send you," the second bouncer gasped, clearly amazed. Drake used the staircase's newel posts to swing forward and plant both feet into the man's chest, sending him toppling backward into the noisy pit.

The other man leapt up the last step and came at Drake, arms swinging. The Englishman took a blow in the ribs that would have felled a lesser man. It hurt. His adversary paused, waiting for effect.

But Drake just sighed and delivered a close uppercut, swinging from the very soles of his feet. The bouncer was lifted off his toes, instantly unconscious. The noise as he hit the ground made Pilipo visibly jump.

"You were saying?" Mai traced a perfectly manicured finger nail across the Hawaiian's stubbly cheek. "About your men?"

"Are you crazy? Do you even *know* who this club belongs to?"

Mai smiled. Alicia paced up to them both, unruffled after taking out four bodyguards. "Funny you should say that." She planted a foot over Pilipo's heart and pressed hard. "This guy, Claude. Where is he?"

Pilipo's eyes darted like captive fireflies. "I... I don't know. He never comes here. I run the place but I... I don't know Claude."

"Regrettable." Alicia slammed her foot against Pilipo's heart. "For you."

Drake took a moment to scan their perimeter. All seemed secure. He bent down until he was nose-to-nose with the club owner.

"We get it. You're a lowly minion. I'll even accept that you don't know Claude. But you sure as hell *know* someone who knows him. A man who visits from time to time. A man who ensures you keep yourself in check. Now—" Drake grabbed

Pilipo by the throat, his rage barely concealed. "You tell me that man's name. Or I'll twist your fuckin' head off."

Pilipo's whisper went unheard even up here, where the pounding beats were subdued by the heavy acoustic walling. Drake shook his head like a tiger shakes the head of a felled gazelle.

"What?"

"Buchanan. The man's name is Buchanan."

Drake squeezed harder as the rage began to take over. "Tell me how you contact him." Images of Kennedy filled his vision. He barely felt Mai and Alicia pulling him off the dying club owner.

EIGHTEEN

The Hawaiian night was still young. It was barely after midnight when Drake, Mai and Alicia slipped out of the club and hailed a parked taxi. Alicia had covered their way out by gleefully striding up to the DJ, grabbing his mic, and doing her best rock-star impression. "Hey, Honolulu! How the fuck are ya? So glad to be here tonight. You guys are fucking beautiful!" Then she'd sashayed off, leaving a thousand speculations on a thousand lips behind her.

Now they talked freely around the cab driver. "How long you think before Pilipo warns Buchanan?" Alicia asked.

"With good fortune they might not discover him for a while. He's well trussed. But if they do—"

"He won't talk," Drake said. "He's a coward. He won't draw attention to the fact that he ratted out Claude's man. I'd put my mortgage on it."

"The bouncers might talk." Mai said quietly.

"Most of 'em are unconscious." Alicia laughed, then said more seriously. "But the sprite's right. When they can walk and talk again, they're gonna squeal like pigs."

Drake clicked his tongue. "Damn, you're both right. So we have to do this quick then. Tonight. There's no other choice."

"North Kukui Street," Mai told the cab driver. "You can drop us off near the mortuary."

The cab driver flicked a glance at her. "For real?"

Alicia drew his attention with a feisty smile. "Keep it down, five-o. Just drive."

The cab driver muttered something that sounded like

"Fuckin' haole," but switched his eyes to the road and went silent. Drake thought about where they were going. "If this really is Buchanan's office, he's unlikely to be there at this time."

Alicia snorted. "Drakey, Drakey, you just don't listen hard enough. When we finally realized that the silly man, Pilipo, had jammed his throat so hard into your hands he was turning purple we set about saving his ridiculous life, and he told us that Buchanan has a house."

"A house?" Drake made a face.

"Of business. You know these dealers. They live and eat there, play there, organize their local jobs from there. Keeps it neat. He'll even keep his men around. It's a nonstop hard-core party, dude."

"Which will help keep the nightclub events quiet, for now." Mai said as the cab stopped outside the mortuary. "Remember when we infiltrated that shipping magnet's office in Hong Kong? Fast in, fast out. That's what this should be."

"Just like when *we* hit that place in Zurich." Alicia said loudly to Drake. "It's not all about you, Kitano. Not by a long shot."

*****

Hayden entered the apartment she'd been assigned within the Honolulu CIA facility and stopped dead in surprise. Ben was waiting for her, perched on the bed, legs swinging.

The young man looked tired. His eyes were bloodshot from days of staring at a computer screen, and his forehead looked a little scrunched from concentrating so hard. Hayden was pleased to see him.

She made a show of looking around the room. "You and Karin finally got the umbilical snipped?"

"Har, har. She's family." He said it as if their closeness was the most obvious thing. "And she sure knows her way around a computer."

"Genius-level IQ will help you with that." Hayden slipped her shoes off. The thick carpet felt like a foamy cushion beneath her aching feet. "I have absolute faith that tomorrow you will find what we need in Cook's logs."

"If we can even locate them."

"Everything's online. You just have to know where to look."

Ben frowned at her. "Does... does it feel like we're being manipulated here? First finding the Tomb of the Gods and then the displacement devices. Now we discover that the two are linked. And—" He paused.

"And what?" Hayden planted herself next to him on the bed.

"The devices might to be linked to the Gates of Hell in some way," he reasoned. "If Kovalenko wants them, they must be."

"That's not true." Hayden leaned in close. "Kovalenko is a madman. We can't presume to understand his thinking."

Ben's eyes showed he was fast losing track of his thoughts and flirting with others. He kissed Hayden when she dipped her head against his. She pulled away as he began to fumble with something in his pocket.

"I'm more comfortable with it coming out through the zipper, Ben."

"Uh? No. I wanted this." He pulled out his mobile, flicked the screen to the MP3 player and selected an album.

Fleetwood Mac began to sing 'Second Hand News' from the classic *Rumours.*

Hayden blinked in surprise. "Dinorock? Really?"

Ben flung her onto her back. "Some of it's better than you'd think."

Hayden didn't miss the poignant sadness in her boyfriend's tone. She didn't miss the theme of the song apparent in the title. For the same reasons as Ben it made her think of Kennedy Moore and Drake and all that they had lost. Not only had they both lost a great friend in Kennedy, but her violent death had reduced every one of Drake's friends to mere background noise.

But when Lindsey Buckingham began to sing about tall grass and doing his stuff, the mood soon changed.

*****

Mai asked the cab driver to wait but the man wouldn't listen. As soon as they cleared the car, he revved the engine and set off in a spray of gravel.

Alicia stared after him. "Wanker."

Mai motioned toward the intersection ahead of them. "Buchanan's house is to the left."

They walked in comfortable silence. A few months ago, Drake knew such a thing would never have happened. Today, they had a common enemy. They had all been touched by the Blood King's lunacy. And, if allowed to stay at large, he could still hurt them dearly.

Together, they were one of the best teams in the world.

They cut across the intersection and slowed as Buchanan's property came into view. The place was ablaze with light. Curtains drawn. Doors were open so music could spill out into the neighborhood. The *thud, thud* of rap music could be heard even from across the road.

"A model neighbor," Alicia commented. "Someone like that—I'd just have to mosey on round and smash their Goddamn music center to pieces."

"But most people aren't like you," Drake said. "That's what these people thrive on. At heart, they're bullies. In real life, they carry shotguns and have no compassion or conscience."

Alicia grinned at him. "They won't expect a full-frontal assault then."

Mai acquiesced. "Fast in, fast out."

Drake thought about how the Blood King had ordered the murder of so many innocents. "Let's go fuck 'em up."

*****

Hayden was naked and sweating when her cellphone rang. If it hadn't been the distinctive ringtone of her boss, Jonathan Gates, she would have blocked it out.

Instead, she groaned, pushed Ben away, and jabbed at the *answer* button. "Yes?"

Gates didn't even notice her breathlessness. "Hayden, apologies for the late hour. Can you talk?"

Hayden immediately snapped back to reality. Gates deserved her attention. The horror he had endured for his country was way beyond the call of duty.

"Of course, sir."

"Dmitry Kovalenko holds captive members of the families of eight United States Senators, fourteen Representatives and one mayor. This monster will be brought to justice, Jaye, by any means necessary. You have all resources."

The connection went dead.

Hayden sat there staring into the semi-dark, her ardor completely extinguished. Her thoughts were with the prisoners. The innocent were suffering yet again. She wondered how many more would suffer before the Blood King was brought to justice.

Ben crawled over the bed to her and just held her like she wanted.

*****

Drake went inside first and found himself in a long hallway with two doors opening off to the left and an open kitchen at the end. A man was coming down the stairs, eyes suddenly registering shock as he saw Drake enter the house.

"What the—?"

Mai's hand moved faster than the eye could see. One second the man was drawing breath to shout warning, the next he was tumbling down the stairs with a tiny dagger in his throat. When he hit the bottom, Mai finished the job and retrieved her dagger. Drake advanced up the hall. They turned left into the first room. Four sets of eyes looked up from the plain boxes they were packing with explosives.

Explosives?

Drake recognized the C4 instantly, but had no time to think as the men grabbed carelessly abandoned weapons. Mai and Alicia danced around Drake.

"There!" Drake pointed to the quickest. Alicia felled him with an ungraceful kick to the groin. He went down burbling. The man in front of Drake came at him fast, leaping over the table to get some height and power to his attack. Drake angled his body underneath the man's flight, and when he landed, kicked out both his knees from behind. The man screeched in rage and spittle flew from his mouth. Drake brought a devastating axe-kick down on the top of his head, all brute-force and power.

The man collapsed without another sound.

To his left Mai had jabbed two men in swift succession. Both doubled-over with stomach wounds, surprise plastered across their faces. Drake swiftly used a stranglehold to incapacitate one whilst Mai knocked out the other.

"Go." Drake hissed. They might not know it, but these were still the Blood King's men. They were lucky Drake was in a hurry.

They moved back into the hallway and down to another room. As they slipped inside, Drake caught sight of the kitchen. Men were crammed in there, all staring at something on a low table. The sound of rap music pounding from inside was so loud, Drake almost expected it to come walking out to greet him. Mai bounded ahead. By the time Drake entered the room, she had already felled one man and was on to the next. A guy with a thick beard confronted Drake, revolver already in hand.

"What did you do—?"

Training was everything in the art of fighting, and Drake's was returning faster than a politician could dodge a key question. Instantly, he snapped his foot up, struck the revolver from the man's hands, then stepped in and caught it in mid-air.

He reversed the weapon.

"Live by the sword." He fired. Buchanan's man fell backward in an artistic spray. Mai and Alicia immediately scooped up other discarded firearms as someone shouted from the kitchen. "Hey, fools! What the fuck you doin?"

Drake grinned. The discharge of firearms was not unheard of in this house it seemed. Good. He approached the door.

"Two," He whispered, indicating that the door space afforded just two of them the space to maneuver. Mai fell in behind.

"Let's put these dogs down." Drake and Alicia stepped out firing, aiming for the forest of legs that surrounded the table.

Blood sprayed and bodies folded to the floor. Drake and Alicia moved forward, knowing   shock and awe would confuse and intimidate their opponents. One of Buchanan's guards leapt over the low table and barged into Alicia, sending her flying. Mai stepped into the breach, defending as the guard jabbed at her twice. Mai caught each blow on a forearm before bringing her gun down hard on the bridge of his nose.

Alicia was back in the fray. "I had him."

"Oh, I'm sure you did, sweetie."

"Blow me." Alicia trained her gun on the groaning, weeping men. "Anyone else want to try? Hmm?"

Drake was staring at the low table and its contents. Piles of C4 littered the surface in various stages of preparation.

What on earth was the Blood King planning?

"Which one of you is Buchanan?"

No one answered.

"I have a deal for Buchanan." Drake shrugged. "But if he's

not here, then I guess we'll have to shoot you all." He shot the nearest man in the stomach.

Uproar filled the room. Even Mai stared at him in astonishment. "Matt—"

He snarled at her. "No names."

"I'm Buchanan." A man with his back against the big fridge gasped as he pressed hard on a bullet wound. "C'mon, man. We ain't hurt you."

Drake's finger tightened on the trigger. It required a massive amount of self-control not to fire. "You haven't hurt me?" He jumped forward and deliberately knelt on the leaking wound. "You haven't *hurt* me?"

Bloodlust filled his vision. Inconsolable grief stabbed at his brain and heart. "Tell me," he said thickly. "Tell me where Claude is or, so help me, I will blow your brains all over this fucking fridge."

Buchanan's eyes didn't lie. Fear of death rendered his ignorance transparent. "I know Claude's friends," he whimpered. "But I don't know Claude. I could give you his friends. Yes, I can give you them."

Drake listened as he spilled two names and their whereabouts. Scarberry and Peterson. Only when that information was fully extracted did he indicate the table full of C4.

"What are you doing here? Getting ready to start a war?"

The answer stunned him. "Well, yes. The battle of Hawaii's about to begin, man."

NINETEEN

Ben Blake walked into the tiny office he shared with his sister to find Karin standing by the window. "Hey, sis."

"Hi. Just look at this, Ben. A Hawaiian sunrise."

"We should be at the beach. Everyone goes there for sunrise and sunset."

"Oh, *do they?*" Karin eyed her brother with a little sarcasm. "Look that up on the internet did you?"

"Well, now we're here I'd like to get out of this stuffy place and meet some locals."

"What for?"

"I never met a Hawaiian."

"Mano's a friggin' Hawaiian, dumbo. Jeez, sometimes I wonder if I got both our allowance of brain cells."

Ben knew it was useless to start a battle of wits with his sister. He drank in the glorious sight for a few minutes before heading out the door to pour them both a coffee. When he returned, Karin was already booting their computers up.

Ben placed the mugs next to their keyboards. "You know, I'm looking forward to this." He rubbed his hands. "Searching for Captain Cook's logs, I mean. This is real detective work because we're looking for what's hidden away, not what's obvious."

"We do know there are no references on the web that tie Cook to Diamond Head, or *Leahi,* to the Hawaiians. We know that Diamond Head is but one of a series of cones, vents, tunnels and lava tubes that run underneath Oahu."

Ben sipped the hot coffee. "We also know that Cook landed

at Kauai, in the town of Waimea. Points to note about Waimea—there's a canyon there awesome enough to rival the Grand Canyon. The locals of Kauai coined the phrase *Hawaii's original visitor destination*, as a cheeky taunt toward Oahu. Cook's statue stands in Waimea near a very small museum."

"The other thing we know," Karin responded. "Is that Captain Cook's logs and journals are right here." She tapped her computer. "Online."

Ben sighed and started flicking through the first of the extensive journals. "Let the fun begin." He plugged his earphones in and sat back.

Karin stared at him. "Turn it down. Is that the Wall of Sleep? And another cover? Someday, little brother, you're going to have to get those new tracks down and stop wasting away your five minutes of fame."

"Don't talk to me about wasting your time away, sis. We all know you're the master of that."

"You intend to bring that up again? Now?"

"It's been five years." Ben turned the music up and concentrated on his computer. "Five years of ruin. Don't let what happened back then wreck the next ten."

*****

Running on no sleep and minimal rest, Drake, Mai and Alicia decided to take a short break. Drake had been receiving calls from Hayden and Kinimaka since about an hour after the sun came up. The mute button soon resolved that problem.

They rented a room in Waikiki. It was a big Outrigger hotel, packed with tourists, allowing them a high level of anonymity. They ate quickly at a local Denny's, then headed to their hotel where they took an elevator to their room on the eight floor.

Once inside, Drake relaxed. He knew the benefits of fuelling up on food and rest. He curled into an easy chair near the window, basking as the clear Hawaiian sun bathed him through the French windows.

"You two can fight over the bed," he murmured without looking around. "Someone set an alarm for two hours."

With that, he allowed his thoughts to drift away, calm with the knowledge that they had an address on two men who were as close to Claude as anyone could be. Calm with the knowledge that Claude led straight to the Blood King.

Calm with the knowledge that bloody vengeance was only hours away.

*****

Hayden and Kinimaka spent the morning at the local Honolulu PD. The news was that some of Claude's 'associates' had been taken out during the night, but no real news was forthcoming. A club owner called Pilipo was saying very little. Several of his bouncers were in hospital. It also appeared his video feed had miraculously *gone down* when a man and two women had assaulted him sometime before midnight.

Add to that a bloody gun-battle somewhere in downtown that involved more of Claude's known associates. When armed officers had arrived at the scene, all they found was an empty house. No men. No bodies. Just blood on the floor and a kitchen table that, when dusted, revealed traces of C4.

Hayden tried Drake. She tried Alicia. She pulled Mano to one side and whispered furiously in his ear. "Damn them! They don't know we have the backing to proceed as we see fit. They need to know."

Kinimaka shrugged, his big shoulders rising and falling. "Maybe Drake doesn't want to know. He'll do this his way, government backing or not."

"He's a liability now."

"Or a poisonous arrow shooting straight for the heart." Kinimaka smiled when his boss glanced at him.

Hayden was momentarily fazed. "What? Are those song lyrics, or something?"

Kinimaka looked hurt. "Don't think so, boss. So"—he flicked a glance toward the assembled cops—"what does the HPD know about Claude?"

Hayden sighed deeply. "Not surprisingly, very little. Claude's the shady owner of a few clubs that may or may not be involved in illegal activities. They're not high on the HPD's watch list. Hence, their silent owner stays anonymous."

"With everything no doubt engineered by Kovalenko."

"No doubt. It always pays for a criminal to be several times removed from the real world."

"Maybe Drake's making progress. If he wasn't, I think he'd be with us."

Hayden nodded. "Let's hope so. In the meantime, we have a few locals to shake down. And you should make contact with anyone you know who might be able to help us. Kovalenko's started a bloodbath already. I hate to think how it might all end up."

*****

Ben fought hard to keep the focus at a high level. His emotions were in disarray. It was months now since his life had been normal. Before the 'Odin thing' his idea of being adventurous was keeping his modern rock band, The Wall of Sleep, a secret from his mum and dad. He was a family man, a good-hearted nerd with a talent for all things technical.

Now he'd seen fighting. He'd seen men killed. He'd fought for his life. His best friend's girlfriend had died in his arms.

The adjustment between worlds was wrenching him apart.

Add to that the pressure of coping with his new girlfriend, an American CIA agent, and he wasn't the least bit surprised to find himself floundering.

Not that he'd ever tell his friends. His family, yes, he could tell them. But Karin wasn't ready for it yet. And she had troubles of her own. He'd just told her that after five years she should have moved on, but he knew that if the same thing ever happened to him, it would destroy the rest of his life.

And the remaining members of the Wall of Sleep were texting him constantly. *Where the f*** are you, Blakey? Get together tonight? At least text me back, wanker!* They had new tracks ready to lay down. It was his bloody dream!

Placed in jeopardy now by the very thing that had given him his big break.

He thought of Hayden. When the world came down, he could always switch his thoughts to her and everything felt a little easier. His mind drifted. He kept on scrolling down the pages of the online eBook that someone had transcribed from Cook's own scribblings.

He almost missed it.

For suddenly, right there amidst the weather reports and the longitude and latitude notations and the brief details about who was punished for refusing daily rations of beef and who had been found dead in the rigging, was a short reference to the Gates of Pele.

"Sis." Ben breathed. "I think I've found something." He read a short paragraph. "Wow, it's a man's accounting of their journey. You ready for this?"

*****

Drake went from lightly sleeping to wide awake in the time it took to open his eyes. Mai was pacing up and down behind him. It sounded like Alicia was in the shower.

"How long have we been out?"

"Ninety minutes, give or take. Here—check this." Mai threw him one of the handguns they had liberated from Buchanan and his men.

"What's the count?"

"Five revolvers. All serviceable. Two .38's and three .45s. All with three quarter full mags."

"More than enough." Drake stood up and stretched. They had decided they were likely to be hitting more serious opposition—men close to Claude— so carrying weapons was imperative.

Alicia padded out of the bathroom, hair wet, shrugging on a jacket. "Ready to roll?"

The information they had obtained from Buchanan was that both Scarberry and Peterson owned an exotic car dealership on the outskirts of Waikiki. Called Exoticars, it was both a sales outlet and repair shop. It also rented most types of high-end vehicles.

A very lucrative front, Drake thought. No doubt developed to help conceal all sorts of criminal enterprise. Scarberry and Peterson were undoubtedly close to the top of the food chain. Claude would be next.

They climbed into a cab and gave the driver the dealership's address. It was about twenty minutes away.

*****

Ben and Karin read through Captain Cook's log with wonder.

To see through another man's eyes events that happened to a famous seafaring Captain over two-hundred years ago was remarkable enough. But to read an account of Cook's recorded but still highly secretive journey beneath Hawaii's most famous volcano was almost overwhelming.

"This is amazing." Karin flicked through her copy on the computer screen. "One thing you don't realize is the brilliant foresight Cook had. He took men from every field with him to record his discoveries. Scientists. Botanists. Artists. Look—" She tapped the screen.

Ben leaned over to see an exquisitely rendered drawing of a plant. "Cool."

Karin glared. "It *is* cool. These plants were undiscovered and undocumented until Cook and his crew logged them and returned to England with these fantastic drawings and descriptions. They *mapped our world, these men.* They painted the landscapes and the coastlines like we would just snap a photo today. Think about it."

Ben's voice betrayed his excitement. "I know. I know. But listen to this—"

"Whoa." Karin was engrossed in her own yarn. "Did you know that one of Cook's crew was William Bligh? The man who went on to captain the *Bounty*? And Benjamin Franklin sent a message out to all his sea captains to leave Cook alone, despite the fact that the American's were at war with the British at the time. Franklin called him a 'common friend to mankind.'"

"Sis." Ben hissed. "I've found something. Listen—landfall was made on Owhyhee (Hawaii) near the high point on the island. Latitude 21degrees 15 minutes North, Longitude 147 degrees North, 48 minutes West. Height 762 feet. We were obliged to make anchor near Leahi and go ashore. The natives we employed looked like they might strip the cloths from our backs for a bottle of rum, but were in fact both tolerable and knowledgeable."

"Give me the abridged version," Karin barked. "In English."

Ben growled at her. "God, girl, where's your Indiana Jones? Your Luke Skywalker? You just got no sense of adventure. Okay, well, our narrator, a man called Hawksworth, went with Cook, six other seamen and a handful of natives to investigate something the natives referred to as the Gates of Pele. This was done without the local king's knowledge and at great risk. If they were found out, the king would kill them all. The Hawaiians venerated the Gates of Pele. The native guides demanded great rewards."

"The Gates of Pele must have kindled some major excitement for Cook to take such a risk," Karin pointed out.

"Well, Pele was the god of fire, lightning, wind and volcanoes. Arguably the most popular Hawaiian deity. She was big news. Much of her legend centered round her controlling the oceans. The way the Hawaiians must have talked about her probably peaked Cook's interest. And, allegedly, he was an arrogant man on a great voyage of discovery. He wouldn't have balked over worrying a local king."

"A man like Cook wouldn't fear much."

"Exactly. According to Hawksworth, the natives led them through a dark passage beneath the deep heart of the volcano. Once lights had been struck and, as Gollum would say, a few tricksy bends had been negotiated, they all stopped and stared in wonder at the Gates of Pele."

"Geek. Is there a drawing?"

"No. The artist was left behind for this trip. But Hawksworth does describe what they saw. A great arch that soared so high it peaked above the topmost range of our flames. A craftsman's frame inlaid with tiny symbols. Notches at each side, missing two smaller items. The wonder of it stole our breath away and we did stare, until the dark centre began to draw our eye."

"So, in the spirit of all men, he means that they had found what they were seeking, but then realized that they wanted more." Karin shook her head.

Ben rolled his eyes at her. "I think you mean—in the spirit of all *adventurers*, they wanted more. But you're correct. The Gates of Pele were just that. A gate. It had to lead somewhere."

Karin pulled her chair over. "Now I'm interested. Where did it lead?"

At that moment Ben's cell-phone began to ring. He checked the screen and rolled his eyes. "Mum and Dad."

TWENTY

Mano Kinimaka loved the heart of Waikiki. Born and raised Hawaiian, he had spent his early childhood on Kuhio beach before his family upped sticks and moved to the quieter north shore. The surf there was world class, the food authentic even when you ate out, the life as loose as you were ever going to get.

But his enduring early memories were of Kuhio: the great beach and the free luau's, the Sunday beach barbecues, the effortless surf and the easy-going locals and the nightly glory of the setting sun.

Now, as he drove down Kuhio Avenue and then Kalakaua, he noticed the old, poignant things. Not the fresh-faced tourists. Not the locals carrying their morning helping of Jamba Juice. Not even the shaved ice vendor outside the Royal Hawaiian. It was the long black torches they lit every night, the now mostly empty shopping complex where he'd once cried laughing at a simple A-frame warning sign blocking off one of the walkways that read: *Unless you're Spiderman, the bridge is out.* So simple. So Hawaiian.

He passed the old Lassen store where he'd once gawped at their magnificent paintings and fantastic cars. It was gone now. His early childhood, moved on. He passed the King's Village shopping center, which his mother had once told him used to be the residence of King Kalakaua. He passed the most auspicious police station in the world—the one situated right on Waikiki Beach in the shadow of a hundred surfboards. And he passed the enduring statue of Duke Kahanamoku, covered as always in fresh lei's, the same one he'd stared up at as a young boy with a million dreams bouncing around his head. His family was now being guarded around the clock. Crack members of the US Marshall Service and select marines were watching over them. The family home was empty, being used as bait for hired killers. He himself was a marked man.

Hayden Jaye, his best friend and boss, sat next to him in the passenger seat, perhaps seeing something in the set of his face, for she said nothing. She had been stabbed, but was almost recovered now. People around him had been murdered. Colleagues. New friends.

Now here he was, returned to his home, the place of his childhood. Memories crowded him like long lost friends, eager to reclaim his acquaintance. Reminiscences tugged at him from every street corner.

The beauty of Hawaii was that it lived in you forever. It didn't matter if you spent a week there or twenty years. Its character was eternal.

Hayden at last broke the mood. "This guy, this Kapua. Does he really sell shaved ice from a van?"

"It's a good business over here. Everybody loves shaved ice."

"Fair enough."

Mano smiled. "You'll see."

As they drove the beauty of Kuhio and Waikiki, beaches opened up intermittently to the right. The sea glistened and the white-tops rolled invitingly. Mano saw a few Outriggers being prepared on the beach. Once upon a time, he'd been part of an outrigger team that had won trophies.

"We're here." He pulled in to a curving parking area with railings at one end that looked upon the Pacific. Kapua's van was situated right at the end, a prime spot. Mano spotted his old friend straight away, but paused for a moment.

Hayden smiled at him. "Old memories?"

"Great memories. The kind of thing you don't want to spoil by reimagining something new, ya know?"

"I know."

She didn't sound certain. Mano took a long look at his boss. She was a good person— straight, fair, tough. You knew where you stood with Hayden Jaye and what employee could ask for more from his boss? Since they'd first met, he had gotten to know her well. Her father, James Jaye, had been a star of the force, a true legend and worthily so. Hayden's goal had always been to live up to his promise, to his legacy. It was her driving force.

So much so that Mano had been stunned when she had announced how serious she was about the young geek, Ben Blake. He had thought it would be a long, long time before Hayden stopped making herself step up, to live up to a legacy that, in Mano's eyes, she had already surpassed. At first, he'd thought the long-distance thing would kill the flame, but then the pair were thrown back together again. And now they seemed tighter than ever. Would the geek give her a new purpose, a new direction in life? Only the next few months would tell.

"Let's go." Hayden nodded toward the van. Mano cracked the door open and took a deep breath of pure local air. Diamond Head rose to his left, a striking shape imposing itself upon the skyline, always present.

For Mano, it had always been there. It didn't take him aback that it might sit atop some great wonder.

Together, they approached the shaved ice van. Kapua was leaning out, staring at them. His face creased in surprise and then in genuine delight.

"Mano? Mano! Hey!"

Kapua disappeared. After a second, he came running around the side of the van. He was a broad, fit individual with dark hair and a swarthy complexion. Even at first glance, Hayden could tell he spent at least two hours every day on a surfboard.

"Kapua." Mano embraced his old friend. "Been a few, brah."

Kapua stepped back. "What you been doing? Say, how's the Hard Rock shot glass collection coming?"

Mano shook his head and shrugged. "Ah, some blah-blah, and more. You know. You?"

"True. Who da *howlie?*"

"The haole..." Mano switched back to comprehensible American, much to Hayden's relief. "...is my boss. Meet Hayden Jaye."

The local straightened himself up. "Pleased to meet you," he said. "You are Mano's boss? Wow. Lucky Mano, I say."

"You got no woman, Kapua?" Mano tried hard to deflect the slight affront.

"I got me a *poi-dog*. She one hot Hawaiian-Chinese-Phillipino, haole, Got me pitching tent all night long, dude." Most Hawaiian's were of mixed race.

Mano drew a breath. A *poi-dog* was a person of mixed race. A *haole* was a visitor, and not necessarily a derogatory term.

Before he could say anything, Hayden had turned to him and said sweetly, "Pitching tent?"

Mano cringed. Hayden knew perfectly well what Kapua meant and it had nothing to do with camping. "That's... great. She sounds lovely. Look, Kapua, I need to ask you a few questions."

"Shootz."

"Ever hear of a big shot underworld figure who goes by the name of Kovalenko? Or the Blood King?"

"All I hear is what's in the news, brah. He on Oahu?"

"Maybe. How about Claude?"

"Nah. Howlie name like that, I'd remember." Kapua hesitated.

Hayden saw it. "But you *do* know something."

"Maybe, boss. Maybe I do. But your *friends* over there"—he bobbed his head in the direction of the Waikiki Beach Police Station—"they don't wanna know. I told them already. They done nothin'.'"

"Try me." Hayden held the man's eyes.

"I hear things, boss. That's why Mano came to see me, right? Well, new money been handing out some fat wads lately, man. New players, all over the scene, partying like they ain't never gonna see next week."

"New money?" Mano echoed. "From where?"

"Nowhere," Kapua said seriously. "I mean, right here, man. Right here. They always been fringe people, but now they rich people."

Hayden ran a hand through her hair. "What does that say to you?"

"I ain't plugged into that scene, but I know this. Something's going down or about to. A lot of people have been paid a lot of money. When that happens, you learn to keep your head down 'til the bad blows over."

Mano stared at the sparkling ocean. "You sure you know nothin', Kapua?"

"On my *poi-dog*, I swear."

Kapua took his *poi* seriously. Hayden indicated the van. "Why don't you fix us a couple, Kapua."

"Sure."

Hayden made a face at Mano as Kapua moved away. "Worth a shot, I guess. Do you have any idea what he's talking about?"

"I don't like the sound of something about to go down in my home town," Mano said and held out a hand for his shave ice. "Kapua. Give me a name, brah. Who *would* know something?"

"There's this local boy, Danny, lives over on the hill." His eyes flicked toward Diamond Head. "Rich. His folks, they bring him up like a *howlie.*" He smiled at Hayden. "Say, like an American. Nothin' wrong with that, I guess. But he more serious with the lowlife. He gets off on knowing shit, you get me?"

Mano used his spoon and dug out a great hunk of rainbow colored ice. "Guy likes to pretend he's a big shot?"

Kapua nodded. "But he ain't. He just a boy playin' a man's game."

Hayden touched Mano's arm. "We'll pay this Danny a visit. If there's some kind of new threat around, we need to know that too."

Kapua nodded at the ice cones. "They on the house. But you don't know me. You never came to see me."

Mano nodded at his old friend. "Goes without saying, brah."

*****

Kapua gave them an address, which they programmed into the car's nav. Within fifteen minutes, they were pulling up just beyond a set of black, wrought iron gates. The property sloped down back toward the ocean so they could only make out the upstairs windows of a big house.

They got out of the car, springs squealing on Mano's side. Mano put a hand on the big gates and pushed. The front garden made Hayden stop and stare.

A surf board rack. A brand new open-back truck. A hammock slung between two palm trees.

"Oh my God, Mano. Are all Hawaiian gardens like this?"

Mano grimaced. "Not exactly, no."

As they were about to ring the bell, they heard noises coming from the back. They walked around the house, hands close to their weapons. When they came around the last corner, they saw a young man cavorting in the pool with an older woman.

"Excuse me!" Hayden shouted. "We're with the Honolulu PD. Quick word?" Under her breath she whispered, "I hope that's not his mother."

Mano choked. He wasn't used to his boss cracking jokes. Then he saw her face. She was deadly serious. "Why would you—?"

"What the hell do you want?" The young man was striding toward them, gesticulating wildly. As he came closer, Mano saw his eyes.

"We got a problem," Mano said. "He's strung out."

Mano let the guy swing wildly. A few big haymakers and he was panting, shorts starting to slide. He showed no awareness of his predicament.

Then the older woman was running at them. Hayden blinked in disbelief. The woman launched herself onto Kinimaka's back and began to ride him like a stallion.

What on earth had they walked into here?

Hayden let Kinimaka take care of himself. She surveyed the house and the grounds. There was no sign anyone else was home.

At last, Mano managed to shrug the she-beast off. She landed with a wet slap on the gravel that surrounded the pool and began to wail like a banshee.

Danny, if it was Danny, gawped at her open-mouthed, shorts now sliding past his knees.

Hayden had had enough. "Danny!" she shouted in his face. "We   need   to   speak   to   you!" She pushed him back into a lounge chair. Jeez, if only her father could see her now. She turned around and emptied the couples' cocktail glasses and then filled them both with water from the pool.

She flung the water into Danny's face and slapped him lightly. He immediately started to grin. "Hey, baby, you know I like—"

Hayden stepped back. If handled right, this could be turned to their advantage. "You alone, Danny?" She smiled a little.

"Tina's here. Somewhere." He spoke in short breathy sentences as if his heart was working to support a man five times his size. "My girl."

Hayden breathed an inner sigh of relief. "Good. Now, I hear you're the man to see if I want information."

"That I am." Danny's ego shone through the haze for a second. "I am that man."

"Tell me about Claude."

The stupor took him again, making his eyes appear heavy. "Claude? The black guy who works at Crazy Shirts?"

"No." Hayden gritted her teeth. "Claude, the guy who owns clubs and ranches all over Oahu."

"I don't know that Claude." Honesty was probably not one of Danny's strong points, but Hayden doubted he was faking it now.

"How about Kovalenko? Heard of him?"

Nothing leapt in Danny's eyes. No signs or tells of awareness.

Behind her Hayden could hear Mano trying to sooth Danny's girl, Tina. She decided it couldn't hurt to try a different tack. "Alright, let's try something else. There's fresh money in Honolulu. Lots of it. Where's it coming from, Danny, and why?"

The kid's eyes opened wide, suddenly lit with so much horror Hayden almost reached for her gun.

"It could happen any time!" he cried. "D'you see? *Anytime!* Just… just stay at home. Stay right at home, boy." He sounded disturbingly like he was repeating something that had been said to him.

Hayden felt a deep chill creep the length of her spine even as the heat of paradise warmed her back. "What might happen soon, Danny. C'mon, you can tell me."

"The attack," Danny said dully. "It can't be called off because it's been bought and paid for." Danny grabbed her arm, suddenly looking frighteningly sober.

"Terrorists are coming, Miss HPD. Just do your damn job and stop the bastards from coming here."

TWENTY-ONE

Ben Blake recited from the logs of Captain Cook and his man, Hawksworth, describing the most treacherous journey a man had ever taken.

"They walked through the Gates of Pele," Ben said with wonder, "into total darkness. At this time, Cook still refers to the arched entrance as the Gates of Pele. It is only after he experiences what lies beyond—it says here—that he later changes the reference to the Gates of Hell."

Karin turned to Ben with wide eyes. "What could possibly make a man like Captain Cook express such raw fear?"

"Almost nothing," Ben said. "Cook discovered cannibalism. Human sacrifice. He voyaged into utterly unknown waters."

Karin motioned toward the screen. "Read the damn thing."

"Beyond the black Gates lie the most damnable paths known to Man—"

"Don't narrate," Karin snapped. "Summarize."

"I can't"

"What? Why?"

"Because it says here—the following text has been deleted from this conversion due to doubts as to its authenticity."

"What?"

Ben frowned thoughtfully at the computer. "I guess if it were out there for all to see then someone would have tried exploring by now."

"Or maybe they did and died. Maybe the authorities decided the knowledge was too dangerous to be aired to the public."

"But, how do *we* view the deleted document?" Ben stabbed randomly at a few keys. There were no hidden links on the page. Nothing untoward. He Googled the author's name and found several pages that referenced Cook's chronicler, but no more mentions of the Gates of Hell, Pele, or even Diamond Head.

Karin turned to stare out at the heart of Waikiki. "So Cook's journey through the Gates of Hell was expunged from history. We could keep trying." She waved at the computers.

"But futile it will be, " Ben said in his best Yoda impression. "Waste our time we should not."

"What Hayden sees in you I'll never know." Karin shook her head before turning slowly round. "The problem is, we have no way of knowing what we're going to find down there. We'd be walking into hell, blind."

*****

Hayden and Kinimaka managed to squeeze a few more sentences out of Danny before deciding it was wise to leave the two of them to their drug-infused party. With luck, they would both think the CIA's visit was a bad dream.

Kinimaka climbed back into the car, placing his hand on the soft, leather steering wheel. "A terrorist attack?" he repeated. "On Waikiki? I don't believe it."

Hayden was already dialing her boss. Gates answered immediately. She recited in a few short sentences the information they had gleaned from Danny.

Mano listened to Gates's reply by speakerphone. "Hayden, I'm inbound. A few hours and I'll be there. The Police are leaning very heavily on all known criminals to get a location for the ranches. We'll have it soon. I'll alert the relevant bodies about this alleged attack, but keep digging."

The line went dead. Hayden exhaled in quiet surprise. "He's coming here? He can hardly cope as it is. What good will he do?"

"Maybe the work will help him cope."

"Let's hope. They think they'll get the ranches location soon. We're on terrorist watch. It's positive, direct people we need now. Hey, Mano, you think this terrorist thing is a part of the Blood King conspiracy?"

Mano nodded. "It crossed my mind." His eyes were taking in the breathtaking view as if storing it to help fight against the coming dark.

"Speaking of direct people, Drake and his two cronies still haven't returned my messages. And neither has the HPD."

Her cellphone sang out, startling her. It was Gates. "Sir?"

"This thing just went apeshit," he shouted, clearly alarmed. "The Honolulu cops just got three more legitimate terrorist threats. All on Waikiki. All happening soon. There are links established to Kovalenko."

"Three!"

Gates suddenly went offline for a second. Hayden swallowed as she felt the pit of her stomach churn. The fear in Mano's eyes made her start to sweat.

Gates came back on the line. "Make that *four*. Another piece of intel just got authenticated. Contact Drake. You're about to be in the fight of your life, Hayden. Get mobilized."

*****

The Blood King stood on an elevated deck, the briefest glimpse of a wintry smile on his face, a few of his trusted lieutenants stood before and below him. "It is time," he said simply. "This is what we have been waiting for, what we have worked for. This is the result of all my endeavors and all your sacrifices. This" —he paused for effect— "is where it all ends."

He surveyed faces for any signs of fear. There were none. Indeed, Boudreau looked practically ecstatic at being allowed back into the bloody fray.

"Claude, destroy the ranch. Kill all the captives. And…" He

grinned. "Let loose the tigers. They should keep the authorities busy for a while. Boudreau, just do what you do, but more brutally. I invite you to fulfill your every desire. I invite you to impress me. No, shock me. Do that, Boudreau. Go to Kauai and shut down the ranch over there."

The Blood King gave one last glance at his few remaining men. "As for you… go unleash hell in Hawaii."

He turned away, dismissing them, and cast a final, critical eye over his transport and the hand-picked men who were to accompany him into the death-defying depths below Diamond Head.

"No man has done this since Cook and lived to tell the tale. No man has seen beyond the fifth level of hell. No man has ever discovered what the trap system was built to conceal. *We will.*"

Death and devastation were both behind and before him. The onset of chaos was imminent. The Blood King was happy.

*****

Matt Drake walked across the parking lot that fronted Exoticars, arm in arm with his 'girlfriend,' Alicia Myles. A basic Dodge rental was the only car parked there, probably belonging to a tourist couple who had rented one of the new Lamborghini's for an hour. By the time Drake and Alicia had entered the fancy showroom, a thickset man with a crew cut was already in their face.

"Good afternoon. May I help you?"

"Which one of these is the fastest?" Drake put on an eager face. "We have a Nissan back home and the girlfriend here wants to appreciate some real speed." Drake winked. "Might get me some bonus points, if you know what I mean."

Alicia smiled sweetly.

Drake hoped Mai was currently skirting around the back of the big showroom, keeping out of sight of the rear garage and making her way toward the fenced-off side compound. She would try to gain entry from that direction. Drake and Alicia had about six minutes.

The man's smile was big and not surprisingly, false. "Well, most folks choose the new Ferrari 458 or the Lamborghini Aventador, both of which are fine cars." The smile actually broadened as the salesman pointed toward said vehicles, both positioned in front of the full-length showroom windows. "But, in terms of legendary accomplishments, if that's what you're looking for, I might recommend the Ferrari Daytona or the McLaren F1." He waved a hand toward the rear of the showroom.

Back there and to the right were the offices. To the left were a series of secluded booths where credit card details would be taken and keys handed over. The office was windowless, but Drake heard figures moving around.

He counted down the seconds. Mai was due in four minutes.

"Are you Mr. Scarberry or Mr. Petersen?" he asked with a smile. "I saw their names on the sign outside."

"I'm James. Mr. Scarberry and Mr. Petersen are the owners. They're out back."

"Oh." Drake made a show of looking the Ferrari and the Lamborghini over. The showroom's air-conditioning blasted down on his back. No noise came from the far office. Alicia stayed apart, playing the easy-going wife and at the same time creating space.

One minute until Mai was due to come through the side doors.

Drake readied himself.

*****

Time was passing them by at an alarming rate, but Ben was hopeful that Karin's crazy idea would bear fruit. The first step had been to find out where the original logs of Captain Cook where being stored. This proved an easy task. The documents were kept in the National Archives, near London, a government building, but not exactly as secure as the Bank of England.

So far so good.

The next step was to enlist Hayden. It took a long time to get their point across. At first, Hayden seemed hugely distracted without being rude, but when Karin, backed up by Ben, presented their plan, the CIA agent went deadly quiet.

"You want to *what?*" she asked suddenly.

"We want you to send a world-class thief into the National Archives at Kew to *photograph*—not steal—and then email me a copy of the relevant part of Cook's logs. The part that's missing."

"Have you been drinking, Ben? Seriously—"

"The hardest part," Ben pressed, "will not be the theft. It will be making sure the thief finds and sends me the right part."

"What if he's caught?" Hayden fired off a question without thinking.

"That's why he has to be a world class thief the CIA might own through this deal. And why he ideally would already be in custody. Oh, and Hayden, it all has to be done in the next few hours. This really can't wait."

"I'm aware of that," Hayden snapped, but then her tone softened. "Look, Ben, I know you two have been stuffed away in that little office, but you might want to stick your head out the door and get some up-to-date intel. You need to be prepared in case—"

Ben glanced worriedly at Karin. "In case what? You sound like the world's about to end."

Hayden's silence told him all he needed to know.

After a few moments, his girlfriend spoke up again, "How badly do you need these records, these logs? Is it worth pissing the Brits off?"

"If the Blood King reaches the Gates of Hell and we have to go in after him," Ben said, "they're likely to be our only source of navigation. And we all know how good Cook was with his maps. They might save our lives."

*****

Hayden laid her cell on the hood of the car and tried to calm her turbulent thoughts. Her eyes met Mano Kinimaka's through the windshield and she clearly sensed the horror churning through his mind. They had just received the most terrible news, again from Jonathan Gates.

Not that terrorists were about to strike multiple points in Oahu.

Now they knew it was much worse than that.

Mano climbed out, clearly shaking. "Who was that?"

"Ben. He says we need to break into the National Archives in England to get him a copy of Captain Cook's logs."

Mano frowned. "Do it. Just do it. This fucking Kovalenko is trying to destroy everything we love, Hayden. You do everything you can to protect the things you love."

"The British—"

"Screw 'em." Mano forgot himself in his stress. Hayden didn't mind. "If the logs will help us kill this bastard, get 'em."

Hayden sorted through her thoughts. She tried to clear her mind. It would take several calls to the CIA offices in London and a big shout from her boss, Gates, but she thought she could probably get the job done. Especially in light of what Gates had just told her.

And she knew quite well there was a particularly charming CIA asset based in London who could pull the job off without breaking a sweat.

Mano still stared at her, still in shock. "Can you believe that call? Can you believe what Kovalenko is about to do just to divert people's attention?"

Hayden couldn't, but stayed quiet, still preparing her speech for Gates and the London office. After a few minutes, she was ready.

"Well let's follow one of the worst calls of our lives with one that's gonna help us turn the tables," she said and jabbed in a speed-dial number.

Even as she spoke to her boss and arranged help from overseas to break into the British National Archives, the previous words of Jonathan Gates scorched her mind.

It's not just Oahu. The Blood King's terrorists are about to hit multiple islands at once.

TWENTY-TWO

Drake took a breath as Mai slipped through a side door, in full view of the salesman.

"What the—"

Drake smiled. "It's Mai-time," he whispered, and then broke the man's jaw with a haymaker. Without a sound, the salesman spun and hit the ground. Alicia strode past the Lamborghini, readying her weapon. Drake leapt over the motionless salesman. Mai stepped quickly along the rear wall, passing behind the pristine McLaren F1.

They were up against the office wall in seconds. The lack of windows worked both for and against them. But there would be security cameras. It was just a matter of—

Someone came running in from the back, overalls smothered in oil and grease, long black hair tied back in a green bandana. Drake pressed his cheek right up against the thin plywood partition, listening to the sounds coming from within the office as Mai took the mechanic out with practiced movements.

Still they hadn't made a sound.

But then more men burst through the door, and someone inside the office let out a yell. Drake knew the game was up.

"Let 'em have it."

Alicia growled "Fuck, yeah" and kicked the office door in just as it opened, sending it slamming against a man's head. Another man stepped out, eyes widening in shock as they locked on to the beautiful woman with the gun and the fighters poise waiting for him. He raised a shotgun. Alicia shot him through the stomach.

He collapsed in the doorway. More shouts came from within the office. Shock was beginning to turn into understanding. Soon, they would figure that it might be wise to phone a few friends.

Drake fired at one of the mechanics, hitting him mid-thigh and taking him down. The man slid full-length down the McLaren, leaving a bloody smear in his wake. Even Drake grimaced. Mai engaged the second man and Drake turned back to Alicia.

"We need to get inside."

Alicia inched closer until she had a good view of the interior. Drake crab-walked along the floor until he reached the door. On his nod, Alicia fired a few shots. Drake almost dived in through the doorway, but at that moment half a dozen men came bursting out of it, weapons up and firing hard.

Alicia spun away, taking cover behind the Lamborghini. Bullets pinged off its flanks. The windshield shattered. Drake slipped away quickly. He could see the hurt in the man's eyes as he fired upon the supercars.

Another saw him too. Drake opened fire a split second before he did and saw him drop hard, taking one of his colleagues with him.

Alicia popped up from behind the Lamborghini and laid down a couple of covering shots. Drake ran for the Ferrari, ducking behind its huge tires. Every bullet counted now. He could see Mai, hidden from view by the corner of the office wall, peering into the back where the mechanics had come from.

Three of them lay at her feet.

Drake cracked a little smile. She was still the perfect killing machine. For a moment he worried about the inevitable meeting of Mai and Alicia, and the reckoning to come over the death of Wells, but then he locked his worry away in the same remote compartment as the love he felt for Ben and Hayden and all his other friends.

This was not a place to let his civilian emotions thrive.

A bullet slammed into the Ferrari, flying through the door and out the other side. With a deafening crash, the front window exploded, glass raining down in a mini waterfall. Drake used the distraction to pop up and shoot another of the men who was bunched up around the office door.

Amateurs, for sure.

Then he saw two hard-looking men exit the office holding machine-pistols. Drake's heart skipped a beat. He had a brief image of two *more* men behind them—almost certainly Scarberry and Petersen being protected by hired mercenaries—before he made his body as small as possible behind the massive tire.

The sound of bullets spewing forth blasted his eardrums. This would be their strategy then. Keep Alicia and him grounded whilst the two owners made their escape through the back.

But they hadn't planned for Mai.

The Japanese agent scooped up a couple of discarded guns and came around the corner, blasting at the men with the machine-pistols. One flew backward as if he'd been hit by a car, firing his pistol crazily and making confetti of the ceiling as he fell. The other herded his bosses behind his own bulk and switched his aim toward Mai.

Alicia burst upward and fired one shot that went through the bodyguard's cheek, felling him in an instant.

Now Scarberry and Petersen pulled out weapons of their own. Drake cursed. He needed them alive. At that moment two more men came through the back and side doors, forcing Mai to take cover behind the McLaren again.

A bullet blasted through the precious car's shell.

Drake heard one of the owners squeal like a Hawaiian Kalua pig .The few remaining men gathered around their bosses and, firing wide of the cars and thus their assailants, ran at breakneck speed for the rear garage.

Drake was momentarily taken aback. Mai took out two of the bodyguards, but Scarberry and Petersen vanished quickly through the back door amidst a hail of covering fire.

Drake rose and fired as he walked forward. Advancing all the while, he bent over to scoop up two more weapons. One of the guards by the back door fell, holding his shoulder. The other vanished backward in a hail of blood.

Drake ran to the door, Mai and Alicia at his side. Mai fired whilst Drake took a few quick peeks, trying to assess the layout of the back rooms and garage.

"Just a big open space," he said. "But one big problem."

Alicia squatted at his side. "What?"

"They've got a Shelby Cobra back there."

Mai rolled her eyes at him. "Why is that a problem?"

"Whatever you do, don't shoot it."

"Is it loaded with explosives?"

"No."

"Then why can't I shoot it?"

"Because it's a Shelby Cobra!"

"We just shot up a showroom full of stupid supercars." Alicia elbowed him aside. "If you ain't got the stomach for it, piss off."

"Damn." Drake jumped in front of her. A bullet whizzed by his forehead and embedded into the plaster wall, spraying Gypsum shavings past his eyes. As he'd expected, the bad guys were firing as they ran. If they hit anything, it'd be blind luck.

Drake aimed, took a deep breath, and dropped the men on either side of the two bosses. As their last remaining bodyguards fell, both Scarberry and Petersen seemed to realize they were fighting a losing battle. They stopped, guns hanging by their sides. Drake ran at them, finger already tensioned on the trigger.

"Claude," he said. "We want Claude, not you. Where is he?"

Up close the two bosses were oddly similar. They both had tired faces, etched all around with hard lines born of years of ruthless decision making. Their eyes were cold, the eyes of feasting piranhas. Their hands, still holding the guns, flexed cautiously.

Mai pointed at the guns. "Drop them."

Alicia fanned out wide, making the target harder. Drake could almost see the defeat enter the bosses' eyes. The guns clattered to the floor almost simultaneously.

"Bloody hell," Alicia muttered. "They look the same and act the same. Does being a bad guy in paradise turn you all into clones? And whilst I'm at it—why would anyone turn into a bad guy out here? This place is better'n a vacay on cloud nine."

"Which one of you is Scarberry?" Mai asked, leading with an easy one.

"I am," the lighter-haired one said. "You the guys' been looking for Claude all over town?"

"That's us," Drake whispered. "And this is our last stop."

A faint *click* echoed through the stillness. Drake spun, knowing Alicia would stay on target as she always used to. The garage looked empty, the silence suddenly as heavy as a mountain.

Scarberry gave them a sallow smile. "We're in a workshop. Sometimes things fall over."

Drake didn't look at Alicia but signaled her to keep constant lookout. Something was off. He stepped in, took hold of Scarberry. With a quick judo move, Drake lifted him and threw him over his shoulder, slamming the man hard onto the concrete. By the time the pain in Scarberry's eyes had cleared, Drake had jammed the gun under his chin.

"Where's Claude?"

"Never heard—"

Drake broke the man's nose. "You get one more chance."

Scarberry was hyperventilating. His face was set like

granite, but the muscles in his neck worked hard, betraying nerves and fear.

"Let's start shooting bits off." Mai's light voice drifted past them. "I'm bored."

"Fair enough." Drake pushed up, stepped away, and squeezed the trigger.

"NOO!"

Scarberry's scream stopped him at the last possible instant. "Claude lives on a ranch! Inland from the north shore. I can give you coordinates."

Drake smiled. "Then go ahead."

Another click. Drake saw the briefest of movements and his heart sank.

Oh no.

Alicia fired. Her bullet killed the last bad guy instantly. He had been hiding inside the Shelby's trunk.

Drake glared at her. She smiled back with a bit of the old mischief. Drake saw that she, at least, would find herself again. She was a strong character, able to deal with loss.

He wasn't so sure about himself. He nudged Scarberry to get a move on. "Be quick. Your friend, Claude, is in for a big surprise."

TWENTY-THREE

Hayden and Kinimaka hadn't even started the car engine when Drake's call came in. She saw his number on her screen and breathed a sigh of relief.

"Drake. Where have—"

"No time. I have Claude's location."

"Yeah, so do we, smartass. It's amazing what some criminals give up for a quieter life."

"How long have you known? Where are you?" Drake fired off the questions like a drill sergeant barking orders.

"Slow down, tiger. We just got word about a minute ago. Listen, we're gearing up for an immediate strike. And I mean right *now*. You game?"

"Damn right I am. We all are. That bastard is one step removed from Kovalenko."

Hayden filled him in on the terrorist alerts, as she signaled Kinimaka to drive. When she'd finished, Drake went quiet.

After a moment he said, "We'll meet you at the HQ."

Hayden speed dialed Ben Blake. "Your op is a go. We're hoping our asset in London will get you what you need in the next few hours, then he'll send the copies straight over to you. I hope it's what you need, Ben."

"I hope it's actually there." Ben sounded as nervous as she'd ever heard him. "It's sound guesswork, but it's still guesswork."

"I hope so too."

Hayden threw her cell on the dash and stared blankly at the streets of Waikiki as Kinimaka drove the back to the HQ.

"Gates thinks if we can take Claude down quickly we may be able to stop the attacks. They hope Kovalenko might even be there."

Mano gritted his teeth. "Everyone's on it, boss. Local PD, special forces. Everything's being squeezed until it pops. Problem is—the bad guys are already in place. They must be. It's gotta be nigh impossible to stop any attack that's imminent, let alone half a dozen on three different islands."

The overwhelming belief among everyone in authority was that Kovalenko had indeed commissioned the multiple attacks to keep everyone busy whilst he embarked on his dream quest—the journey he'd devoted the latter part of his life too.

To follow in Captain Cook's footsteps. To go one better. To explore beyond the Gates of Hell.

Hayden snapped back as the HQ loomed outside. Time for action.

*****

Drake led Mai and Alicia into the CIA building and were immediately escorted upstairs. They were shown to a room bristling with activity. At the far end, Hayden and Kinimaka stood amidst a gaggle of police and military officers. Drake could see SWAT and a HPD crack team. He could see uniforms undoubtedly belonging to CIA special-ops teams. Maybe even some Delta around.

The Devil was surely on the Blood King's tail now and baying for blood.

"You remember when the Blood King sent his men to attack that Destroyer to steal the device?" he said. "And they tried to kidnap Kinimaka at the same time? I bet that was a chance snatch. They just wanted Kinimaka's Hawaiian knowledge."

Then Drake remembered that neither Mai nor Alicia had been present when Kovalenko's men had attached the destroyer. He shook his head. "Doesn't matter."

Drake spied Ben and Karin parked over by the window. They each had a drink in their hand and looked like wallflowers at a school disco.

Drake thought about losing himself in the crowd. It would be easy. Kennedy's loss still ran hot in his blood, making it impossible for him to discuss. Ben had been there. Ben had held her as she died. It should have been Drake. Not only that. Drake should have prevented her death. It was what he did. Time blurred and for a moment he was back home in York with Kennedy, and they were cooking something in the kitchen. Kennedy was splashing dark rum in the frying pan and raising her eyes when it sizzled. Drake was marinating a steak with garlic butter. It was mundane. It was fun. The world was normal again.

Stars flashed before his eyes like fireworks gone wrong. The world abruptly returned and the voices clamored around him. Someone pushed by his elbow. Another man spilled hot coffee on one of his superiors and took off for the toilets like a bat out of hell.

Alicia was staring at him. "What gives, Drakey?"

He pushed through the crowd until he came face to face with Ben Blake. It was the perfect moment for a quick Dinorock comment. Drake knew it. Ben probably knew it. But they both stayed quiet. Light streamed through the window behind Ben; Honolulu stood framed by sunlight and bright blue skies and a few ribbed clouds outside.

Drake found his voice at last. "Those CIA computers prove useful?"

"We hope." Ben reeled off a quick version of the story behind Captain Cook's journey underneath Diamond Head and finished with the revelation about the CIA using a British asset to rob the National Archives.

Alicia inched forward at the young lad's news. "A British super thief? What's his name?"

Ben blinked at the sudden attention. "Hayden never told me."

Alicia cast a quick glance at the CIA operative, then broke out into a cheeky smile. "Oh, I bet she didn't."

"What does that mean?" Karin spoke up.

Alicia's smile was turning a little wicked. "I'm not best known for my diplomacy. Don't push it."

Drake coughed. "Just another international criminal that Alicia's shagged. The trick has always been finding one she hasn't."

"It's true," Alicia said with a grin. "I've always been popular."

"Well, if it's the asset I'm thinking of," Mai cut into their conversation, "he's known to Japanese intelligence. He is... a player. And a very, very good operative."

"So the chances are he will take care of his end." Drake studied the bliss of the Pacific city laid out before him, longing for a bit of peace himself.

"That's never been a problem for him," Alicia said. "And yes, he will deliver your logs."

Ben was still staring between Alicia and Hayden, but held his tongue. Discretion was the better part of disclosure at this stage. "It's still an educated guess," he said. "But if we do end up at the Gates of Hell, I'm positive that these records could save our lives."

"Hopefully"—Drake turned and scanned the mayhem—"It won't come to that. The Blood King will still be at the ranch. But if these pricks don't hurry it up, Kovalenko will do a runner."

"Kovalenko." Alicia licked her lips as she said it, savoring her vengeance. "Will die for what happened to Hudson. And Boudreau? He's another that's truly marked." She too looked over the bustling throng. "Who's in charge here, anyhow?"

As if in response a voice rose from out of the gaggle of officers surrounding Hayden Jaye. When the din subsided and the man could be seen, Drake was pleased to see Jonathan Gates. He liked the senator. And grieved with him.

"As you know, we have a location for Kovalenko's Oahu ranch," Gates said. "Therefore, our mission must be fourfold. First, secure all the hostages. Second, secure intel on the alleged terrorist attacks. Third, find this man Claude and Kovalenko. And fourth, find the location of the other two ranches."

Gates paused to let that sink in and then somehow managed to make every man and woman in the room think he was looking at them with a single sweep of his eyes. "This must be done by any means necessary. Kovalenko has willingly endangered many lives in the course of his mad quest. It will end today."

Gates turned away. All of a sudden, the chaos inside the room died away and everyone began to walk quickly to their designated areas. The details had been thrashed out.

Drake caught Hayden's eye. She waved him over.

"Tool up and saddle up, guys. We're hitting Claude's ranch in thirty."

TWENTY-FOUR

Drake sat with his friends in one of the light Hawaiian Police Department helicopters and tried to clear his mind as they flew fast toward Claude's ranch. The skies were littered with similar choppers and heavier, military ones. Hundreds of men were in the air. More were en route across land, traveling as fast as they could. A large part of the police and military had had to remain behind in Honolulu and the Waikiki area just in case the terrorist attacks actually materialized.

The Blood King was dividing their forces.

The satellite image showed a lot of movement at the ranch, but much of it was camouflaged so it was impossible to tell what was really going on.

Drake was determined to put his feelings for Kovalenko on hold. Gates had been right. The hostages and their safety were the crucial points here. Some of the most astonishing sights he would ever see opened up below and around him as they flew toward the North Shore, but Drake was using every last bit of his will to focus. He was the soldier he had once been.

He couldn't be anything else.

To his left, Mai was talking briefly to her sister, Chika, double-checking her safety and sharing a few quiet words whilst they could. It was no secret that they could be starting an all-out war or heading into a prepared war-zone.

To Drake's right, Alicia spent the time checking and re-checking her weapons and equipment. She had no need of explaining herself. Drake had no doubt she would extract her vengeance.

Hayden and Kinimaka sat opposite, constantly keying their throat mics and firing off or receiving updates and orders. The good news was that nothing had happened on Oahu or any other island. The bad news was the Blood King had had years to prepare for this. They had no clue as to what they were walking into.

Ben and Karin had been left back at HQ. Their orders were to wait for the asset's email and then prepare for the somewhat terrifying eventuality that they might have to journey beneath Diamond Head and perhaps breach the Gates of Hell.

A tinny voice came over the choppers sound system. "Five minutes to target."

Like it or not, Drake thought. We're in it now.

The helicopter swept low over a deep valley, an incredible sight as it flew flanked by dozens of other choppers. This was the first wave, made up of Special-ops soldiers. Every other US military marque was ready to assist. Air force. Navy. Army.

The voice came once more. *"Target."*

They rose as a unit.

*****

Drake's boots hit the soft grass and he was instantly under fire. He had been the next to last man out the door. The unlucky marine still repelling down took a full burst in the chest and died before he hit the ground.

Drake flattened himself. Bullets whizzed over his head. Dull impacts struck logs next to him. He fired a salvo. Men to either side of him crawled through the grass, using the natural undulating terrain as cover.

Ahead he saw the house, a two-story, brick affair, nothing fancy but no doubt serviceable for Kovalenko's local needs. To the left he spied the ranch area. *What the —?*

Scared, unarmed figures were running toward him. They were running to left and right, every which way. He heard a hiss over his earpiece

"Friendlies."

He snaked forward. Mai and Alicia branched off to his right. At last the marines got their act together and began to announce a coordinated fire pattern. Drake started to advance faster. The men facing them began to retreat, moving away from their concealment and running for the house.

Easy targets

Drake now rose with the attack force and picked off men as he ran, gun up. He saw a captive leaping through the grass, heading for the house. They didn't know the good guys had arrived.

The captive suddenly twisted and fell. The Blood King's men were taking pot shots at them. Drake snarled, lined the shooter up in fine targets and blew the bastard's head off. He fired intermittently, either pinning down or routing men so others could finish them off.

He was searching for Claude. Before they had vacated the chopper, they had all been shown a photo of the Blood King's second-in-charge. Drake knew he would be directing things from behind the scenes with an escape plan worked out. Probably from the house.

Drake ran now, still scanning the area, firing occasionally. One of the bad guys rose up from behind a hillock and charged at him with a machete. Drake simply dropped his shoulder, let the man's momentum carry him right over and sent him crashing to the ground. The man grunted. Drake's boot smashed his jaw. Drake's other boot stood on the hand clutching the machete.

The ex-SAS man leveled his gun and fired. And then moved on.

He didn't look back. The house was ahead, looming large, the door slightly ajar as if inviting entry. Clearly not the way to go. Drake blasted the windows out as he ran, aiming high. Glass exploded into the house.

More captives were streaming in from the ranch now. Some stood in the tall grass, simply screaming or looking shell-shocked. As Drake glance at them, he noticed that most of them were sprinting at pace, flying along as if fleeing something.

And then he saw it, and his blood turned to ice.

The head, the unbelievably huge head of a Bengal tiger, bounced through the grass in easy pursuit. Drake couldn't let the tigers catch their prey. He ran toward them.

Pressed his earpiece. *"Tigers in the grass."*

A flurry of chatter came back. Others had spotted the beasts too. Drake watched one of the animals leap onto the back of a running man. The thing was enormous, savage, and in flight, the perfect image of mayhem and slaughter. Drake forced his legs to go faster.

Another gigantic head broke the grass a few yards ahead. The tiger was on him, leaping, its face one huge snarl, its teeth bared and already slicked with blood. Drake hit the deck and rolled with every nerve in his body alive and screaming. Never before had he rolled so perfectly. Never before had he risen so quickly and accurately. It was as if the fiercer opponent had brought out the better warrior in him.

He whipped the gun came around and fired a bullet point-blank into the tiger's head. The beast fell instantly, shot through the brain.

Drake didn't take a breath. He leapt quickly through the grass to help the man he had seen brought down seconds earlier. The tiger was poised above him, roaring, its huge muscles straining and rippling as it dipped its head down to bite.

Drake shot at it hindquarters, waited for it to turn, and then shot it between the eyes. It landed, all five hundred pounds of it, atop the man it was about to eat.

Not good, Drake thought. But better than being mauled and eaten alive.

Screams and shouts blasted through his earpiece. "Fuck me, these bastards are huge!" "Another, Jacko! Another at your six!"

He studied the surrounds. No signs of tigers, just terrified captives and spooked troops. Drake sprinted back through the grass, ready to take cover if he caught sight of any adversary, but in a matter of seconds, he was back at the house.

The front windows had been breached. Marines were inside. Drake followed, his wireless Bluetooth beeper marking him as a friendly. As he stepped across the broken sill, he wondered where Claude would have situated himself. Where would he be right now?

A voice whispered in his ear. "Thought you'd left the party early, Drakey." Alicia's silky tones. "At your two."

He saw her. Partially hidden by the wall cabinet she was pawing through. Christ, was she checking out his DVD collection?

Mai was behind her, gun in hand. Drake watched as the Japanese woman raised her weapon and pointed it at Alicia's head.

"*Mai!*" His desperate tones shrieked in their ears.

Alicia jumped. Mai's face twitched into a slight smile. "It was a gesture, Drake. I was pointing at the alarm interface, not Alicia. Not yet."

"Alarm?" Drake grunted. "We're already inside."

"The grunts seem to think it's also connected to the big warehouse out back."

Alicia stepped back and aimed her gun. "Fuck if I know." She fired a salvo into the cabinet. Sparks flew.

Alicia shrugged. "That oughta do it."

Hayden, closely followed by Kinimaka, came back into the room. "Barn is shut tight. Signs of booby traps. Tech boys are working on it now."

Drake smelled the wrongness of it all. "And yet we stroll in here so easily? This—"

At that moment there was a commotion at the top of the stairs and the sound of someone descending. Fast. Drake raised the gun and glanced up.

And froze in shock.

One of Claude's men was coming down the stairs, slowly, one arm locked around the throat of a female captive. The other arm had a Desert Eagle pointed at her head.

But that wasn't the extent of Drake's shock. The sinking feeling came when he recognized the female. It was Kate Harrison, the daughter of Gates' ex-aid. The man who had been partly to blame for Kennedy's death.

This was his daughter. Still alive.

Claude's man jammed the gun hard against her temple, making her screw her eyes up in pain. But she did not cry out. Drake, along with a dozen others in the room, leveled their guns at the man.

And still it felt wrong to Drake. Why the hell was this guy upstairs with one captive? It almost seemed as if—

"Go back!" the man screamed, eyes pin-balling wildly in every direction. Sweat ran from him in thick droplets. The way he half-carried, half-pushed the woman meant all his weight was on his back foot. The woman, to her credit, wasn't making it easy for him.

Drake calculated that the pressure on the trigger was already half way there. "Move away! Let us out!" The man heaved her down another step. The special forces soldiers moved alright, but only to slightly more advantageous positions.

"I'm warning you, assholes." The sweaty man breathed heavily. "Get out of the fucking way."

And this time Drake could see he meant it. There was a desperate look in his eyes, something that Drake recognized. This man had lost everything. Whatever he was doing, whatever he had done, had been done under terrible coercion.

"Back!" the man screamed again and roughly pushed the woman down another step. The arm around her neck was a rod of iron. He kept every part of his body behind her so as not to present a target. At one time he had been a soldier, most likely a good one.

Drake and his colleagues saw the wisdom of retreat. They gave the man a bit more room. He moved down a few more steps. Drake caught Mai's gaze. She gave a slight shake of her head. She knew too. This wasn't right. This was. . .

A diversion. Of the most atrocious kind. Claude, no doubt under the order of Kovalenko, was using this man to distract them. Archetypal Blood King behavior. There could be a bomb in the house. The real prize, Claude, was probably making good his escape from the barn.

Drake waited, perfectly poised. Every nerve in his body stilled. He lined up the shot. His breathing stopped. His mind went blank. Now there was nothing, not the rigidly tense room full of soldiers, not the terrified hostage, not even the house and the valet that surrounded it.

Just a millimeter. A crosshair. Less than an inch of target. One move. That's all he needed. And stillness was all he knew. Then the man pushed Kate Harrison down another step, and in that split second of movement, his left eye peered around the woman's skull.

Drake burst it apart with one shot.

The man whipped back, collided with the wall, and slithered past the shrieking woman. He landed with a bang, headfirst, gun clattering behind him, and then they saw his vest, his stomach.

Kate Harrison screamed, "He's wearing a *bomb!*"

Drake leapt forward, but Mai and a big marine were already leaping over the side of the staircase. The marine grabbed Kate Harrison. Mai leapt past the dead mercenary. Her head swiveled at the vest, at the readout.

"Eight seconds!"

Everyone ran for the window. Everyone except Drake. The Englishman sprinted farther into the house, darting down the narrow hallway toward the kitchen, praying that someone had left the back door open. This way he would be closer to Claude when the bomb went off. This way, he stood a chance.

Through the hallway. Three seconds gone. Into the kitchen. A quick look around. Two more seconds. The back door—closed.

Time up.

TWENTY-FIVE

Drake opened fire even as he heard the initial explosion. It would take a second or two to reach him. The kitchen door shattered under multiple impacts. Drake ran straight at it, firing all the time. He didn't slow, just hit it shoulder first and tumbled out into the air.

The explosion zoomed after him like a striking snake. A tongue of fire blasted out of the door and the windows, exploding up into the sky. Drake was rolling. The fire's breath touched him for an instant and then receded.

Without breaking stride, he was up and running again. Bruised and battered, but terribly determined, he dashed for the big barn. The first thing he saw were dead bodies. Four of them. The techs Hayden had left behind to gain entry. He stopped by them, checked each one for signs of life.

No pulse and no bullet wounds. Were the damn walls electrified?

In another moment it didn't matter. The front of the barn exploded, shards of timber and tongues of fire shooting out in a spectacular detonation. Drake hit the deck. He heard an engine roar and looked up just in time to see a yellow blur blast through the shattered doors and fly powerfully down the makeshift driveway.

Drake jumped up. It was probably heading for a hidden chopper, plane, or some other bloody booby trap. He couldn't wait for backup. He ran into the half-demolished barn and looked around. He shook his head in disbelief. The deep shine of polished supercar glimmered in every direction.

Choosing the nearest, Drake wasted valuable seconds looking for a key and then saw a set of them hanging outside an interior office. The Aston Martin Vanquish started with a key and power button combination, which though unfamiliar to Drake, spiked his adrenalin when the crazy roar of the engine kicked in.

The Aston Martin shot out of the barn with a squeal of tires. Drake aimed it in the direction of what he hoped was Claude's speeding car. If this was another round of misdirection, Drake was fucked. As might be the whole of Hawaii. They desperately needed to capture the Blood King's second-in-command.

Out of the corner of his eye, Drake spied Alicia skidding to a stop. He didn't wait. In his rearview, he saw her run purposefully into the barn. Jesus, this could get messy.

The yellow blur ahead began to look like a high-end supercar, something reminiscent of the old Porsche Le Mans winning coupes. Near to the ground, it hugged the curves of the road, bouncing like it ran on springs. Unfit for the rough terrain, but then the makeshift road became fully paved a few miles up.

Drake gunned the Vanquish, setting his weapon carefully on the seat behind him and listening to the Bluetooth squawks hopping around his brain. The operation at the ranch was still in full swing. Hostages were being recovered. Some were dead. Several pockets of Claude's men were still holed up in strategic positions, pinning the authorities down. And there were still half-a-dozen tigers prowling around causing mayhem.

The gap between the Aston Martin and the Porsche closed to nothing. The English car was far superior on the bumpy road. Drake nudged up right behind it, contemplating pulling alongside when, in his rearview mirror, he saw *another* supercar closing in.

Alicia, at the wheel of an old Dodge Viper. Trust her to go for something with muscle.

The three cars blasted across the rough terrain, hugging the bends and slewing back out onto the long straights. Gravel and dirt plumed around and behind them. Drake saw the paved road coming up and made a decision. They wanted Claude alive, but first they had to catch him. He was very careful to keep listening to the earpiece chatter just in case someone broadcast they had caught Claude, but the longer this chase went on, the more confident Drake became that the man in front was the Blood King's second.

Drake picked up the gun and blew out the Aston's windshield. After a moment of dangerous skidding, he regained control and fired a second burst at the fleeing Porsche. Bullets strafed its rear end.

The car barely slowed. It flew onto the new road. Drake opened fire as the Le Mans racer accelerated, bullet casings littering the leather seat beside him. It was time to aim for the tires.

But right then one of the choppers blasted past them all, two figures hanging out of the open doors. The chopper swung round ahead of the Porsche and hovered sideways. Warning shots dug chunks out of the road in front of it. Drake shook his head in disbelief when a hand came out of the driver's window and started shooting up at the helicopter.

Instantly, simultaneously, he took his foot off the accelerator and his hands off the wheel, took aim, and loosed a shot of ambition, skill, and recklessness. Alicia's Viper slammed into his own car. Drake regained control, but saw the gun fly out through the windshield.

But his crazy shot worked. He shot the fleeing driver through the elbow and now the car was slowing. Stopping. Drake brought the Aston to a crunching halt, jumped out and ran swiftly to the Porsche's passenger door, pausing to pick up his gun and keeping his sights leveled at the figure's head the whole time.

"Throw your weapon out! Do it!"

"Can't," came the reply. "You shot my arm to fuck, you dumb grunt."

The chopper hovered ahead, rotors blasting as its thunderous engine made the very ground shake.

Alicia advanced and shot out the Porsche's side mirror. As a team they swung around from left and right, both covering the man behind the wheel.

Despite the man's grimace of agony, Drake recognized him from the photo. It was Claude.

Time to pay.

*****

Ben Blake jumped in shock when his mobile started to ring. Mimicking Drake, he had also switched to Evanescence. Amy Lee's chilling vocals on the track "Lost in Paradise" firmly matched everyone's mood of the moment.

The screen read *International*. The call wouldn't be from a member of his family. But, in light of the National Archives operation, it could be from any number of government offices.

"Yes?"

"Ben Blake?"

Fear scratched his spine with sharp fingers. "Who's this?"

"Tell me." The voice was cultured, English and fully assured. "Right now. Do I speak to Ben Blake?"

Karin came over to him, reading the dread in his face. "Yes."

"Good. Well done. Was that so hard? My name is Daniel Belmonte."

Ben almost dropped the phone. "What? How the hell did you—"

A stream of refined guffaws stopped him. "Relax. Just relax, my friend. I'm surprised, to say the least, that Alicia Myles and your lady friend haven't mentioned my... prowess."

Ben gaped, unable to speak. Karin was mouthing the words, *the thief? From London? That's him?*

Ben's face said it all.

"Cat got your tongue, Mr. Blake? Maybe you should put your lovely sister on. How is Karin?"

The mention of his sister's name galvanized him a little. "Where did you get my number?"

"Don't patronize me. Do you really think it would take two hours to complete the simple operation you asked of me? Or have I spent the last forty minutes learning a little about my... benefactors? Hmm? Take your time with that one, Blakey."

"I know nothing about you," Ben said defensively. "You were suggested by—" He paused. "By—"

"Your girlfriend? I'm sure I was. She knows me rather well."

"And Alicia?" Karin shouted, trying to unbalance the man. They were both so surprised and so green it hadn't even occurred to them to alert the CIA yet.

There was a moment's silence. "That girl actually scares me, truth be told."

Ben's brain stared to function. "Mr. Belmonte, the item you were asked to copy is very valuable. So valuable—"

"I understand that. It was written by Captain Cook and one of his men. Cook made more discoveries in his three voyages than any man in history."

"I don't mean historical value," Ben snapped. "I mean it might save lives. Now. Today."

"Really?" Belmonte sounded genuinely interested. "Please tell."

"I can't." Ben started to feel a little desperate. "Please. Help us."

"It's already on your email," Belmonte said. "But I wouldn't be the man I am if I didn't show you my worth, now would I? Enjoy."

Belmonte ended the call. Ben threw the mobile on the table and clicked away on the computer for a few seconds.

The missing pages from Cooks logs came right up in full, glorious color.

"The levels of hell," Ben read aloud. "Cook only got to the fifth level and then turned back. My God, do you hear that, Karin? Even Captain Cook didn't get past the fifth level. It's... it's..."

"A massive trap system." Karin was speed reading over his shoulder, photographic memory working overtime. "The biggest and most insane trap system ever imagined."

"And if it's that big, that dangerous and elaborate..." Ben turned to her. "Imagine the enormity and significance of the wonder that it leads to."

"Beyond belief," Karin said and read on.

*****

Drake dragged Claude out of the shot-up car and deposited him roughly in the road. His screams of pain rent the air, piercing even the roar of the chopper.

"Fools! You will never stop this. He always wins. Fuck, my goddamn arm hurts, you bastard!"

Drake placed his machine gun at arm's length and knelt on Claude's chest. "Just a few questions, mate. Then the medics will pump you full of some really good shit. Where is Kovalenko? Is he here?"

Claude gave him a stony face, almost petulant.

"Okay, we'll try an easier one. Ed Boudreau. Where is he?"

"He took the wiki-wiki shuttle back to Waikiki."

Drake nodded. "And where are the other two ranches?"

"Gone." Claude's face broke out into a smirk. "All gone."

"That's enough." Alicia had been listening over Drake's shoulder. She came around, gun leveled at Claude's face, and gently placed a boot on Claude's shattered elbow. An instant shriek split the air.

"We can take this as far as you want," Drake whispered.

"Nobody here is on your side, mate. We know about the terrorist attacks. Either talk or scream. It makes no difference to me."

"Stop!" Claude's words were almost unintelligible. "Puh... please."

"That's better." Alicia eased up the pressure a little.

"I have... been with the Blood King for many, many years." Claude spat. "But now he leaves me behind. He leaves me behind to die. To rot in the land of the pig. To cover his ass. Maybe not." Claude struggled to sit up. "Damn."

Every wary, Drake pulled out a handgun and lined Claude's skull up in the sights. "Steady."

"He will regret this." Claude was practically fuming. "I don't care anymore about his terrible retribution." The sarcasm dripped in his tone. "I don't care. There's no more life for me now."

"We get it." Alicia sighed. "You hate you're fucking boyfriend. Just answer the sexy soldier's questions."

Drake's earpiece squawked. A tinny voice said, "Found the first portal device. Seems Kovalenko left it behind."

Drake blinked and sent a fleeting look at Alicia. Why would the Blood King leave the portal device behind at a time like this?

Easy answer. He didn't need it.

"Kovalenko's headed beneath Diamond Head, right? To the Gates of Pele or Hell or whatever. That's his end game, yes?"

Claude screwed his face up. "That legend he found became an obsession. A man rich beyond dreams. A man who can have whatever he wants. What does he do?"

"Obsess about something he can never have?" Alicia suggested.

"A man so clever, so resourceful, reduced to a neurotic idiot in a day. He knows there's something under that friggin' volcano. He always muttered that he would best Cook. That Cook had actually turned back in fear. But not Dmitry Kovalenko, not the *Blood King;* he would go farther."

Even Drake felt a rush of apprehension. "Cook turned back? What the hell is down there?"

Claude shrugged, then groaned in pain. "Nobody knows. But my guess is that Kovalenko will be the first to find out. He's on his way there now."

Drake's heart leapt on that information. On his way there now. There was time.

By now Mai and half-a-dozen of soldiers had drifted over to them. Everyone listened with avid attention.

Drake remembered the business at hand. "We want the ranch locations. And we want Ed Boudreau."

Claude reeled off the information. Two more ranches, one on Kauai, the other on the Big Island. Boudreau was en route to Kauai.

"And the terrorist attacks?" Mai asked quietly. "Is that just another ruse?"

And now Claude's face actually fell with such despair and misery that Drake's stomach plummeted through the floor.

"No." Claude moaned. "They're real. They'll hit any moment now."

TWENTY-SIX

Ben and Karin drifted over to the window, each holding a copy of Captain Cook's classified logs. As they read and reread the craziness therein, Ben quizzed his sister about the Blood King's strange behavior.

"Kovalenko must have been about to embark on this journey when the portable devices were found. He's too well prepared to have organized everything in the last few weeks."

"Years," Karin murmured. "Years of planning and practice and greasing the right wheels. But why did he risk this huge operation to go on a little side-jaunt to Bermuda?"

Ben shook his head at one of the passages he was reading. "Crazy stuff. Just crazy. Only one thing would make him do that, sis."

Karin looked out at the distant ocean. "He saw something about the devices that was relevant to Diamond Head."

"Yes, but what?"

"Well, clearly nothing too important after all." They had been following the shaky head-cam images being broadcast from the Blood King's ranch. They knew that the megalomaniac had left the portal device behind. "He doesn't need it."

"Or he believes he can just take it back at will."

Behind them, coming from the operation uplink, they heard Drake shouting out the information he had gleaned so far from Claude.

Ben blinked at Karin. "He's saying the Blood King's already at Diamond Head. That means—"

But Karin's unexpected scream froze the next words in his throat. He followed her gaze, narrowed his eyes, and felt his world collapse.

The black smoke of many explosions was streaming from hotel windows along Waikiki Beach.

Ignoring the tumult erupting from the offices around him, Ben raced over to the wall and turned the TV on.

His mobile rang. This time it was his father. They, too, must be watching TV.

*****

Drake and the soldiers who weren't engaged in rounding up hostages or routing the few remaining pockets of resistance saw the coverage on their iPhones. The commander of their unit, a man called Johnson, broke out the military Android devices and spoke directly to the mobile command post back in Honolulu as events unfolded.

"Bombs have exploded in three Waikiki hotels," the commander repeated. *"Repeat. Three.* Outrigger West on the beach. Kalakuau Waikiki. Ohana Wave." The commander listened for a minute. "Seems they exploded in empty rooms, causing panic... evacuation... pretty much... chaos. Honolulu's emergency services are stretched to breaking."

"Is that it?" Drake actually felt some relief. It could have been much worse.

"Wait—" The commander's face fell. "Oh no."

*****

Ben and Karin watched in horror as the TV screen switched from scene to scene. The hotels were swiftly evacuated. Men and women ran and pushed and fell. They screamed and shielded their loved ones and wept whilst hugging their children tight. Hotel staff came after, looking hard-faced and terrified, but remaining in control. The police and firemen swept in and out of lobbies and hotel rooms and made their presence felt in front of every hotel. The TV picture panned away as a helicopter was brought in, showing the glorious view of Waikiki and the sprawling hills at its rear, the majesty of Diamond Head volcano and the world-famous sweep of Kuhio Beach, now spoiled by the stunning sight of high-rise hotels belching smoke and flames from their shattered walls and windows.

The TV screen flicked once more. Ben gasped and Karin's heart flipped. They couldn't even speak to each other.

A fourth hotel, in view of the world, was being invaded by masked terrorists. Anyone who stood in their way was gunned down on the sidewalk. The last man turned around and waved a fist at the hovering helicopter. Before he walked into the hotel and secured the door behind him, he shot a civilian who had been crouched down near a parked cab.

"Oh my God." Karin's voice was small. "What about the poor people inside?"

*****

"The Ala Moana Queen has been invaded by armed individuals," the commander told them. "Determined. Masked. Not afraid to kill." He turned a murderous look onto Claude. "How many more attacks are there going to be, you evil bastard?"

Claude looked terrified. "None," he said. "On Oahu."

Drake turned away. He had to think. He had to refocus. This was what Kovalenko wanted, for them all to be distracted. The fact was—Kovalenko knew something staggering was hidden deep below Diamond Head and was on his way to claim it.

Something that might even eclipse the terror of these attacks.

His concentration crept back. Nothing had changed here. The attacks had been timed to perfection. They had disrupted the soldiers and the army and the emergency services all at the same time. But *nothing had changed.* They hadn't found the Blood King so—

Plan B was now in operation.

Drake signaled Mai and Alicia. Hayden and Kinimaka were already close. The big Hawaiian looked shell-shocked. Drake spoke pointedly at him, "Are you up for this, Mano?"

Kinimaka almost growled. "Fucking right I am."

"Plan B," Drake said. "Kovalenko's not here, so we stick to it. The rest of these soldiers will catch on in a minute. Hayden and Mai, you join the Kauai assault. Mano and Alicia, you join the Big Island assault. Get to those ranches. Save as many as you can. And Alicia…" His face turned to chiseled ice. "I'm counting on you to do murder. Make that bastard Boudreau die hard."

Alicia nodded. It had been Drake's idea to keep Mai and Alicia apart when they realized they would have to split their team up. He didn't want the death of Wells and other secrets to come between saving lives and stopping the enemy.

Claude's high-pitched voice drew Drake's attention. "Kovalenko funded attacks on Oahu, Kauai and the Big Island just to draw your attention. To divide and conquer you. You cannot beat this man. He's prepared for years."

Matt Drake lifted his weapons. "That's why I'm gonna follow him through the Gates of Hell and feed him to the fucking Devil." He walked toward the supply chopper. "C'mon, people. Load up."

*****

Ben spun quickly as his mobile rang. It was Drake

"Ready?"

"Hi, Matt. Are you sure? Are we really going?"

143

"We're really going. Right now. Did you get what you need from Daniel Belmonte?"

"Yes. But he's a bit of a wan—"

"Good. Did you pinpoint the nearest lava tube entrance?"

"Yes. There's a fenced-off compound about two miles from Diamond Head. The Hawaiian government fenced off every known entrance the same way. Most times, it doesn't stop even a determined kid from getting in."

"Nothing does. Listen, Ben. Grab Karin and get someone to drive you to that lava tube. Text me the coordinates. Do it now."

"Are you serious? We don't have a clue what's down there. And this trap system? It's beyond brutal."

"Man up, Ben. Or, as Def Leppard put it—*Let's get rocked.*"

Ben put his cell on the table and let out a long breath. Karin put a hand on his shoulder. They both looked at the TV. The presenter's voice was strained.

"*. . .this is terrorism on a scale never seen before.*"

"Drake's right," Ben said. "We're at war. We need to take down our enemies' Commander-in-Chief."

TWENTY-SEVEN

Drake rounded up the eight Delta Team members who'd been assigned to him in the event a deep-cave exploration became necessary. They were the relative veterans of the squad, the most experienced, and every man had at one time, in some godforsaken place, run his own op.

Before they loaded onto the chopper, Drake took a moment out with his friends. The Blood King had already divided the Hawaiian and government forces and now he was about to divide them.

"Stay safe." Drake met everyone's eyes in turn. Hayden. Mai. Alicia. Kinimaka. "We have to spend one more night in hell, but we'll all be free tomorrow."

There were nods and a grunt from Mano.

"Believe it," Drake said and held out his hand. Four other hands bumped it. "Just stay alive, guys."

With that, he turned and jogged over to the waiting chopper. The Delta squad had been finalizing equipment preparations and now took their seats as he climbed aboard. "Ay up, lads." His Yorkshire accent was strong. "Ready to take this vodka-swilling pig apart?"

"Booyah!"

"Shag it." Drake motioned to the pilot who lifted them into the air. He took a last look back at the ranch and saw his friends still standing in the same circle, watching him go.

Would he ever see them all alive again?

If he did, there would be some major reckonings to have. Some apologies he would have to make. Some terrible realities he would have to accept. But with Kovalenko dead—it would be easier. Kennedy would be avenged, if not saved. And now that he was firmly on the Blood King's trail, his spirits were already soaring that little bit higher.

But the final reckoning between Mai and Alicia might well yet turn all that upside down. Something huge was between them, something terrible. And whatever it was, it involved Drake. And Wells.

It didn't take long for the chopper to arrive at Ben's coordinates. The pilot landed them on a flat piece of land about a hundred yards shy of the tiny compound. Drake saw Ben and Karin already sat with their backs against the high fence. Their faces were pure white with strain.

He needed to be the old Drake for a while. This mission needed Ben Blake at his best, at his frostiest, and if Ben was firing on all four cylinders, then Karin would feed off that. The mission's success depended on all of them being on the best form of their lives.

Drake signaled the Delta soldiers, exited the chopper surrounded by violent buffets of air, and jogged up to Ben and Karin. "All good?" he shouted. "You brought the logs?"

Ben nodded, still a bit unsure how to treat his old friend. Karin started tying her hair back. "We're fully loaded, Drake. I hope you've brought some bloody good back up."

Delta soldiers crowded all around them. Drake clapped one man—a big, bearded individual with neck-tattoos and arms like a biker. "This is my new friend, call sign- Komodo, and this is his team. Team, meet my old friends, Ben and Karin Blake."

There were nods and grunts all around. Two of the soldiers got busy breaking through the token padlock that prevented folk from taking a trip down one of Hawaii's famous lava tubes. In a few minutes, they stepped back, and the gates stood open.

Drake strode into the compound. A concrete platform led up to a metal door, securely locked. A high stanchion stood to the right, at the top of which a rotating CCTV camera surveyed the area. Komodo waved the same two soldiers forward to take care of the door.

"You guys got any clue to what me and my men are about to walk into?" Komodo's gravelly voice made Ben start.

"In the words of Robert Baden-Powell," Ben said. "Be prepared."

Karin added, "For anything."

Ben said, "It's the boy scout motto."

Komodo shook his head and muttered "Geeks" under his breath.

Ben fell in behind the rough-looking soldier. "Why do they call you Komodo anyway? Is your bite poisonous?"

Drake interrupted before the Delta captain could reply. "They may call this a lava tube, but it's still a plain, old-fashioned tunnel. I won't insult you by stating the usual protocols, but I will tell you this. Watch for booby traps. The Blood King is all about big displays and separation techniques. If he can isolate us, we're dead."

Drake led the way, motioning for Ben to come next and Karin to follow Komodo. The small guardhouse held nothing but a pair of large lockers and a dusty phone. It smelled of must and dampness and resonated with a deep, primordial silence that hung in the air ahead. Drake walked forward and soon found out why.

The lava tube entrance was at their feet, a vast hole leading down into the creeping darkness.

"How far down is that?" Komodo came forward and dropped a glow stick. The device flickered and rolled for a few seconds before clunking onto solid rock. "Not far. Secure a few ropes, men. Hustle."

Whilst the soldiers worked, Drake listened as best he could. No sounds echoed up from the inky blackness. He guessed they were a few hours behind Kovalenko, but he intended to catch up quick.

Once they had descended and had planted their feet firmly on the lava tube's smooth floor, Drake got his bearings and led the way toward Diamond Head. The tube narrowed and dipped and undulated. Even the Delta team sometimes lost their footing or scraped their heads due to the unpredictability of the volcanic shaft. Twice, it turned sharply, making Drake panic until he realized the gentle curve was always in the direction of Diamond Head.

He kept his eye on the rangefinder. The subterranean dark closed in on them from all sides. "Lights forward," Drake suddenly said and stopped.

Something had rushed out of the darkness. A blast of cold air from below. He paused and studied the gargantuan hole ahead. Komodo came up and dropped another glow stick.

This time it fell for about fifteen feet.

"All right. Komodo, you and your team get set up. Ben, Karin, let's have a look at those logs."

Whilst the Delta team erected a sturdy tripod over the jagged hole, Drake swiftly read through the footnotes. His eyes widened before he had finished the first page and he let out a long breath.

"Bloody hell. I think we need bigger guns."

Ben raised an eyebrow. "It's not bullets we'll need down there. It's brains."

"Well, luckily, I have both." Drake lifted his gun. "I guess if we need to listen to some crappy music along the way, we'll turn to you."

"Balls. I have Fleetwood Mac on my iPod now."

"I'm shocked. Which version?"

"There's more than one?"

Drake shook his head. "I guess all babies have to start their education somewhere." He winked at Karin. "How we doing, Komodo?"

"All done."

Drake stepped forward, grabbed the rope attached to the

tripod, and repelled down the strangely glowing tube. Once his boots hit the bottom, he tugged and the others came sliding down one by one. Karin, a trained athlete, managed the descent with ease. Ben struggled a little, but he was fit and young and eventually landed without breaking too much of a sweat.

"Onward." Drake set off quickly in the direction of Diamond Head. "Stay alert. We're getting close."

The passageway began to slope down. Drake wondered for a moment how a lava tube might incline against the natural flow, but then realized the magma itself would shoot through the path of least resistance with hellish force behind it. The lava would take whatever angle it wished.

A few minutes more and Drake stopped again. There was another hole in the floor ahead, this time, smaller and perfectly rounded. When Komodo dropped the glow stick they guessed the shaft to be about thirty feet deep.

"More dangerous," Drake said. "Take care you two."

Then he noticed that the glow stick's light wasn't being reflected by any rock walls. Its orangey light was eaten up by the surrounding dark. Below them was a large chamber.

He signaled for quiet. As one, they all listened intently for any kind of sounds echoing up from below. After a minute of utter silence, Drake took hold of the drop-rope and swung out over the empty shaft. Quickly, he slid down its length until he emerged under the ceiling.

Still no noise. He snapped half a dozen more glow sticks and threw them into the chamber below. Gradually, the unnatural light began to bloom.

And Matt Drake finally beheld that which few men before him had ever seen. A large, rectangular room about fifty meters long. A perfectly smooth floor. Three curved walls etched with some kind of ancient markings, indistinguishable at this distance.

And dominating one wall—the curved archway that had so

fascinated Captain Cook. The doorway inside it that so obsessed the Blood King. And the terrors and wonders that might lie beyond that filled Matt Drake and his companions with so much dread.

They had found the Gates of Hell.

TWENTY-EIGHT

Hayden held on tight as the chopper banked through the sky in a rapid change of course. Her last view of Kinimaka had been of him being goosed onto another chopper by the ever-playful Alicia Myles. The sight made her wince, but the practical side of her knew that when it came to battle, Mano had some of the best back-up in the business in the form of the crazy Englishwoman.

As did Hayden. Mai sat beside her, quiet and reposed, as if they were heading over to the Napali Coast for a bit of world-class sightseeing. Crack troops filled the rest of the seats. Kauai was about twenty minutes out. Gates had just contacted her to say there had been a terrorist attack at the open-air Kukui Grove shopping center on Kauai. A man had chained himself to a railing outside the joint Jamba Juice/Starbucks unit on the north side of the complex. Someone with wads and wads of cemtex strapped to his body and a finger on the trigger of a crude detonator.

The man also toted two automatic weapons and a Bluetooth earpiece, and he wouldn't allow any of the restaurant's patrons to go free.

In Gates's own words. "The dickhead's clearly going to hold out there as long as he can, then when the authorities make their move, he'll detonate. A large part of the Kauai police force have been diverted to the scene, and away from you."

"We'll secure the ranch, sir," Hayden assured him. "We expected this."

"That we did, Miss Jaye. I guess we'll see what Kovalenko's plans are for the Big Island next."

Hayden closed her eyes. Kovelenko had been planning this assault for years, but questions remained. Why abandon the portal device? Why go out with such a bang? Could it be his Plan B? That, with all his efforts being rapidly exposed by the authorities and the instigation of his Blood Vendetta against Drake and his friends and families, he had chosen this route to gain the most notoriety.

Or, she thought, he might be using the old, old strategy— create a big enough bang over here, that your deeds might go unnoticed over there.

Never mind, she thought. Her mind was on Ben and the dangerous task he was undertaking. She would never say it on duty, but she was growing to love him dearly. The duty she felt to her father had not faded, but it had become less imperative with the terrible death of Kennedy Moore. Real life trumped old promises any day.

As the chopper swooped through the bright blue Hawaiian skies, Hayden offered up a prayer for Ben Blake.

Then her cell phone began to ring. When she glanced at the screen, her eyebrows shot up in surprise.

"Hi," she answered immediately. "How've you been?"

"Most excellent, thank you, but this tomb exploration business has one serious side-effect. My tan has almost faded away."

Hayden smiled. "Well, Torsten, there are salons for that sort of thing."

"Between the command post and the tomb? Not really."

"I'd sure love to chat, Torsten, but you Swede's do pick your moments."

"Understood. I tried Drake first but went straight to voicemail. Is he okay?"

"Better than he was, yes." Hayden saw the shape of Kauai looming off to the right. "Listen—"

"I'll be quick. The op was proceeding well here. Nothing

untoward. All as expected and in a timely manner. But..." Torsten paused and Hayden heard him draw breath. "Something happened today. I would say something feels 'off.' You American's might term it differently."

"Yes?"

"I received a call from my government. From my go-between to the Statsminister. A high-level call. I—" Another hesitant pause, most unlike Dahl.

The jagged Kauai coast swept past below them. The call came over the radio. "Eight minutes to target."

"I was told that our operation—our Scandinavian operation was about to be taken over by a new agency. A joint task force made up of high-level, but unnamed, members of the American CIA, the DIA and the NSA. Now, Hayden, I'm a soldier and I'll follow a command from my highest superior, but does that sound right to you?"

Hayden was shocked despite herself. "It sounds like bullshit to me. What's the name of the man in charge? The one you will hand over to."

"Russell Cayman. Do you know him?"

Hayden searched her memory. "I know the name, but I know very little about him. I'm sure he's DIA, Defense Intelligence Agency, but they mainly look after weapon systems acquisition. What on earth would this Russell Cayman want from you and the Tomb?"

"You read my mind."

From the corner of her eye, Hayden saw Mai's head snap around as if she'd been shot through the skull. But when Hayden turned questioningly toward her the Japanese agent looked away.

Hayden thought for a few seconds and then asked in a quiet voice, "Do you trust all your men, Torsten?"

Dahl's overlong pause answered her question.

"If the DIA have been tipped off about something, then they have a very long reach. Their priority might even exceed the CIA's. Tread softly, buddy. This guy, Cayman, he's nothing short of a ghost. A troubleshooter for black ops, Gitmo, 9/11. If something huge and sensitive goes wrong, he's the sort of man you turn to."

"Fuck me. I wish I hadn't asked."

"I have to go now, Torsten. But I promise you I'll speak to Jonathan about this bullshit as soon as I can. Hang in there."

Torsten signed off with the world-weary sigh of a professional soldier who had already seen it all and was loathe to be assigned as some lackey to an American upstart. Hayden felt for him. She turned to Mai, about to ask what she knew.

But the call came over the radio, *"Target."*

Ahead and below the fields were burning. As the chopper swept lower, tiny figures could be seen running haphazardly in every direction. Ropes deployed from the cabin and men leapt for them, slithering quickly to the blasted landscape below. Hayden and Mai awaited their turn, Mai's expression blank, as they heard their own men open fire.

Hayden checked the readiness of her Glock for the third time and said, "Boudreau's down there."

"Don't worry," the Japanese woman said. "He's about to find out what Mai-time really means."

The two women rappelled together, landing at the same time, and moving off in a classic one-two cover advance. This practice required absolute trust in each other as, whilst one person ran, the second person watched their peripherals. One, two, like a leapfrog formation. But it was a fast and devastating way to advance.

Hayden surveyed the area as she ran. Some rolling hills ended at a gated and fenced compound wherein stood a vast house and several big outbuildings. That would be Kovalenko's second ranch. Judging by the fire and chaos, Boudreau hadn't arrived too long before them.

Or, more likely, he had been taking his sadistic time about the whole thing.

Hayden ran, firing with her loaned marine-issue M16 assault rifle at muzzle flashes and men she saw in concealment. Two minutes and her turn was up and she shouted, "Reload!" and took an extra few seconds to slam a new mag into her weapon. Fire was rarely returned at them, and when it was, it was so disorganized that it missed them by several feet.

To either side, the crack marine teams were advancing at a similar rate. The fence loomed ahead now, the gates left invitingly open, but the teams drifted to the left. A well-thrown grenade made the fence supports collapse, leaving the team a clear run into the ranch.

Bullets now whizzed dangerously close.

Hayden took cover behind a generator outhouse. Impact sparks fizzed off the brickwork as Mai dived for cover. Clay and metal shards splintered everywhere.

Mai wiped a line of blood from her cheek. "Boudreau's soldiers were trained at your Kindergartens."

Hayden breathed for a moment, then took a quick glance at the house. "Twelve feet. You ready?"

"Yes."

Hayden ran. Mai stepped out and laid down a wall of lead, making their enemy duck for cover. Hayden reached the corner of the house and flattened herself against the wall. She threw a stun grenade through a window and then covered Mai.

But at that moment, a stunning amount of chatter burst through her earpiece. The team leader was urging men to make for the far warehouse. Something terrible was about to happen there. As Hayden listened, she managed to glean that Boudreau's men had half-circled the building and were about to open fire at whatever might be within.

Captives no doubt. Hostages.

Hayden raced behind Mai, running out into the clearing and firing together. Other soldiers joined them, fanning out to either side, forming a deadly, charging wall of courage and death.

The senseless slaughter about to be committed was the trademark of Boudreau. He would be there.

The running soldiers never stopped firing. Bullets laced the air, pinged and zipped off walls and machinery, and found at least a half-dozen enemy targets. Boudreau's men recoiled and squirmed away in shock and fear. As the soldiers passed their hiding places, they tried to sneak gutless shots off from the side, but the marines were ready and tossed grenades at them.

Explosions shot high into the air to either side of the runners. Shrapnel fizzed away from the blasts; tongues of fire spread hot death so rapidly the eye could barely follow. Screaming men lie in their wake.

Hayden saw the barn ahead. Her heart clenched in utter horror. It was true. At least fifteen of Boudreau's men were stood around a locked barn, aiming their weapons at the paper thin walls and, as Hayden lined the first man up in her sights, they all opened fire.

*****

Alicia Myles hit the ground running and firing as the Hawaiian forces and their allies launched their attack on Kovalenko's Big Island ranch. The terrain was rough. All deep canyons, high hills and forested flats. Before they had even gotten near the ranch, an RPG had been launched at one of the attack choppers, catching it but not destroying it, forcing them all to make an early landing.

Now they hurried on as a team, negotiating the dense forestation and the rugged hillsides. Already, they had lost one man to a booby trap. The advance had been prepped by the Blood King's men. RPG's rocketed through the trees aimlessly.

Mercenaries having fun.

But the marines were gaining ground, only about thirty feet and one final steep-sided valley away from the fence now. Alicia could make out the grinning faces of their enemy. Her blood began to boil. At her side, the big CIA agent, Kinimaka, loped along quite nimbly for a giant. He was turning out to be quite an asset.

The communication devices in their ears kept the news of atrocities coming. The hotel on Oahu, the Ala Moana Queen, had been sealed off. A tourist had been thrown to his death from a tenth floor window. Grenades had been hurled out into the street. A SWAT team was being readied for an operation that was likely to be quickly green-lit on account of the death and mayhem the mercenaries were causing. On Kauai, the lone suicide bomber had let loose a few rounds at gathering news vans, winging a reporter. And now, on the Big Island, a coach load of tourists had been abducted and their coach fitted with a bomb. They had been locked inside whilst their captives sat around outside in deck-chairs, drinking beer and playing cards. It wasn't known which one of them had the detonator, or how many there were.

Alicia leapt down the side of the valley. An RPG exploded in front of her, raining dirt and rock high into the air. She jumped through it, laughing, and turned when she sensed Kinimaka's hesitancy.

"C'mon, tubby," she said with a playful curl of her mouth. "Stick with me. This is where things really get dirty."

*****

Hayden fired again and again, trying to stay calm and thus maintain her accuracy. Three heads exploded in her sights. Mai still ran beside her, saying nothing. Other soldiers dropped to one knee, squeezing off shots and felling the mercenaries before they could spin around.

Then Hayden was among them. One man turned and she smashed her rifle across the bridge of his nose. He went down with a scream, but kicked her legs, sending her tumbling headlong over him.

David Leadbeater

She quickly scrambled up, but his bulk was on top of her, bearing her down. When she looked up, she stared straight into his hate-filled, pain-soaked eyes. With a bear-like growl he punched her and clamped thick hands around her throat.

Instantly she saw stars, but she didn't try to stop him. Instead, her two free hands found weapons of their own. In the right, her Glock. In the left, her knife. She shoved the barrel of the gun into his ribs, letting him feel it.

His grip relaxed, eyes going wide.

Hayden fired three dull shots. The man rolled off her. As the view above her cleared, another mercenary's face came into view. Hayden shot at the nose, saw the man fly back and vanish.

She sat up and saw Mai. The last remaining mercenary facing her. Hayden blinked. The man was a ruin. His face looked like it had been painted red. Teeth were missing. His jaw looked out of line. One arm had been dislocated, the other broken at the elbow. He stood on shaking legs and then collapsed to his knees in the bloody dirt.

"You picked the wrong person to challenge," Mai said with a sweet smile, aimed her borrowed Glock, and blew his head off.

Hayden gulped despite herself. That was some serious piece of woman.

The barn door was being opened by marines shouting out their presence. Hayden's heart sank at the amount of puncture holes in the fabricated walls. Hopefully, the hostages had taken cover.

Amidst her rapidly clearing thoughts something became apparent above all else. Boudreau wasn't here. She looked back at the house. It was the last place she would expect him to hide, but still—

A sudden commotion caught her attention. Marines were stumbling back out of the barn, one holding his shoulder as if he'd been stabbed.

Then Boudreau and a horde of mercenaries poured out of the barn, guns firing, screaming like demons. Did that mean the other mercenaries had given their lives to be decoys? Had they been firing blanks or at a designated position? Reality hit her like a nuclear payload. The Blood King's men were among the marines now, fighting, and Boudreau was pounding toward Hayden, knife raised in challenge.

*****

Alicia spurred the team on with her ingenuity and spirit under fire. Within minutes, they had reached the top of the final rise and were laying down a halo of fire at the entrenched defenders. Alicia spied a big house, a big barn and a double garage. The property backed onto a wide river, no doubt a means of escape, and a helipad stood near the barn, complete with one shabby-looking chopper.

She glanced behind her. "Grenade launchers."

The team leader frowned. "Already on it."

Alicia pointed to enemy positions. "The low wall there. The backside of the house. Behind the Rolls. To the right of the fountain."

The team leader licked his lips. "Flush the bastards out."

Multiple explosions made the ground shake. The attackers fired three rounds of grenades and then rushed forward in one-two formation, still firing as a unit but fanning out in a deadly arc.

With a devastating severity, they stormed the Blood King's ranch.

TWENTY-NINE

Drake's booted feet touched the floor of the chamber. Before the others started to descend, he set of a luminescent flare to brighten their way. Immediately, the walls came to life, their etchings now standing out starkly to Drake's shocked eyes.

Whorls, like the ones on the two portable devices. Now confirmed as being exactly the same as the ones Torsten Dahl and his team had discovered in the Tomb of the Gods back in Iceland.

What manner of ancient civilization had they stumbled onto lately? And where would it all end?

Ben and Karin and the rest of the Delta team repelled down the drop rope until they all crowded around the huge archway of the Gates of Pele. Drake tried hard not to look too deeply into the inky blackness beyond.

Ben and Karin fell to their knees. The actual arch itself consisted of some kind of dull metal, perfectly smooth and symmetrical. Upon the surface of the metal were etched the same tiny markings as the rest of the cave.

"These markings"—Karin touched them carefully—"are not random. Look. I see the same whorl repeated time after time. And the rest of the cave…" She glanced around. "Is the same."

Ben fumbled out his phone. "This is the pic that Dahl sent us." He held it up to the light. Drake leaned forward, confident that the Delta team would be alert for intruders.

"So the Tomb of the Gods has some link to the Gates of Hell," Drake thought aloud. "But what do the whorls mean?"

"Repeated patterns," Karin said quietly. "Tell me. What kind of markings, ancient or

Modern, consists of many repeated patterns?"

"Easy." The big Komodo hunkered down next to them. "A language."

"That's right. So if this is a language—" She indicated the chamber walls. "Then they tell quite a story."

"As do the ones Dahl found." Drake nodded. "But we don't have time to analyze it now. Kovalenko's through that gateway."

"Wait." Ben gripped the bridge of his nose. "These markings..." He touched the archway. "Are *exactly* the same as the ones on the devices. To me, that says this gateway is a fixed version of the same contraption. A time travel machine. We've already concluded that the gods may have used the portable devices to flit through time and influence fate. Maybe this thing is the master system."

"Listen," Drake said quietly, "that's fine. You'll figure it out. But beyond that gate—" He jabbed a finger into the pitch black. "Is the Blood King. The man responsible for Kennedy's death, among hundreds of others. It's time to stop talking and start walking. Let's go."

Ben nodded and stood up, looking a bit guilty as he brushed himself off. Everyone in the chamber drew a deep breath. There was something else beyond the gate that none of them wanted to mention:

The reason Captain Cook had changed the archway's name from the Gates of Pele to the Gates of Hell.

THIRTY

The state of Hawaii shuddered in the grip of a madman.

If a helicopter could sweep by, one capable of offering a wide, panoramic view of the dark, immoral events that were unfolding across the islands, it would swoop first across Oahu to take in the besieged hotel, the Ala Moana Queen, where expert members of several SWAT teams had just started to move against a well-armed, well-motivated force of mercenaries who held all the high ground and countless hostages. It would zoom past at pace, avoiding the hellish clouds of black smoke that poured from at least a dozen shattered windows, warily pinpointing the openings where masked men with rifles and grenade launchers could be seen herding helpless men, women and children into groups that would be easier to slaughter.

And then it would roll away, up and to the right in a great arc, at first toward the sun, that fat yellow ball inching its way toward an uncertain and possibly disastrous future, and then dipping beneath and to the left on its terrible journey of discovery toward Kauai. It would pass near Diamond Head, oblivious of the heroes and villains searching for secrets and chasing terrible dreams through the extinct volcano's darkest and most dangerous subterranean caverns.

On Kauai, it would plunge toward the sweat-drenched man who had chained himself to the railings of a coffee shop, sealing its patrons inside and clearly showing off a vest packed with dynamite and the shaking hand that clutched a dead-man's detonating device. If the picture panned in close, it would see the desperation in the man's eyes. It would clearly reveal the fact that he couldn't possibly hold out much longer. And then it would soar high, rising again over the rooftops to follow the graceful curve of the exotic coast. On to the burning ranch where Hayden Jaye had just faced off with Ed Boudreau whilst Mai Kitano and the rest of the marines fought in close hand-to-hand combat with dozens of Boudreau's mercenaries. Amidst the appalling din of death and battle, the injured hostages wept.

And onward. The past and the future were already colliding. The ancient and avant-garde locked in conflict.

Today was a day gods might die, and new heroes might flourish and rise.

The helicopter would make one last fly-by, tearing across the contrasting landscapes and dynamic ecosystems that made up the Big Island. Racing over one more ranch, it would focus for a few moments as Alicia Myles, Mano Kinimaka and their team of marines stormed a well-defended compound where hostages and mercenaries and men wearing necklaces made of dynamite came together in one almighty clash. Around the edges of the battle, powerful vehicles revved and made ready to evacuate the Blood King's men by land and air and water. The camera would start to zoom away as Alicia and Kinimaka lifted their heads, aware of the absconders and already making tracks to intercept and eradicate them.

And at last the helicopter would veer away, just a machine but still a machine teeming with images of man's folly, of the courage they can display and discover, and of the worst evil that they can do.

THIRTY-ONE

Drake stepped beneath the archway Captain Cook had christened the Gates of Hell to find himself in a rough-hewn, narrow passageway. He switched on a rifle light and attached it to the barrel. He also strapped on a shoulder light and adjusted it so that it illuminated the walls. For a while there was a plethora of light and no obvious peril.

As they traversed the winding passage, Drake spoke over his shoulder. "Tell me, Ben, about Cook's logs."

Ben exhaled quickly. "It's nothing more than an overview of this huge trap system. Cook called it the Gates of Hell because of the nature of the traps. He didn't even see what's at the end."

"So who built the traps?" Drake asked. "And why?"

"Nobody knows. The markings we found outside and the ones from the Tomb of the Gods aren't on these interior walls." He coughed and added, "Yet."

Komodo's voice boomed from behind them. "Why did Cook not see the end?"

"He ran," Karin said quietly. "In fear."

"Oh, crap."

Drake paused for a moment. "So, since I'm just a dumb soldier and you two are the brains of this op, let me get this straight. Essentially, the logs are the key to the trap system. And you two have copies with you."

"We have one copy," Ben said. "Karin's got the other in her head."

"Then we have one copy," Komodo grumbled.

"No—" Ben began, but Drake stopped him. "He means that

if she dies we have one copy, kiddo. A photographic memory ain't much use when you're dead."

"I didn't. . . yes, well, sorry we don't think like soldiers."

Drake noticed the tunnel start to widen. The faintest of breezes wafted past his face. He held up a hand to slow them down and then poked his head around a corner.

To behold a stunning sight.

He was at the entrance to an enormous chamber, oblong in shape and with a ceiling lost in darkness. The faint light emanated from glow sticks that the Blood King's men must have left behind. Directly opposite him and guarding the tunnel that continued into the depths of the mountain was a sight that made his heart pound.

Carved into the very rock face above the tunnel was a giant face. With slanted eyes and hooked nose and what could only be described as horns sprouting from its head, Drake's immediate conclusion was that this was the face of the Devil, or a demon.

Ignoring the face for now, he scouted the area. The walls were curved, their bases shrouded in darkness. They needed to get some extra light in here.

He beckoned the others slowly forward.

And then, suddenly, a noise blasted through the cavern, a noise like a hundred flamethrowers firing at once or, as Ben put it, *'sounds like the bloody Batmobile.'*

Fire shot down through the carving's nostrils, creating a furnace around the rock floor. Two separate licks of flame blazed from each nostril, and then a few seconds later one blast from each eye.

Drake studied it uneasily. "Maybe we set off some kind of mechanism. A pressure sensitive trip switch or something." He turned to Ben. "Hope you're ready, mate, cos as one of my favorite Dinorock bands, Poison, used to say—this ain't *nothin' but a good time.*"

Ben's mouth twitched into a brief smile as he consulted his

notes. "This is level one of hell. According to the writer, a man called Hawksworth, they named this level Wrath. I guess the reason's obvious. They later cross-referenced it to the devil, Amon, the demon of wrath."

"Thanks for the lesson, kid." Komodo growled. "Does it happen to mention a way past?"

Ben laid the text on the floor and spread it out. "Look. I saw this before but didn't understand it. Maybe it's a clue."

Drake squatted next to his young friend. The copied logs were elaborately penned and illustrated, but Ben's finger drew his eye toward to an odd line of text.

1(||)—MOVE TO 2(||||)—
MOVE TO 3 (||)—MOVE TO 4(|||||)

And the single inscription that followed it, "With Wrath, have patience. A careful man will plan his route if the lines of navigation lie before him."

"Cook was the greatest navigator of all time," Ben said. "That line tells us two things. That Cook navigated the route past the demon and that the way through needs careful planning."

Karin was watching the bursts of fire. "I count four," she said speculatively. "Four eruptions of flame. The same total as—"

A shot rang out, shocking through the stillness. A bullet ricocheted off the wall by Drake's head, making sharp fragments of rock fracture the air. In a millisecond Drake had his gun up and fired a shot off, and in another millisecond he understood that if he ducked back into the passageway, the sniper might keep them pinned down indefinitely.

With that in mind he ran, firing, into the chamber. Komodo, clearly having come to the same conclusion, followed him. The joint fire struck sparks off the surrounding wall. The hidden man ducked in shock, but still managed to fire another bullet which sizzled between Drake and Komodo.

Drake fell to one knee, aiming.

The man jumped out of his hiding place, weapon high, but Komodo fired first—a blast that sent their assailant flying backward. There was a high scream and the man landed in a tangle, rifle clattering to the floor. Komodo walked over and made sure the man was dead.

Drake cursed. "As I thought, Kovalenko left snipers to slow us down."

"And to thin us out," Komodo added.

Karin poked her head back around the corner, blond hair falling around her eyes. "If I'm right, the odd sentence is the keyhole and the word 'patience' is the key. Those two tram lines that look like two 'I's'? In music and poetry and old literature they can signify a pause. Therefore—patience means to 'pause.'"

Drake looked at the sentence as the Delta team fanned out around the cavern, urged by Komodo and determined not to make any more mistakes.

Komodo shouted, "And men? Watch out for booby traps. I wouldn't put it past that Russian prick to jury-rig something."

Drake rubbed his sweaty palm against a rough wall, feeling the uneven stone as cold as the inside of a fridge beneath his hand. "So it's, 'wait for the first blast, then pause two and move to two. After the second blast, pause four and move to three. After the third blast, pause two and move to four. And after for the fourth blast, pause six and then out.'"

"Easy." Ben winked. "But how long's a pause?"

Karin shrugged. "A brief spell."

"Oh, that's helpful, sis."

"And how do you number the blasts?"

"My guess is the one that reaches farthest first is number one, with number four the shortest."

"Well, that makes some sense, I suppose. But it's still a—"

"That's it." Drake had had enough. "My *patience* has been tested already listening to this debate. I'll go first. Let's do this before my caffeine high runs out."

He walked past Komodo's crew, coming to a stop a few yards short of the reach of the longest tongue of fire. He sensed each man turn to watch. He sensed Ben's anxiety. He closed his eyes, feeling the temperature rise as another superheated discharge roasted the air before him.

Kennedy's face swam before his inner eye. He saw her as she used to be. The severe bob in her hair, the featureless pantsuits—one for every day of the week. The conscious effort to detract everything away from the fact that she was female.

And then Kennedy let her hair down, and he remembered the woman he had spent two glorious months with. The woman who had started to help him move on from the crushing death of his wife, Alyson, and the pain caused by that fateful car crash so many years ago.

Her eyes flared right through his heart.

Before him, the fire burned.

He waited for the heat of the blaze to wane and paused for two seconds. As he waited, he was conscious of the burst of fire from the second eye already flashing down. But after two seconds he moved to that point, though every fiber of his being screamed that he shouldn't.

The fire blasted him—

But died away the instant he finished his movement. The air around him was still hot, but bearable. Drake breathed, sweat pouring off him in waves. Unable to relax for a second, he began the count again.

Four seconds.

Flames crackled near him, trying to ignite the very spot he was about to occupy.

Drake made his move. The fire died away. The inside of his mouth felt like a salt-flat. Both his eyeballs stung as if they'd been scraped with sandpaper.

Counting, though. Thinking, always thinking. Two more seconds and move. On to the final maneuver. The confidence built in him now.

Pause six seconds, and then—

At six he moved, and the fire didn't relent! His eyebrows singed. He fell to his knees, threw his body back. Ben shouted his name. The heat grew so intense he tried to scream. But at that moment it abruptly faded away. He slowly became aware of his hands and knees scraping the rough stone floor. Lifting his head, he quickly crawled through the tunnel at the rear of the chamber.

After a moment, he turned and shouted to the others, "Best make that last pause seven seconds, guys. 'less you wanna find out what a Kentucky Fried feels like."

There was a bit of subdued laughter. Komodo immediately stepped up and asked both Karin and Ben when they would like to take their turn. Ben opted for a few more soldiers to go before him, but Karin was up for following Drake. It took Komodo himself taking her aside and having a quiet word about the prudence of ensuring Drake hadn't just gotten lucky with the timings before they risked losing one of the brains of their op.

Drake saw Karin relent and even smile a little. It was good to see someone having a calming effect on the wild-child of the Blake family. He checked the tunnel around him and threw a glow stick into the shadows. Its expanding amber hue illuminated nothing but more hewn-out tunnel vanishing into the blackness.

The first Delta soldier fell in beside him, soon to be followed by a second. Drake wasted no time in sending them down the tunnel on a scouting mission. When he turned back to the chamber of wrath, he saw Ben Blake making his move.

Ben clutched his satchel almost like a schoolboy, made sure his long hair was tucked into the top of his T-shirt, and stepped forward. Drake watched his lips move as he counted the seconds off. Without betraying any outward signs of emotion, Drake's heart literally leapt into his mouth and stayed there until his friend collapsed puffing by his feet.

Drake offered him a hand. Ben looked up, "What you

gonna say, dickhead? *If you can't stand the heat?*"

"I don't quote Bucks Fizz," Drake said in an exasperated tone. "If you want—no, wait—"

Drake had caught sight of Karin approaching the first jet of fire. Ben's mouth instantly clamped shut and his eyes followed his sisters every move. When she wobbled, Ben's teeth grated so hard Drake thought about tectonic plates grinding together. And when she slipped between one safe haven and the next Drake had to grab Ben hard to stop him rushing out to grab her.

"Wait! You can't save her."

Karin faltered. Her fall had completely disoriented her. She was staring the wrong way with about two seconds before another eruption incinerated her.

Ben fought against Drake, who grabbed the lad roughly by the back of the head and used his body to shield his friend from witnessing the next, terrible event.

Karin closed her eyes.

Then Komodo, the Delta team leader, scooped her up in one big arm as he skipped deftly between the pauses. He never missed a beat, just carried Karin headfirst over his shoulder and deposited her gently to the ground beside her enraged brother.

Ben dropped down beside her, babbling, hugging her to him. Karin stared over Ben's shoulder straight at Komodo and mouthed two words. "Thank you."

Komodo nodded gruffly. Within a few minutes, the rest of his men arrived safely and the two Drake had dispatched down the tunnel returned.

One of them addressed both Drake and Komodo. "Another trap, sir, about a klick ahead. No obvious signs of snipers or booby traps, but we didn't hang around to double-check. Figured we should get back here."

Karin brushed herself off and stood up. "What's the trap look like?"

"Miss, it looks like one major motherfucker."

THIRTY-TWO

Up the narrow passage they ran, urged on by the acts of violence that may be happening in the world above them and by the malicious intentions of the man who crept through the subterranean dark before them.

A roughly formed archway admitted them to the next cavern. Again glow sticks illuminated part of the huge space, both fresh and slowly fading, but Drake quickly fired two amber flares against the far wall.

The space before them was stunning. The walkways were shaped like a trident. The main shaft was made up of a walkway wide enough to accommodate three men abreast. It finished at the far wall in another exit archway. Branching off the main shaft and making up the other two tines of the trident were two more walkways, only these ones were much narrower, little more than ledges. These ledges ended up against the broad curve of the cavern wall.

The spaces between the paths of the trident crawled with deep, treacherous darkness. When Komodo dropped a stone into the nearest absence of light, they never heard it strike bottom.

Carefully, they inched their way forward. Tension made their shoulders go rigid and their nerves begin to fray. Drake felt a thin sliver of sweat slide the length of his spine, itching all the way down. Every set of eyes in the company flicked around and searched every shadow, every nook and cranny, until Ben finally found his voice.

"Wait," he said faintly, then cleared his throat and shouted, "Wait."

"What is it?" Drake froze with a foot still in the air.

"We should check Cook's logs first, just in case."

"You pick your bloody times."

Karin spoke up. "They called this one Greed, the second deadly sin. The demon associated with greed is Mammon, one of the seven princes of hell. He was referred to in Milton's *Paradise Lost,* and has even been called Hell's Ambassador to England."

Drake stared at her. "That's not funny."

"It's not meant to be. It's something I once read and retained. The only clue Hawksworth gives here is the sentence: *Opposite Greed sits Charity. Let the next man have what you desire.*"

Drake considered the cold, damp cavern. "There's not much I desire in here, 'cept a Krispy Kremes maybe."

"It's a straight run to the exit." Komodo stopped one of his men from pushing by. "Nothing's ever that easy. Hey! What the fuck, man—"

Drake turned to see the Delta man push Komodo aside and walk right past his commanding officer.

"Wallis! Get your ass in line, soldier."

Drake noticed the man's eyes as he approached. Glazed. Fixed on a point off to the right. Drake followed his gaze.

And saw the niches immediately. Funny how he hadn't noticed them before. At the end of the right-hand tine, where it ended against the cavern wall, Drake now saw three deep niches had been carved into the black rock. Inside each niche something sparkled. Something precious made of gold and sapphires and emeralds. The object caught the weak and diffused light that flickered about the cavern and returned it tenfold. It was like staring into the heart of a shiny disco-ball made of ten-carat diamonds.

Karin whispered, "There's an empty one on the other side."

Drake felt the pull of the promised wealth. The harder he looked, the clearer the objects became and the more he wanted them. It took a moment for Karin's comment to sink in, but when it did, he beheld the empty niche with both jealousy and trepidation. Had some fortunate soul dared the ledge and walked away with a prize? Or had he been clutching it when he plunged screaming into the incalculable depths below?

One way to find out.

Drake put one foot in front of the other and then stopped himself. *Damn.* The lure across the ledges was strong. But his pursuit of Kovalenko held a stronger attraction. He snapped back to reality, wondering how a set of lights could be so mesmerizing. At that moment, Komodo jogged past him and Drake reached out to stop him.

But the Delta team commander just fell on his own colleague and wrestled him to the ground. Drake turned to see the rest of the team on their knees, rubbing their eyes or generally avoiding the enticements. Ben and Karin stood spellbound, but Karin's quick brain soon wrenched itself free.

She turned quickly to her brother. "You okay? Ben?"

Drake considered the young lad's eyes. "We could be in trouble. It's the same glazed look he gets when Taylor Momsen walks on stage."

Karin shook her head. "Boys," she muttered and slapped her brother hard.

Ben blinked and brought a hand up to his cheek. "Ow!"

"Are you okay?"

"No I'm bloody not! You just nearly broke my jaw."

"Stop being a pussy. Tell Mum and Dad next time they call."

"Too damn right I will. Why the hell did you hit me anyway?"

Drake shook his shoulder as Komodo lifted his man bodily off the floor and hurled him back into line. *"Rookie."*

Karin watched admiringly.

Drake said, "Don't you remember? The pretty lights? They almost had you, mate."

"I remember..." Ben's eyes suddenly snapped back to the rock wall and its cunning niches. "Oh, wow, what a rush. Gold and diamonds and riches. I remember that."

Drake saw the sparkling objects begin to reassert their pull. "Let's move," he said. "Double time. I see what this cave does, and the faster we get through it, the better."

He moved off at pace, keeping an arm around Ben's shoulder and nodding at Karin. Komodo followed soundlessly, watching his men closely as they passed close by the ledges that stretched out to either side.

As they passed closer to the niches, Drake risked a quick look. A small chalice-shaped object stood in each niche, its surface encrusted with precious stones. But that alone wasn't enough to make the spectacular light show that so drew the eye. Behind each chalice the rough walls of the niches themselves had been lined with row upon row of rubies, emeralds, sapphires, diamonds and countless other gemstones and jewels.

The chalices might be worth a fortune, but the niches themselves were of inestimable value.

Drake paused as he neared the exit archway. Cold breezes tugged at him from left and right. The whole place reeked of ancient mystery and hidden secrets. Water trickled somewhere, just a small stream, but enough to augment the immensity of the cavern system they were exploring.

Drake gave everyone the once over. The trap had been overcome. He turned to walk through the exit archway.

And a voice yelled, "Stop!"

Instantly, he froze. His faith in the shout and his instinct born of old SAS training saved his life. His right foot barely touched the thin wire, but any more pressure would release the booby trap.

This time Kovalenko hadn't left a sniper. He'd judged correctly that the group behind him would be hauling ass through the chamber of Greed. The trip wire led to a concealed M18 Claymore Mine, the one that bore the famous legend *Front Toward Enemy.*

The front was aimed toward Drake and would've blasted him apart with steel ball bearings along with Ben and Karin if Komodo hadn't shouted the warning.

Drake dropped and quickly disarmed the device. He passed it along to Komodo. "Many thanks, mate. Keep it handy and we'll shove it up Kovalenko's arse later."

THIRTY-THREE

The next passage was short and descended rapidly downhill. Drake and the others had to walk on their heels with their bodies' angled backward to stay upright. At any moment, Drake thought he might slip and slide helplessly down to God only knew what dreadful fate waited below.

But in only a few minutes, they spied the now-familiar archway. Drake readied a glow stick and paused at the entrance. Mindful of snipers, he quickly ducked his head in and out.

"Oh, balls," he breathed to himself. "It gets worse."

"Don't tell me," Ben said. "There's a giant concrete ball poised over our heads."

Drake stared at him. "Life's not a movie, Blakey. God, you're a geek."

He took a deep breath and led them into the third gargantuan cavern. The awesome site they beheld stopped every one of them in their tracks. Mouths fell open. *If the Blood King could have chosen any point in their journey so far to lay a trap, this was it,* Drake thought a few minutes later, *the perfect chance.* But, luckily for the good guys, nothing lie in wait. Maybe there was a good reason for that. . .

Even Komodo gawped in awe and disbelief, but he did manage to croak out a few words. "I guess this one's *lust* then."

Coughs and grunts were his only response.

The path before them ran in a single straight line to the exit archway. The hindrance was the path was lined on both sides

176

by short pedestals topped with statues, and by high pedestals topped with paintings. Every statue and every painting presented several erotic forms, ranging from the surprisingly tasteful to the downright obscene. Beyond that, cave-drawings filled every available inch of the cavern walls, but not the primitive depictions normally found in ancient caves—these were stunning representations, easily the equal of any renaissance or modern-day artist.

The subject matter was shocking in another way. The images portrayed one mass orgy, every man and woman drawn in excruciating detail, committing every lustful sin known to man… and many more.

All in all, it was a stunning blow to the senses, a blow that didn't let up as more and more dramatic pictures unfolded to strike the human eye and mind.

Drake almost shed a crocodile tear for his old pal Wells. That old perv would be in his element down here. Especially if he'd discovered it with Mai.

The thought of Mai, his oldest living friend, helped divert his mind from the pornographic sensory overload all around. He glanced back at the group.

"Guys. *Guys!* This can't be everything. There has to be some kind of trap system here. Keep your eyes peeled." He coughed. "And I mean for traps."

The path ran on ahead. Drake now noticed that even staring at the ground wouldn't help you. Exquisitely detailed figures writhed there too. But it was all surely a diversion.

Drake took a deep breath and stepped forward. He noticed that, to either side of the pathway, a four-inch raised edging ran for about a hundred yards.

Komodo spoke up at the same time. "See that, Drake? Could be nothing."

"Or everything." Drake placed one foot gingerly in front of the other. Ben followed a step behind, then a couple of soldiers and then Karin, watched carefully by Komodo. Drake heard the big, tough Komodo whisper a quiet apology to Karin for the insolent images and the rudeness of his gawping men, and stifled a smile.

At that moment, as his lead foot touched the ground at the start of the raised edgings, the air filled with a deep, rumbling sound. Immediately before him, the floor began to move.

"Ay up." His broad Yorkshire came out in times of stress. "Wait, folks."

The path was divided into a series of wide, horizontal stone shelves. Slowly, each shelf began to move sideways so that anyone standing on it would fall off if they didn't step onto the next. The sequence was quite slow, but Drake guessed they had now found the reason for the chambers audacious distractions.

"Step carefully," he said. "In pairs. And keep your minds off the filth and on the way ahead, 'less you wanna try that new sport 'abyss-diving.'"

Ben joined him on the first moving shelf. "It's so hard to concentrate," he moaned.

"Think of Hayden," Drake told him. "That'll get you through."

"I *am* thinking of Hayden." Ben blinked at the nearest statue, a writhing threesome of tangled heads, arms and legs. "That's the problem."

"With me." Drake stepped warily onto the second sliding shelf, already gauging the movement of the third and fourth. "You know, I'm so glad I spent all those hours playing Tomb Raider after all."

"Never thought *I'd* end up being the sprite in the game though," Ben muttered back and then thought of Mai. Most of the Japanese intelligence community likened her to a character in a video game. "Hey, Matt, ya' don't think we're really asleep, do ya? And this is all a dream?"

Drake watched his friend tread carefully onto the third shelf. "I never had a dream this vivid." He didn't need to nod at their surroundings to make his point.

Now, behind them, a second and third group of men had started their painstaking journey. Drake counted twenty shelves before he reached the end and jumped off, thankfully, onto solid ground. Thank God, his pounding heart could take a breather. He watched the exit archway for a minute then, satisfied they were alone, he turned back to check the others' progress.

Just in time to see one of the Delta men wrench his gaze away from the gaudily painted ceiling—

And miss the shelf he was about to step on to. He was gone in a split second, the only reminder that he'd ever been there was the terrified shriek that followed his fall.

The entire company stopped and the air trembled with shock and fear. Komodo gave them all a moment and then urged them on. They all knew how to survive this. The fallen soldier had been a fool to himself.

Again, and more warily now, they all started to move. Drake fancied for a moment that he could still hear the soldiers scream, falling forever into that limitless chasm, but shrugged it away as hallucination. He focused on the men once more just in time to see the big Komodo take the same fall.

There was one desperate moment of flailing, one angry, regretful cry about his terrible lapse of concentration and the big Delta team leader slipped over the edge of the shelf. Drake cried out, almost ready to leap to his aid but woefully sure he couldn't possibly make it in time. Ben screamed like a girl—

But this was because Karin simply dived after the big man!

Without hesitation, Karin Blake left all the highly-trained Delta team staring in her wake and leapt headlong at Komodo. She had been in front of him, so her momentum should help push him back onto the concrete slab. But Komodo was a big man, and heavy, and Karin's point-blank leap barely moved his bulk.

But she *did* move him slightly. And that was enough to help. Komodo managed to turn, as Karin gave him an extra two seconds of air-time, and clamp hold of the edge of the concrete with vice-like fingers. He clung, desperate, unable to haul himself up.

And the sliding shelf moved agonizingly slow toward its left-hand perimeter, at which point it would disappear, taking the Delta team leader with it.

Karin took firm hold of Komodo's left wrist. At last, the other members of his team responded and grabbed his other arm. With a huge effort, they hauled him up and over the slab just as it disappeared into its hidden runner.

Komodo shook his head into the dusty concrete. "Karin," he said. "I will never look at another woman again."

The blond ex-student dropout genius grinned. "You guys with your straying eyes, you will never learn."

And cutting through Drake's admiration came the realization that this third level of 'hell,' this chamber called *lust*, was nothing more than a depiction of man's age-old affliction with the wandering eye. The cliché that if a man was sitting in a café with his wife or girlfriend, and another pair of pretty legs walked by—he would almost certainly look.

Except down here, if he looked he died.

Some women would have no problem with that, Drake mused. And not unreasonably, either. But Karin had saved Komodo and now the pair were even. It took another five minutes of anxious waiting, but at last the remainder of the team made it across the sliding shelves.

They all took a breather. Every man in the company made a point of shaking Karin's hand and commending her bravery. Even Ben.

Then a shot rang out. One of the Delta soldiers fell to his knees, clutching his stomach. All of a sudden, they were under attack. Half a dozen of the Blood King's men poured out of the archway, guns blazing. Bullets fizzed through the air.

Already on their knees, Drake and his team hit the deck, reaching for weapons. The man who had been hit stayed kneeling and took another four rounds to the chest and head. In less than two seconds he was dead, another victim to the Blood King's cause.

Drake dragged his loaned M16 assault rifle up and fired. To his right one of the statues was riddled with lead, alabaster chips sent zipping through the air. Drake ducked.

Another bullet whistled past his head.

The entire team was prone, calm, and able to take careful aim with their rifles balanced on the ground. When they opened fire it was a massacre, dozens of bullets riddling Kovalenko's running men and making them dance like bloodied marionettes. One man bulldozed his way through, miraculously unharmed, until he met Matt Drake.

The ex-SAS man leapt to meet him head-on, leading with a devastating head-butt and a quick series of knife-strikes to the ribs. The last of Kovalenko's men slipped into that place all evil men ended up.

Hell.

Drake motioned them on, sparing a regretful look for the fallen Delta team member. They would collect his body on the way back.

"We must be catching the bastard up."

THIRTY-FOUR

Hayden faced off against Ed Boudreau and the world melted away.

"Pleased to kill you," Boudreau repeated the words he'd said to her once before. "Again."

"You failed last time, psycho. You'll fail again."

Boudreau flicked a glance down to her leg. "How's the thigh?"

"All better." Hayden stayed on the balls of her feet, expecting the lightning attack. She tried to steer the American so his ass was against the barn wall, but he was too wily for that.

"You're blood." Boudreau mimed licking his knife. "Tasted good. I think my baby here wants more."

"Unlike your sister," Hayden growled. "She really couldn't take any more."

Boudreau exploded toward her. Hayden had been expecting it and sidestepped neatly, leaving her blade for his cheek to run into. "First blood," she said.

"Foreplay." Boudreau lunged and retreated, then came at her with several short slices. Hayden parried them all and finished with a palm strike to his nose. Boudreau staggered, tears coming to his eyes.

Hayden instantly pressed the advantage, thrusting and slicing with her knife. She backed Boudreau up against the wall, then retreated for one beat—

Boudreau lunged.

Hayden ducked under and jabbed the knife into his thigh. She withdrew as he screamed, unable to keep the sly grin from creeping into her eyes.

"Ya feel that, fuckstick?"

"Bitch!" Boudreau went crazy. But it was the crazy of a fighter, of a thinker, of a seasoned warrior. He drove her back with thrust after thrust, taking crazy chances, but retaining just enough power and speed to make her think twice about stepping in. And now, as they ploughed backward, they collided with other knots of fighting men and Hayden lost her balance.

She fell, scrambling across a fallen man's knee, rolled and came up, knife ready.

Boudreau melted away through the crowd, the grin on his face turning to a leer as he tasted his own blood and brandished the knife.

"Be seeing you," he shouted over the din. "I know where you live, Miss Jaye."

Hayden kicked one of the Blood King's men out of the way, snapping the man's leg like a twig as she cleared a path to Boudreau. Out of the corner of her eye, she saw Mai, clearly the game-changer in this battle, fighting unarmed against men with sharp weapons, the battle too close up for gunplay, and leaving them heaped at her feet. Hayden gaped at the dead and dying that twitched all around her.

Even Boudreau, she saw, did a double-take when he followed Hayden's gaze and saw the legendary Japanese agent in action.

Mai eyeballed Hayden. "Right behind you."

Hayden sprinted at Boudreau.

The Blood King's top psycho took off as if a Hawaiian mongoose was snapping at his heels. Hayden and Mai pursued. Mai dealt a devastating blow to another of Kovalenko's men as she passed, thus saving another soldier's life.

Beyond the barn lay an open field, a helipad complete with chopper, and a narrow jetty where several boats lay at anchor. Boudreau sped past the chopper, heading for a big speedboat and didn't even break stride when he leapt on board, tumbling through the air. Before Hayden could even make it past the chopper, the big boat was already burbling away and starting to inch ahead.

Mai began to slow. "That's a Baja. Very fast, and with three men already waiting inside. Those other boats are sedate by comparison." Her eyes drank in the chopper. "Now that's what we need."

Hayden ducked as a bullet whizzed by them, barely noticing. "Can you fly it?"

Mai favored her with a 'are you *really* asking me that question?' look, before stepping onto a skid and jumping inside. Before Hayden got there, Mai already had the main rotor spinning and Boudreau's boat let out a mighty roar as it surged off down the river.

"Have faith," Mai said softly, displaying the legendary patience she was known for as Hayden ground her teeth in frustration. In a minute, the machine was ready to fly. Mai finessed the collective. The skids left the ground. A bullet thudded into the pillar beside Hayden's head.

She flinched away, then turned to see the last of the Blood King's men collapse under fire. One of the Hawaiian special forces soldiers gave them a big thumbs up as the chopper began to dip and turn in preparation to pursue the speedboat. Hayden waved back.

Just another crazy day in her life.

But she was still here. Still surviving. The old Jaye motto crept back into her head. *Survive another day. Just live.* Even at moments like this, she sorely missed her dad.

In a minute the chopper wobbled and swooped off in hot pursuit. Hayden's stomach was left somewhere back at the camp and she gripped the handholds until her knuckles hurt. Mai didn't miss a beat.

"Keep your pants on."

Hayden tried to take her mind off the hair-raising ride by checking the state of her weapons. Her knife was back in its holder. Her only remaining gun was a standard-issue Glock, not the Caspian she had favored lately. But, what the hell, a gun's a gun, right?

Mai flew low enough to catch spray on the windscreen. The big yellow boat powered through the wide river ahead. Hayden saw figures standing in the back, watching them get closer. No doubt they were armed.

Mai dipped her head and then looked hard at Hayden. "Guts and glory."

Hayden nodded. "All the way."

Mai punched the collective, sending the chopper in a vicious dive, on a collision course for the yellow Baja. Predictably, the men stood around its flank fell back in shock. Hayden leant out of the window and squeezed off a shot. The bullet went hopelessly wide.

Mai passed her a half-empty M9. "Make 'em count."

Hayden fired again. One of Boudreau's men shot back, the bullet pinging off the chopper's canopy. Mai zigzagged the collective, sending Hayden's head crashing off a support pillar. Then Mai dived again, aggressive, giving no quarter. Hayden emptied the clip of her Glock and saw one of Boudreau's men go flying off the boat in a spray of blood.

Then another bullet hit the chopper, followed by a flurry of others. The big machine presented a big target. Hayden saw Boudreau at the wheel of the boat, knife held firmly between his teeth, firing up at them with a machine pistol.

"Oh," Mai's shout was an understatement as black smoke suddenly billowed out of the chopper and the engine note changed drastically from a roar to a whine. Without guidance, the chopper began to weave and jerk.

Mai blinked at Hayden.

Hayden waited until they were over Boudreau's boat and threw open her door as the chopper came down.

She looked into the very whites of Boudreau's eyes, said, *"Fuck it,"* and leapt out of the falling helicopter.

THIRTY-FIVE

Hayden's free fall was short lived. It wasn't far down to Boudreau's boat but she struck the man a glancing blow on the way down before she crashed to the deck. The air whooshed out of her body. The old wound in her thigh screamed. She saw stars.

The chopper spiraled down into the rushing river about thirty feet to the left, the thunderous sound of its death drowning out all cohesive thought and sending a gigantic wave across the speedboat's bows.

A wave powerful enough to alter the very course of the boat.

The vessel lost its velocity, sending everyone flying forward, and began to tip. Then at the end of its forward momentum, it rolled right over to land belly up in the white water.

Hayden held on as the boat tipped. When she went under she kicked hard, aiming straight down, and then struck out in the direction of the nearest bank. Cold water made her head ache, but soothed her aching limbs a little. The tug of the current made her realize just how tired she was.

When she surfaced she found herself near the bank, but facing Ed Boudreau. He still had the knife clamped between his teeth and snarled when he saw her.

Behind him the wreckage of the steaming helicopter began to sink beneath the river. Hayden saw Mai chasing Boudreau's two remaining men to the muddy shore. Knowing she would not survive a water fight, she struck out past the madman and didn't stop until she hit the bank. Thick mud oozed all around her.

There was a heavy splash at her side. Boudreau, gasping. "Stop. Fucking. Running." He panted.

"You got it," Hayden scooped up and flung a heap of mud into his face and scrambled up the bank. The mud and dirt clung to her, tried to drag her down. What should have been an easy crawl to dry ground got her only a couple of feet above the river line.

She turned and smashed a dirty heel into Boudreau's face. She saw the knife he gripped between his teeth slice deep into his cheeks, cutting him a wider smile than the Joker's. With a scream and a spit of blood and ooze, he belly-flopped onto her legs, using her belt as a means of hauling himself up her body. Hayden struck down at his unprotected head but her blows had little effect.

Then she remembered her knife.

With her other hand she reached beneath her, pushing, straining, lifting her body an inch as the mud squelched and tried to hold on to her.

Her fingers clasped around the hilt. Boudreau practically tore her trousers off as he heaved one more time, coming to rest right on her back, head and lips suddenly right beside her ear.

"Nice fuckin' try." She felt blood dripping from his face onto her cheek. "You're gonna feel this one. It's going in nice and slow."

He spread-eagled his weight over her whole body, driving her farther into the mud. With one hand, he pushed her face into the goo, stopping her breath. Hayden struggled madly, bucking and rolling as best she could. Every time her face came up, covered in sticky filth, she could see Mai in front of her, taking on Boudreau's two henchmen alone.

One fell in the three seconds Hayden's face was held under. The other backed away, prolonging the agony. By the time

Hayden's face had come up for air the fourth time Mai had finally cornered him and was about to break his back over a fallen tree.

Hayden's remaining strength was almost gone.

Boudreau's knife pricked her skin around the third rib. With an agonizingly slow and measured thrust, the blade began to slide in deeper. Hayden reared and kicked, but couldn't remove her assailant.

"Nowhere to go." Boudreau's wicked whisper invaded her head.

And he was right, Hayden suddenly realized. She should stop fighting and let it happen. Just lie there. Give herself time—

The blade sank deeper, steel grating against bone now. Boudreau's chuckle was the call of the Grim Reaper, the call of a demon mocking her.

The knife beneath her body came free with a heavy sucking sound. With a single movement, she reversed it in her hand and jabbed it hard behind her into Boudreau's own ribs.

The psycho reared back, screaming, the knife's hilt protruding from his ribcage. Even then Hayden couldn't move. She was jammed too far into the mud, her whole body being sucked down. She couldn't even move her other arm.

Boudreau wheezed and panted atop her. Then she felt the big knife being removed. This was it then. He would kill her now. One rigid thrust to the back of her neck or to her spine. Boudreau had beaten her.

Hayden opened her eyes wide, determined to see the sunlight one last time. Her thoughts were of Ben and she thought, *judge me on how I lived, not how I died.*

Again.

Then, looming large and as terrifying as a charging lion, Mai Kitano came storming in. About three feet from Hayden, she launched herself off the ground, pouring every ounce of momentum into a flying kick. One second later, and all that force shattered Boudreau's upper torso, breaking bones and organs and sending splintered teeth and splatters of blood in a wide arc.

The weight was lifted from Hayden's back.

Someone lifted her out of the mud with seeming ease. Someone carried her and laid her gently on the grassy bank and stood over her.

That someone was Mai Kitano. "Relax," she said easily. "He's dead. We won."

Hayden couldn't move nor speak. She simply stared up at the blue sky and the swaying trees and at Mai's smiling face.

And, after a while, she said, "Remind me never to piss you off. Truly, if you're not the best there's ever been I'll. . ." Her thoughts were still mainly with Ben, so she finished with something that he might say. "I'll show my arse in Asda."

THIRTY-SIX

The Blood King pushed his men to the absolute limit. The fact their pursuers had almost closed the gap made him furious. It was the overlarge contingent of men slowing him down. It was their dim-witted guide, dawdling over trivialities when they could be making strides. The amount of men who died claiming this prize was irrelevant. The Blood King demanded and expected their sacrifice. He expected them all to lay down and die for him. Their families would be looked after. Or at least, they wouldn't be tortured.

The prize was everything.

His guide, a man called Thomas, was babbling on about this being the level some other geek called Hawksworth had named *envy*. It was the fourth chamber, the Blood King fumed. Only the fourth. Standard legend spoke of seven levels of hell. Could there really be three more after this one?

And how did Hawksworth know? The scribe and Cook had turned and fled, balls shrunken to the size of peanuts, when they beheld the trap system after level five. *Dmitry Kovalenko,* he thought, *certainly would not.*

"You are waiting for what?" he growled at Thomas. "We will move. Now."

"I haven't quite worked out the trap system, sir," Thomas started to say.

"Fuck the trap system. Send the men in. They will find it faster." The Blood King curled a lip in amusement whilst studying the chamber.

Unlike the previous three, this chamber sloped down to a central shallow basin that looked like it had been hewn out of

The Bones of Odin

the very rock. Several thick metal stanchions protruded from the hard floor, almost like stepping stones. The sides of the chamber narrowed as they proceeded, until after the basin when they started to widen out again.

The basin appeared to be a 'choke-point.'

Envy? the Blood King thought. How did such a sin translate to real life, to this subterranean world where shadows could as soon kill you as protect you? He watched as Thomas ordered the advance. At first all went well. The Blood King cast a glance back the way they had come, as he heard the distant sounds of gunfire. Damn Drake and his little army. Once he got out of here, he would personally ensure the blood vendetta achieved its cruel aim.

The gunfire galvanized him. "Move!" he cried, just as the lead man stepped on some kind of hidden pressure point. There was a crack like stone falling, a whoosh of air, and suddenly the lead man's head bounced to the stone floor before rolling down the sharp gradient like a football. The headless body collapsed into a bloody heap.

Even the Blood King stared. But he felt no fear. He only wanted to see what had caused such trauma to his lead man. Thomas shrieked beside him. The Blood King pushed him forward, following in his steps, taking great delight in the man's fear. At last, beside the twitching body, he stopped.

With scared men all around him the Blood King studied the ancient mechanism. A razor thin wire had been strung at head height between two metal poles that must have been held in position by some kind of tension device. When his man stepped on the release lever, the poles had released, and the wire swung around with them, severing his man's head at the neck.

Ingenious. *A wonderful deterrent,* he thought, and wondered if he might employ such a device in the servant quarters of his new home.

"What are you waiting for?" he bellowed at the remaining men. "Move!"

191

Three men leapt forward, another dozen followed close behind. The Blood King saw the prudence of leaving another half dozen behind him just in case Drake caught up fast.

"Quick now," he said. "If we go faster we get there faster, yes?"

His men ran, deciding they actually had no choice and there was an outside chance their deranged boss was right. Another trap triggered and a second head went bouncing down the incline. The body fell and the man behind it tripped over it, counting himself lucky when another taut wire sliced open the air right above his head.

When the second group started down, the Blood King joined them. More traps were sprung. More heads and scalps rolled. Then, there was a booming clap that echoed through the cavern. On either side of the narrowing pathway *mirrors* sprung out, positioned so that they reflected the man in front.

At the same time there was the sound of water rushing and the basin at the bottom of the incline began to fill up.

Only this water wasn't just water. Not judging by the way it was smoking.

Thomas shouted as they ran toward it. "It's being fed by an acid lake. That's when the gas sulfur dioxide becomes dissolved in water and produces sulfuric acid. You definitely don't want to touch that!"

"Do not stop," the Blood King bellowed as he saw men begin to slow. "Use the metal poles, idiots."

The entire team hurtled down the incline as a pack. To left and right, random traps flicked open with a sound like a bowshot. Decapitated bodies fell and heads rolled like discarded pineapples among the men, tripping some over, being inadvertently kicked by others. The Blood King noticed early on that there were too many men for the number of poles and understood that the pack mentality would drive the less sharp amongst them to leap without thinking.

They would deserve their fate. An idiot was always better off dead.

The Blood King slowed and held Thomas back. Several other men also checked their pace, affirming the Blood King's belief that the only the brightest and best would survive. The lead man of the pack leapt out onto the first metal upright and then began to skip from pole to pole over the rushing water. At first he made some headway, but then a virulent surge splashed up at his legs. Where the acidic water touched, his clothes and his skin burned.

When his feet touched the next pole the pain made him fold and he fell, splashing down right into the teeming basin. Furious, agonized screams echoed around the chamber.

Another man toppled off a stanchion and fell in. A third man pulled up at the edge of the basin, belatedly realizing there was no free pillar for him to leap to, and was pushed in as another man barreled blindly into his back.

The mirrors reflected the man ahead. Would you envy the man in front of you?

The Blood King saw the purpose of the mirrors and the beating of the trap. "Look down!" Thomas shouted at the same time. "Look down at your feet and not at the man ahead. This simple practice will see you safely over the uprights."

The Blood King came to a stop at the edge of the newly formed lake. By the way the water was still rushing in, he saw the tops of the stanchions would soon be under the swirling surface. He pushed a man on before him and dragged Thomas behind. A trap activated just out of range, so close he felt the wind as the metal post blasted past his shoulder.

Out onto the poles and a quick dance in a haphazard pattern. A brief pause as water splashed ahead. One more pole, and the man in front of him tripped. Screaming, he performed wonders by managing to catch his fall by landing on another pole. The acid-laced water splashed around him, but didn't touch him.

Yet.

The Blood King saw his chance. Without thought or pause

he stepped onto the man's prone body, using him as a bridge to walk over and reach the safety of the far shore. His weight pushed the man farther down, dipping his chest into the acid.

In another second, he was lost beneath the vortex.

The Blood King stared after him. "Fool."

Thomas landed at his side. More men leapt deftly between metal poles to safety. The Blood King looked ahead to the arched exit.

"And so to level five," he said smugly. "Where I will emulate that worm, Cook. And where finally," he snarled. "I will destroy Matt Drake."

THIRTY-SEVEN

The Big Island of Hawaii is so-called to avoid confusion. Its real name is Hawaii, or Hawaii Island, and it is the largest island in the United States. It is home to one of the most famous volcanoes in the world, Kilauea, a mountain that has been continuously erupting since 1983.

Today, on the lower flanks of its sister volcano, Mauna Loa, Mano Kinimaka and Alicia Myles, along with a team of America marines, set about ousting a parasite that had become attached to the island's consciousness.

They broke through the outer perimeter, shot dead dozens of the Blood King's men and stormed the large outbuilding just as the guards released all the hostages. In that same moment there came the throaty roar of vehicles accelerating away behind the building. Alicia and Kinimaka wasted no time racing around the side.

Alicia stopped in dismay. "Damn, the twats are escaping." Four ATV's were speeding away, bouncing around on their outsize tires.

Kinimaka raised his rifle and took aim. "Not for long." He fired. Alicia watched as the last man fell and the ATV rolled quickly to a stop.

"Wow, big guy, not bad for a cop. C'mon."

"I'm CIA." Kinimaka always rose to the bait, much to Alicia's continuing pleasure.

"The only three letter acronyms that matter belong to the British. Remember that."

Kinimaka muttered something as Alicia reached the ATV.

It was still running. Simultaneously they both tried to take the front seat. Alicia shook her head and pointed at the back.

"I prefer my men behind me, mate, if they're not underneath."

Alicia revved the engine and peeled out. The ATV was a big ugly beast, but it ran smooth and bounced comfortably from bump to bump. The big Hawaiian slipped his hands around her waist to hold on, not that he had to. There were handles back where he sat. Alicia grinned and said nothing.

Ahead, the fleeing men realized they were being pursued. The passengers on two of them whirled and fired. Alicia frowned, knowing it was beyond impossible to hit anything that way. *Amateurs,* she thought. *Always I seem to be fighting amateurs.* The last real battle she'd had had been against Drake in Abel Frey's citadel. And even then the man had been rusty, hindered by the trappings of seven years of civility.

Now he might be a different prospect.

Alicia drove cleverly rather than quickly. In short order, she had brought their ATV within an acceptable shooting range. Kinimaka shouted in her ear. "Gonna fire!"

He squeezed a shot off. Another mercenary screamed and bounced badly into the dirt. "That's two out of two," Alicia cried. "One more and you get a blo—"

Their ATV struck a hidden mound and veered crazily to the left. For a moment they were on two wheels, tipping over, but the vehicle managed to gain its balance and crash back to earth. Alicia wasted no time in opening the throttle to shoot it forward.

Kinimaka saw the ditch before she did. "Fuck!" He shouted "Hold on!"

Alicia could only increase her speed as the wide, deep ditch came up fast. The ATV flew over the gap, wheels spinning and engine roaring, and came down on the other side scrambling for purchase. Alicia banged her head against a padded roll-bar. Kinimaka held her so tight he prevented both of them being flung around and, by the time the dust settled, they realized they were suddenly amongst the enemy.

Beside them, a black ATV spun in the dirt, having landed badly, and now trying to get itself straight. Kinimaka leapt without thought, barreling right into the driver and knocking both him and his passenger off the vehicle and into the churned dirt.

Alicia wiped dust from her eyes. The ATV with the single occupant picked up speed in front of her, but was still within range. She scooped up her rifle, aimed and fired and then, without needing to check, swiveled the sight to where her Hawaiian partner struggled in the dirt.

Kinimaka dragged one man through the dirt. "This is my home!" Alicia heard him growl before he twisted and broke his adversary's arm. When the second man came rushing at him, Alicia laughed and lowered the rifle. Kinimaka didn't need her help. The second man bounced off him like instructions bounce off a four-year-old, making no impact whatsoever. The man hit the ground and Kinimaka finished him with a full-face punch.

Alicia nodded at him. "Let's finish this."

The last ATV was struggling up ahead. Its driver must have been hurt in all the bouncing around. Alicia rapidly began to gain ground, now a little disappointed at the ease in which they had retaken the ranch. But at least they had saved all the hostages.

If there was one thing she knew about the Blood King, it was the fact that these men here, these so-called mercenaries, were the dregs of his crew, sent here to hinder and distract the authorities. To divide and conquer.

She slowed as she came closer to the last ATV. Without pause, without even holding onto the steering column, she fired two shots and two men fell.

The battle that had barely begun was over. Alicia stared into the distance for a minute. If everything went as planned, if Mai and Hayden, and Drake and the others, survived their own parts of the battle, then the next battle could well be her hardest, and her last.

Because it would be against Mai Kitano. And she would have to tell Drake it was Mai who had killed Wells.

In cold blood.

Kinimaka patted her on the shoulder. "We should be getting back."

"Ach, give a girl a break," she murmured. "We're in Hawaii. Let me stare into the sunset."

THIRTY-EIGHT

"So that's what envy looks like?"

Drake and his team entered the fourth chamber, taking all precautions. Even then, it took several moments to fully comprehend the scene that lay before them. Headless bodies lay all around. Blood had spattered across the floor and in some places still ran thickly. The heads themselves were scattered around the floor like some child's cast-off toys.

Sprung traps stood on both sides of the narrow pathway. Drake took one look at the thin razor-like wire and guessed what had happened. Komodo whistled in disbelief.

"At some point these traps might reset," Ben said. "We need to move."

Karin made a noise of distaste.

"We should move quickly and stay dead center," Drake said. "No, wait."

Beyond the traps he now saw the wide basin full of water, swirling and churning. At the edges of the basin the water lapped and spilled over.

"That could be a problem. See the metal poles?"

"I bet the Blood King's men used them as stepping stones," Ben said, cryptically. "All we have to do is wait for the water to recede."

"Why not just wade on through." Even as Komodo said the words his face looked dubious.

"That basin could be fed by some kind of acidic lake or well," Karin explained. "Gases can turn water to Sulfuric acid inside or near a volcano. Even a long-extinct one."

"Wouldn't acid rot the metal uprights?" Drake pointed out.

Ben nodded. "Definitely."

They watched the swirling water for a few minutes. As they watched there was an ominous clicking sound. Drake brought his gun up fast. The six surviving Delta men copied him a fraction of a second later.

Nothing moved.

Then the sound came again. A heavy clicking. The sound of a garage door cable running through its metal guides. Only this wasn't a garage door.

Slowly, as Drake watched, one of the traps began to grind its way back into the wall. A time delay? But such technology hadn't been available to the ancient races. Or was that line of thinking akin to the folly a man shows by pronouncing that there is no other intelligent life in the universe?

Such arrogance.

Who knew what civilizations existed before records dated back? It wasn't for Drake to deliberate now. It was time for action.

"The water's receding," he said. "Ben. Any surprises?"

Ben consulted his notes and Karin was hopefully running it through her memory. "Hawksworth doesn't say much." Ben rustled the papers. "Maybe the poor guy was in shock. Remember, back then, they couldn't have expected anything like this."

"The fifth level must be a real shitstorm then," Komodo said gruffly. "Cos it's after that when Cook turned back."

Ben pursed his lips. "Hawksworth says it's what Cook *saw* after the fifth level that made him turn back. Not the chamber itself."

"Yeah, most likely levels six and seven," one of the Delta soldiers said quietly.

"Don't forget the mirrors." Karin pointed them out. "They point forward, obviously toward the man in front. It's most likely a warning."

"Like keeping up with the Joneses." Drake nodded. "Got it. So, in the spirit of Dinorock and in particular, David Coverdale, I'm gonna ask the opening line I always heard him say at every gig I ever went to. *Are you ready?*"

Drake led the way. The rest of the team fell in line the way they had become accustomed too. Taking the central line, Drake expected no difficulties with the traps and faced none, though he did step on several spent pressure points. By the time they approached the lip of the basin the water was draining away at a rapid pace.

"Poles look okay," he said. "Stay alert. And don't look down. There's some nasty stuff floating in here."

Drake went first, careful and precise. The entire team crossed easily within minutes and headed for the exit archway.

"Nice of the Blood King to trigger all the traps for us." Ben scoffed a little.

"We can't be far behind the bastard now." Drake felt his hands clench into fists and his head start to pound at the prospect of coming face-to-face with the most feared underworld figure in recent history.

*****

The next archway opened into a vast cavern. The immediate pathway led down an incline and then along a wide road below a high rock shelf.

But there was a major obstruction completely blocking their path.

Drake stared. "Bloody hell."

He had never even dreamt of anything like it. The blockage was actually an immense figure carved out of the living rock. Lying in repose with its back against the left-hand wall, its huge belly protruded out across the pathway. Sculpted representations of food lay heaped upon its belly and also scattered across its legs and piled in the pathway.

An ominous shape lay near the feet of the sculpture. A dead human body. The torso appeared to be twisted as if in extreme agony.

"This is gluttony," Ben said in awe. "The demon associated with gluttony is Beelzebub."

Drake's eye twitched. "You mean as in 'Bohemian Rhapsody's' Beelzebub?"

Ben sighed. "Not everything's about rock and roll, Matt. I *mean* Beelzebub the demon. Satan's right hand."

"I heard Satan's right hand is overworked." Drake stared at the enormous obstacle. "And whilst I respect your brain, Blakey, stop talking bollocks. Of course everything's about rock and roll."

Karin unfastened her long blond hair and then started to tie it back again, even tighter. Some of the Delta soldiers watched her, Komodo among them. She pointed out that Hawksworth related several interesting details about this particular cavern in his notes. As she spoke, Drake let his eyes wander the chamber.

Beyond the immense figure, he now noticed the lack of an exit archway. Instead, a wide ledge ran along the back wall, twisting its way toward the high ceiling until it gave out onto a high rock plateau. As Drake stared up at the plateau, he saw what looked like a balcony at its far end, almost like a viewing platform that gazed out across—the final two levels?

Drake's thoughts were interrupted when a shot rang out. A bullet ricocheted above their heads. Drake fell to the floor, but then Komodo pointed soundlessly toward the same rock plateau he had just been evaluating and saw over a dozen figures running onto it from the twisting ledge.

Kovalenko's men.

Which meant…

"Work out a way past that fucker," Drake hissed at Ben, nodding toward the overweight sculpture that blocked their way forward and then focused his complete attention on the rocky shelf.

A heavily accented, arrogant and superior voice boomed out. "Matt Drake! My new nemesis! So you seek to stop me yet again, huh? *Me!* Don't you people ever learn?"

"What is it you're after, Kovalenko? What's this all about?"

"What's it all about? It's *about* a lifelong quest. About me beating Cook. About how I learned and trained by killing a man every day for twenty years. I am not like other men. I stepped beyond that before I made my first billion."

"You've already beaten Cook," Drake pointed out evenly. "Why not come back down here? We'll talk, you and I."

"You want to kill me? I wouldn't have it any other way. Even my men want to kill me."

"That's probably because you're a major bell-end."

Kovalenko frowned, but was so far into his self-indulgent tirade now the insult didn't even register properly. "I would kill thousands to achieve my goals. Maybe I already have. Who bothers keeping count? But mark this, Drake, and mark it well. You and your friends will be a part of that statistic. I will wipe your memories from the Earth."

"Stop being so melodramatic," Drake shouted back. "Get down here and prove you've got a set, old man." He saw Karin and Ben consulting closely nearby, both starting to nod vigorously now as they figured something out.

"Do not think I will die so easily, even if we do happen to meet. I grew up on the hardest streets of the hardest city in Mother Russia. And I walked free on them. I *owned* them. The British and the Americans know nothing of real struggle." The hard-looking man spat on the ground.

Drake's eyes were deadly. "Oh, I sincerely hope you don't die easily."

"I will see you soon, *British man.* I will see you burn whilst I claim my treasure. I will see you scream whilst I take another of your women. I will see you rot whilst I become a god."

"For fuck's sake." Komodo had had enough of listening to the tyrants bluster. He loosed a volley toward the stone ledge, sending the Blood King's men into a panic. Even now, Drake saw, nine out of ten men still ran to assist him.

Immediately, shots were fired back. Bullets zinged off the nearby rock walls.

Ben shouted, "All we have to do is climb over the fat guy. Not too tough. . ."

Drake sensed a *but* coming. He raised an eyebrow as rock chips landed on his shoulder.

"But," Karin chimed in, her similarities to Ben becoming more clear the longer Drake spent time with her. "The snag is the food. Some of it is hollow. And filled with a kind of gas."

"I'm guessing it's not laughing gas." Drake eyed the misshapen corpse.

Komodo fired off a conservative volley to keep the Blood King's men at bay. "If it is, then it's really, really good stuff."

"Prepared powders," Karin said. "Released by pressure triggers. Possibly similar to the ones that killed most of the archaeologists who found Tutankhamen's tomb. You know about the supposed curse, right? Well, most people believe certain potions or gases we're left in the tomb by ancient Egyptian priests designed solely to kill grave robbers."

"What's the safe path?" Drake asked.

"We don't know, but if we run quick, one at a time, if anyone does release some powder behind them, it should be a miniscule amount that will evaporate quickly. The trap is there primarily to stop anyone climbing the *sculpture*, not get across it."

"According to Hawksworth," Karin said with a tight smile.

Drake assessed the situation. To him, this looked to be the turning point. If there was an observation balcony up there then they had to be close to the end. He imagined it would be a straight run from there to the sixth and seventh chambers and then on to the fabled "treasure." He took a moment to assess the team.

"This is where we go for it," he said. "All or nothing. Up

there"—he flicked an angry fist toward Kovalenko—"is a blind man shooting bullets at the world. And, Ben, for your information, that's *real* Dinorock. But this is where we go for it. All or nothing. You up for it?"

He was met with a resounding roar.

Matt Drake took off at a sprint, leading his men into the lower levels of hell, on the last leg of his own quest to avenge the woman he loved and rid the world of the most evil man he had ever known.

Time to rock.

THIRTY-NINE

Drake leaped up onto the gigantic sculpture, scrambling for purchase and grabbing the carved food to pull himself up. The sculpture felt cold, rough and foreign beneath his fingers, like touching the egg of an alien. He held his breath as he pulled hard to maintain his balance, but the fruit and loaves and haunches of pork held.

Below him and to the right lay the body of a man who hadn't been quite so lucky.

Bullets zinged around him. Komodo and another member of the Delta team laid down covering fire.

Without more than a wasted second, Drake leapt across the main body of the molded shape and scrambled down the other side. As his feet hit the rock floor, he turned and gave a thumbs-up to the next man in line.

And then he, too, opened fire, picking off one of the Blood King's men with his first shot. The man tumbled down the cliff face, landing near the body of his already dead comrade with a horrible crunch.

The second man in line made it.

Ben came next.

*****

Five minutes later and the entire team crouched safely in the shadow of Gluttony. Only one item of food had been crushed. Drake had watched as a puff of powder seeped into

The Bones of Odin

the air, spiraling like the body of a deadly, charmed snake, but it had evaporated after a few seconds not even touching the guilty man's fleeing boots.

"The ledge."

Drake led the way double-time to the short incline that formed the beginning of the ledge. From this vantage point, they saw it curved gracefully up the wall before giving out onto the rock plateau.

The Blood King's men withdrew. It was a race against time. Up they pounded, single file. The ledge was wide enough to forgive a few mistakes. Drake fired as he ran, picking off another of Kovalenko's men as they vanished through the next exit archway. When they reached the top of the ledge and saw the vast expanse of the rocky shelf Drake saw something else too, lying in wait.

"Grenade!"

In full flight, he flung himself headlong to the floor, using his momentum to twist his body as it slid across the smooth rock and booted the grenade away.

It fell off the plateau, exploding a few seconds later. The blast rocked the chamber.

Komodo helped him up. "Could use you on our soccer team, dude."

"Yanks can't play soccer." Drake started running toward the balcony, eager to see what lay beyond and get after Kovalenko. "No offense."

"Hmm. I don't see the English team bringing home many trophies."

"We'll bring home the gold." Drake put the American right. "At the Olympics. Beckham will make the difference."

Ben had caught them up. "He's right. The team will play for him. The crowd will rise for him."

Karin let out an exasperated cry from behind. "Is there *nowhere* where a man won't talk about bloody football!"

Drake reached the balcony and placed his hand on the low,

broken stone wall. The sight that greeted him made his legs turn weak, made him stagger, made him forget all his woes and wonder again just what manner of creature had actually *built* this awe-inspiring place.

The view they beheld struck both awe and fear into their hearts.

The balcony stood about a quarter of the way up a truly gargantuan cavern. Without doubt, the biggest any of them had ever seen. The light came from the countless deep amber flares the Blood King's men had fired before they embarked on the sixth level. Even then much of the cavern and its dangers still lay in murk and shadow.

To their left and leading from the exit archway, what appeared to be a covered, zigzag staircase led down about a hundred feet. From deep inside this staircase, Drake and his team now heard a heavy rolling sound followed by screams that made fists of dread clutch at their hearts.

Ben took a breath. "Man, do I *not* like the sound of that."

"Yeah. Sounds like the opening to one of your songs." Drake tried to keep the spirits from falling too far, but it was still hard to drag his jaw up from the ground.

The staircase gave out into a narrow ledge. Beyond this ledge, the cavern opened into enormity. He could see a narrow, snaking path clinging to the right hand wall, running a short way into the cavern above infinite depths, and a similar one that then continued over to the left, but no bridge or any other means to connect them across a massive gap.

At the farthest end of the cavern rose an enormous black, jagged rock face. When Drake squinted, he thought he might just be able to make out a shape about half way up that rock face, something big, but distance and darkness thwarted him.

For now.

"One last push," he said, hoping it was true. "Follow me."

Once a soldier always a soldier. That's what Alyson had said to him. Right before she left him. Right before she...

He brushed the memories away. He couldn't contend with them now. But she had been right. Scarily right. If she had lived, things might be different, but pumping through him now was the blood of a soldier, a warrior; the true mettle had never left him.

Into the narrow passage they walked: two civilians, six Delta soldiers, and Matt Drake. At first, the tunnel differed little from the previous ones, but then, in the light of the amber flares they kept firing ahead, Drake saw the passageway suddenly divide and expand to a two-car width and noticed that a channel had been delved into the rock floor.

A guidance channel?

"Look out for ankle-breakers." Drake noticed a wicked little hole ahead positioned just where a man might place his foot. "Shouldn't be too hard to avoid at this pace."

"No!" Ben cried, without humor. "You're a friggin' soldier. You should know better than to say things like that."

As if in affirmation, there came a mighty *boom* and the ground shook beneath them. It sounded like something big and heavy had dropped into the passage that divided the one they had walked down. They could turn back and be blocked or—

"Run!" Drake shouted. "Just bloody run!"

A deep thunder began to fill the passage as though something heavy was heading toward them. They took flight, Drake firing flares as he ran and hoping to hell that neither Ben nor Karin stepped in one of the nasty trap-holes.

At this speed...

The roar grew louder.

They kept running, not daring to look back, keeping to the right of the wide channel and hoping Drake didn't run out of flares. After a minute they heard a *second* ominous grumble coming from up ahead.

"Jesus!"

Drake didn't slow down. If he did, they were dead. He

raced past a wide opening in the wall to their right. The noise was coming from up there. He risked a quick glance.

NO!

Blakey had been right, the crazy little geek. Rolling stones were rumbling toward them, and not the Dinorock type. These were large spherical balls of rock, let loose by ancient mechanisms and guided by obvious and hidden channels. The one to their right ploughed at Drake.

He put on a huge burst of speed. *"Run!"* He spun, screaming. "Oh, god."

Ben joined him. Two Delta soldiers, Karin and Komodo rushed by the opening with an inch to spare. Two more soldiers squeezed by, falling over their own feet and crashing into Komodo and Karin, ending up in a groaning tangle.

But the last Delta man was not so lucky. Without a sound, he disappeared as the huge ball came out of the cross-passage, impacted him with the force of a Mack truck and smashed resoundingly into the side of the tunnel. There was another boom as the ball that had been following them smashed into the one that had dissected their escape.

Komodo's face said it all. "If we're quick," he growled, "we might be able to beat the rest of the traps before they reset."

They took off again. They passed three more intersections where the grumbling machinations of immense machinery cracked and boomed. The Delta leader had been right. Drake listened hard, but heard no sound of Kovalenko or his men up ahead.

Then, they came up against the blockage he had been dreading. One of the immense stones stood ahead, impeding the way forward. They bunched together, wondering if perhaps the thing was about to start resetting.

"Maybe it's broken," Ben said. "The trap, I mean."

"Or maybe…" Karin fell to her knees and crawled forward a few feet. "Maybe it's meant to be here."

Drake fell beside her. There, beneath the huge stone was a

small crawlspace. There was just enough room for a man to squeeze underneath.

"Not good." Komodo squatted down as well. "I've lost one man already to this bullshit trap. Find another way, Drake."

"If I'm right," Drake said, looking back over his shoulder, "once those traps reset, they'll trigger again. They must work on the same kind of pressure pad system as the others. We'll be trapped here." He met Komodo's eyes with a hard stare. "We don't have a choice."

Without waiting for a reply, he shimmied his way under the ball. The rest of the team crowded in after him, not wanting to be last in line, but the Delta men held their discipline and placed themselves where their team leader indicated. Drake felt the familiar urge rise inside his chest, that urge to say, *Don't worry, trust me. I'll get you through this,* but he knew he would never say that again.

Not after Kennedy's senseless death.

After a moment of wriggling, he found himself sliding headfirst down a sharp incline and immediately heard the rest following. The bottom wasn't far, but gave him enough room to stand upright beneath the massive stone ball. Everyone else crowded in behind him. Thinking hard, he didn't dare move a muscle. If this thing dropped, he wanted everyone on level ground.

But then the familiar groaning sound of grating machinery shook the silence and the ball shifted. Drake took off like a bat out of hell, shouting at everyone to follow. He slowed and helped Ben along, sensing that even the young student had fitness limits and lacked the endurance training of a soldier. He knew Komodo would be helping Karin, though with her being a martial arts expert, her fitness might well be on a par with the men.

As a group they sprinted along the hewn out passage *beneath* the deadly rolling ball, trying to take advantage of its sluggish start because, up ahead, they might be faced with a tough incline to get them back up in front of it.

Drake spotted an ankle-breaker and yelled out a warning. He leapt over the fiendishly placed hole, almost dragging Ben bodily with him. Then he hit the incline.

It was sharp. He dug in, head down, legs pounding, right arm locked around Ben's waist, heaving with every step. In the end, he beat the ball by some distance, but then he had to give everyone behind him a chance.

He didn't let up, just shifted forward to give the others some room and fired more flares ahead.

They bounced off a solid rock wall!

The immense stone rumbled toward them. The entire team had beaten it, but now faced a dead-end. Literally.

Drake's eyes made out a deeper blackness between the bright flares "There's a hole. A hole in the ground."

Quickly, feet tripping and nerves frayed by desperation, they raced over to the hole. It was small, man-size, and completely black inside.

"A leap of faith," Karin said. "Kind of like believing in a god."

The heavy rumble of the ball of stone grew louder. It was within a minute of crushing them.

"Glow stick," Komodo said, voice tight with tension.

"No time." Drake cracked a glow stick and leapt down the hole in one swift movement. The drop seemed interminable. Blackness flickered, seeming to reach out with twisted fingers. Within a few seconds, he hit rock bottom, allowed his legs to fold and hit his head hard on solid stone. Stars swam before his eyes. Blood seeped across his brow. Conscious of those who had to follow he left the glow stick in place and crawled out of range.

Someone else landed with a crash. Then Ben was beside him. "Matt. Matt! You alright?"

"Oh aye, I'm fuckin' peachy." He sat up, holding his temples. "Got an aspirin?"

"They'll rot your gut."

"Polynesian Mai Tai? Hawaiian Lava Flow?"

"Geez, don't mention the 'L' word down here, mate."

"How about another stupid joke?"

"Never run out of those. Hold still."

Ben checked his gash. By now the rest of the team had landed safely and were crowding around. Drake shrugged the young lad off and rose to his feet. Everything seemed to be in working order. Komodo fired off a couple of flares that struck the roof and bounced down a steep incline.

And tumbled over and over until they exited through an archway at the bottom.

"That's it," Drake said. "I think that's the final level."

FORTY

Drake and the Delta team came out of the tunnel firing hard. There was no choice. If they were going to stop Kovalenko, then speed was vital. Immediately, Drake looked to his right, recalling the layout of the cavern, and saw the Blood King's men had leaped over to the first S-shaped ledge and were congregated around its farthest point. The start of the second S-shaped ledge began a few steps in front of them, but over on the other side of the gargantuan cavern, a yawning chasm of unknown depth separating them. Now that he was closer, and since the Blood King's men seemed to have fired off several more amber flares, he finally got a good look at the far end of the cavern.

A great rock plateau jutted out from the back wall, on the same level as both of the S-ledges. Cut into the back wall itself was a steep staircase, seeming so close to vertical it would give even Maverick vertigo.

At the top of the staircase, the big black shape protruded. Drake only had a second, a glimpse, but. . .was that a colossal chair made of rock? An implausible, extraordinary throne maybe?

Bullets peppered the air. Drake fell to one knee, picking off a man and hearing his terrible scream as he plummeted into the abyss. They ran for the only cover they could see, a broken mass of boulders that had probably crumbled from the balcony above. As they watched one of Kovalenko's men fired a loud weapon, a weapon that expelled something that looked like a bulky, steel dart across the gap. It hit the far wall with a loud crack and lodged into the rock.

As the dart flew, a heavy line unraveled behind it.

The other end of the line was then inserted into the same weapon and fired into the nearer wall, embedding itself several feet higher than the first. The rope was quickly tensioned.

They had created a zip-line.

Drake thought quickly. "If we're gonna stop him, we need that line," he said. "It would take too long to set our own up. So don't shoot it. But we also need to stop them cutting it when they're across."

"Think more like the Blood King," Karin said with distaste. "Think of him cutting the line when the last few of his men are still on it."

"We don't stop," Drake said. "Not for anything."

He burst from behind the cover and opened fire. To his left and right, the Delta force ran, shooting carefully but accurately.

The first of Kovalenko's men zipped across the chasm, picking up speed as he went and landing deftly on the other side. Quickly, he turned and began to lay down a wall of covering fire on full-auto.

A Delta soldier hurtled sideways, shot to pieces. His body crashed in front of Drake, but the Englishman jumped over without breaking stride. As he approached the first S-ledge, a wide gulf of emptiness opened up before him. They would have to leap onto it!

Still firing, he sprang over the chasm. The second of Kovalenko's men flew down the line. Boulders were dislodged from the nearby cavern wall as bullets impacted with devastating force.

Drake's team sprinted and leapt behind him.

A third figure jumped onto the highly-tensioned line. Kovalenko. Drake's brain shrieked at him to take the shot. *Risk it!* Take the fucker out right now.

But too many things could go wrong. He might sever the line and Kovalenko might still fall to safety. He might only wound the bastard. And—biggest of all—they needed the Russian arsehole alive to lift the blood vendetta.

Kovalenko landed safely. Three more of his men made it across. Drake dropped another three as the two forces came together. Three close shots. Three kills.

Then a rifle flew at his head. He ducked, hefted the assailant over his shoulder and heaved him off the ledge into blackness. He turned and fired from the hip. Another man fell. Komodo was at his side. A knife was drawn. Blood sprayed across the cavern wall. Kovalenko's men backed up slowly, driven to the sheer drop at their backs.

The remaining four Delta soldiers knelt at the edge of the chasm, shooting carefully at any of Kovalenko's men who lingered near the line. It was only a matter of time though, before one of them thought to retreat and start taking pot shots.

Speed was all they had.

Two more of the Blood King's men had climbed up to the zip-line and now pushed off. Drake saw another start the ascent up the jagged wall and fired, blasting him off like a swatted fly. A man charged at him, head down, screaming, no doubt seeing that he was cut off. Drake sidestepped toward the wall. Komodo bundled the man off the ledge.

"Up!"

Drake wasted precious seconds casting around. *What the hell had they used to hold the bloody line?* Then he saw. Each man must have been given a small purpose-made pulley, the kind used by professionals. There were several lying around. The Blood King had come prepared for all eventualities.

As had Drake. In their packs they carried professional Caving—spelunking—equipment. Drake quickly dragged a pulley out and attached a harness to his back.

"Ben!"

Whilst the young man crab-walked over, Drake turned to Komodo. "You'll bring Karin?"

"Of course." Gruff, hard-faced and battle-scarred, the big man still could not hide the fact that he was already smitten.

Of all the places. . .

Trusting the Delta men to keep Kovalenko's goons at bay, Drake kept up the pressure by rapidly linking his pulley onto the highly tensioned zip-wire. Ben fastened himself into the harness and Drake passed him the rifle.

"Shoot like our lives depend on it, Blakey!"

Screaming, they pushed off and shot down the zip-line. From this height and at this speed, the distance appeared greater and the far ledge seemed to recede. Ben opened fire, his shots spreading high and wide and sending chunks of rock showering onto the Blood King's men below.

But that didn't matter. It was the noise and the onslaught and the threat that was required. Picking up speed, Drake lifted his legs as the air whipped past and the great, bottomless chasm opened up below. Terror and exhilaration made his heart pound. The sound of the metal pulley whipping across the zip-wire fizzed loudly in his ears.

Several bullets zipped by, splitting the air around the speeding pair. Drake heard return fire coming from the Delta team. One of Kovalenko's men folded noisily. Ben roared and kept his finger on the trigger.

The closer they got, the more dangerous it became. The godsend was that there was no cover for Kovalenko's men and the constant barrage of bullets coming from the Delta team was beyond withering. Even at this speed, Drake could feel the cold rushing up beneath his feet. Centuries of blackness stirred beneath him, roiling, churning, and perhaps reaching up with shadowy fingers to try to pluck him down into an eternal embrace.

The ledge rushed up to meet him. At the last minute, the Blood King ordered the retreat of his men and Drake let go of the pulley. He landed on his feet, but his momentum was not enough to maintain the balance between forward thrust and rearward weight.

In other words, Blakey's weight toppled them over backward. Toward the abyss.

Drake deliberately fell sideways, throwing his entire body into the ungainly maneuver. Ben was grabbing frantically at the unyielding rock, but still gamely holding on to the rifle. Drake heard the sudden whip of the zip-line tautening and knew Komodo and Karin were already on it, zooming down toward him at bone-breaking speed.

The Blood King's men were darting along the ledge toward the rear of the chamber now, almost in a position to make the final leap onto the vast rock plateau where the mysterious staircase began. The good news was he was down to a dozen men.

Drake dragged himself across the ledge before unbuckling Ben, then allowed himself a few seconds respite before sitting up. In a flash of motion, Komodo and Karin flew across his sight, the pair landing gracefully and not without a little sly smile.

"Kid's put on some weight." Drake indicated Ben. "Too many full breakfasts. Not enough dancing."

"The band doesn't *dance.*" Ben hit back instantly as Drake assessed their next move. Wait for the rest of the team or give chase?

"Hayden says when you dance you look like Pixie Lott."

"Bollocks."

Komodo was also staring after Kovalenko's men. The zip-line went taut again and they all moved against the wall. In quick succession, two more Delta soldiers arrived, their boots grating loudly over grit as they decelerated to a quick halt.

"Keep moving." Drake decided. "Best not to give them time to think."

They raced along the ledge, guns ready. The Blood King's

progress was momentarily hidden from sight by the curve of the rocky wall, but when Drake and his team beat the curve, they saw Kovalenko and the remainder his men already on the rock plateau.

He had lost two more men somewhere.

And now it seemed they had been ordered to take extreme measures. Several men were breaking out portable RPG launchers.

"Damn, they're muzzle loaded!" Drake yelled, then stopped and turned, heart suddenly falling through the earth. "Oh no—"

The initial *pop* and whistle of a muzzle-fired grenade rang out. The last two Delta soldiers were whizzing down the zip-line, zeroing in on the ledge when the missile struck. It hit the wall above the zip-line anchors and destroyed them amidst an explosion of rock and dust and shale.

The line sagged. The soldiers flew down into black oblivion without even a sound. Somehow, that was even worse.

Komodo cursed, rage distorting his features. These were good men he had trained and fought with for years. Now the Delta team were only three-strong, plus Drake, Ben and Karin.

Drake shouted and bullied them along the ledge, frantic with the knowledge that more RPG's were about to be launched. The survivors raced along the ledge, guided by glow sticks and the abundance of amber flares. Every step took them closer to the rocky plateau and the strange staircase and the mystifying but incredible sight of the giant throne jutting out of the rock wall.

A second RPG was fired. This one exploded on the ledge behind the runners, damaging but not destroying the pathway. Even as he ran and pushed every ounce of speed from his overworked muscles, Drake could hear Kovalenko screaming at his men to take care—the ledge might be their only way out of there.

Now Drake came to the bottom of the ledge and saw the

gap he had to leap in order to reach the rock plateau and confront the Blood King's men.

It was big.

So big, in fact, that he almost faltered. Almost stopped. Not for himself, but for Ben and Karin. On first sight, he didn't think they'd make the leap. But then he hardened his heart. They *had* to. And there could be no slowing down, no going back. They were the only people capable of stopping the Blood King and putting an end to his crazy plan. The only people capable of taking down an international terrorist leader and making sure he never got the chance to hurt anyone ever again.

But he still half-turned as he ran. "Don't stop," he shouted at Ben. "Believe. You'll make it."

Ben nodded, adrenalin taking his feet and his muscles and firing them with willpower, glory and strength. Drake hit the gap first, leaping with arms spread and feet still pumping, arcing over the gap like an Olympic athlete.

Ben came next, reaching, head all over the place and his sense of balance shot through with nerves. But he landed on the other side with inches to spare.

"*Yes!*" he cried and Drake grinned at him. "Jessica Ennis ain't got nowt on you, matey."

Next, Komodo landed heavily, almost turning his body inside out as he twisted immediately and looked for Karin. Her leap was beautiful. Legs high, back arched, oodles of forward momentum.

And the perfect landing. The rest of the Delta team followed.

Drake spun to see the most shocking sight he'd ever laid eyes on.

The Blood King and his men, screaming and wailing, most covered in blood and gaping wounds, were all charging straight at them and brandishing their weapons, like demons from hell.

It was time for the last stand.

FORTY-ONE

Matt Drake stood strong and met the Blood King head on.

First, his men arrived, cries resounding as rifles clashed and knives flicked and flashed like swords, catching the amber light and glinting their fire in myriad directions. A few shots were fired, but at this range and in this maelstrom of testosterone and fear, none were properly aimed. Yet still there was a sharp cry from behind Drake, another Delta solider fallen.

Drake's muscles ached like he'd fought a three-hundred pound gorilla. Blood and dirt coated his face. Nine men came at him, at them, but he took them all on because the Blood King stood behind them, and nothing would stop him from claiming his revenge.

The old soldier was back, the civilian now diminished, and he was back up there in the top ranks with the baddest motherfucking soldiers alive.

Point-blank, he shot three men, straight through the heart. The fourth, he stepped into with his gun reversed, completely pulverizing the man's nose and breaking part of the cheekbone at the same time. Three seconds had passed. He sensed the Delta crew almost back away from him in awe, giving him space to work. He left them to contend with three mercenaries whilst he advanced on one man and Kovalenko himself.

Komodo head-butted a man and stabbed a second in one movement. Karin was beside him and didn't back down. Not for a second. She used a face-palm to send the stabbed man stumbling back and followed with a jab combination. When the mercenary growled and attempted to rally, she stepped in and used a tae-kwon-do technique to throw him over her shoulder.

Toward the sheer edge.

The man slipped off, screaming, claimed by the abyss. Karin stared at Komodo, suddenly aware of what she had done. The big team leader thought quickly and gave her a thank you sign, instantly saluting her actions and giving them relevance.

Karin took a deep breath.

Drake faced the Blood King.

At last.

The last man had put up a short fight and now lay squirming at his feet, wind-pipe crushed, both wrists broken. Kovalenko gave the man a disdainful stare.

"A fool. And weak."

"All weak men hide behind their wealth and the semblance of power it brings them."

"Semblance?" Kovalenko drew a pistol and shot the writhing man in the face. "Is that not power? Did you think it a semblance? I kill a man in cold blood every single day because I *can*. Is that a semblance of power?"

"Like you ordered the killing of Kennedy Moore? And my friends' families? Some part of the world may have spawned you, Kovalenko, but it was not the sane part."

They moved quickly and simultaneously. Two weapons, a pistol and a rifle, clicking at the same time.

Both empty. Double clicks.

"No!" Kovalenko's shriek was ripe with infantile rage. He had been denied.

Drake thrust with his knife. The Blood King showed his street smarts by dodging to one side. Drake threw the rifle at him. Kovalenko took the blow on the forehead without flinching and, at the same time, drew a knife of his own.

"If I have to kill you myself, Drake…"

"Oh aye, you will," the Englishman said. "I don't see anyone else around. You're not a full fucking shilling, mate."

Kovalenko lunged. Drake saw it coming in slow motion. Kovalenko might think he'd grown up hard, might even think he'd trained hard, but his training was nothing compared to the severe demands and trials endured by the British SAS.

Drake stepped in from the side, striking with a swift knee that temporarily paralyzed Kovalenko and broke some ribs. The gasp from the Russian's mouth was instantly stifled. He backed away.

Drake feigned a rush attack, waited for the Blood King to react and instantly caught the man's right hand between his own. A quick downward twist and Kovalenko's wrist snapped. Again the Russian only hissed.

Around them, Komodo and Karin and Ben and the remaining Delta soldier watched.

The Blood King glared at them. "You can't kill me. All of you. You can't kill me. I am a god!"

Komodo snarled. "We can't kill you, asshole. You got a fuck load of squealin' to do. But I sure am looking forward to helping choose which hellhole you spend the rest of your life in."

"*Prison.*" The Blood King spat. "No prison will hold me. I will *own* it within a week."

Komodo's mouth broadened into a smile. "Some prisons," he said quietly. "Don't even exist."

Kovalenko looked momentarily surprised, but then the arrogant veil cloaked his face again and he turned back to Drake. "And you?" he said. "You might as well be dead without me to chase half way around the world."

"Dead?" Drake echoed. "There are different kinds of dead. You should know that."

Drake kicked him over his cold, dead heart. Kovalenko staggered. Blood leaked from his mouth. With a pathetic cry he fell to his knees. A shameful end for the Blood King.

Drake laughed at him. "He's done. Tie his hands and let's go."

Ben spoke up. "I recorded his speech patterns." He said softly, raising his phone. "We can use special software to reproduce his voice. Matt, we don't actually *need* him alive."

The moment was as loaded as the last second before an explosion. Drake's face changed from resignation to pure hate. Komodo hesitated to intervene, not through fear but through hard-earned respect—the only respect a soldier will acknowledge. Karin went wide-eyed with horror.

Drake raised his rifle and tapped the hard steel against Kovalenko's forehead.

"You're sure?"

"Positive. I saw her die. I was there. He ordered terrorist attacks against *Hawaii*." Ben looked around the chamber. "Even Hell will spit him out."

"This is where you belong." Drake's smile was cold and dark, like the Blood King's soul. "Beyond the Gates of Hell. This is where you should stay and this is where you should die."

Kovalenko's jaw set hard with forty years of death and hardship and bloody decadence behind it. "You will never scare me."

Drake studied the fallen man. He was right. Death wouldn't hurt him. There wasn't a thing on earth that would scare this man.

But there was one thing that would *break* him.

"So we tie you up down here." He lowered the rifle, much to Komodo's relief. "And *we* go on to claim the treasure. It was your life's quest and you'll never know what it was. But remember my words, Kovalenko, *I will*."

"No!" The Russian's yelp was instantaneous. "*Your* claim? No! Never. It is mine. It always has been mine."

With a desperate roar, the Blood King made a last despairing lunge. Pain racked his face. Blood flew from his face and hands. He rose and threw every ounce of will and a life of hate and murder into his leap.

Drake's eyes glowered, his face set hard as granite. He allowed the Blood King to strike him, stood firm as the frantic Russian expended every last ounce of energy in a dozen blows, at first hard, but weakening rapidly.

Then Drake laughed, a sound beyond bleak, a sound both loveless and lost and caught halfway between purgatory and hell. When the last of the Blood King's energy was spent, Drake pushed him over with a palm and stood on his chest.

"It was all for nothing, Kovalenko. You lost."

Komodo rushed over and trussed the Russian up before Drake could change his mind. Karin helped divert him by pointing up at the near-vertical staircase and the mind-boggling sight of the black throne jutting out. From here it was even more staggering. The thing was enormous and perfectly sculpted, poised a hundred feet above their heads.

"After you."

Drake appraised the next hurdle. The staircase ran upwards at a slight angle for about a hundred feet. The underside of the throne was lost in deepest black, despite the numerous amber flares scattered around.

"I should go first," Komodo said. "I have a little rock climbing experience. We should climb a few lengths at a time, inserting carabiners as we go, and then thread a safety line to our team."

Drake let him lead. The fury was still strong in his brain, almost overwhelming. His finger still felt good around the M16's trigger. But to kill Kovalenko now would blight his soul forever, implant a darkness that would never lift.

As Ben Blake might say—it would *turn him to the dark side.*

He started up the wall after Komodo, needing the distraction as the incessant cravings for vengeance rose and tried to take control of him. The sharp climb instantly focused his mind. The Blood King's wails and moans faded away as the throne grew closer and the staircase trickier.

Up they went, Komodo leading the way, carefully placing

each carabiner before testing its weight and then threading the safety rope and dropping it to his team below. The higher they went, the darker it became. Each tread of the staircase had been hewn and shaped out of the living rock. Drake began to get a sense of awe as he climbed. Some incredible treasure awaited them; he could feel it in his bones.

But a throne?

With a sheer void at his back he stopped, braced himself, and looked down. Ben was struggling, eyes wide and scared. Drake felt a rush of sympathy and love for his young friend, something absent ever since Kennedy had died. He saw the remaining Delta soldier trying to help Karin and smiled when she waved him away. He extended a helping hand toward Ben.

"Stop tossing it off, Blakey. Come on."

Ben looked up at him and it was as if a firework went off in his brain. Something in Drake's eyes or in his tone of voice stirred him and a hopeful look fastened onto his face.

"Thank God you're back."

With Drake's help, Ben climbed faster. The deadly void at their back was forgotten and each step became a step toward discovery rather than peril. The underside of the throne grew closer and closer until it was within touching distance.

Komodo climbed cautiously off the staircase and onto the throne itself.

After a minute, his American drawl caught their attention. "Oh my God, guys, you aren't gonna believe this."

FORTY-TWO

Drake swung across a small gap and landed squarely on the wide block of stone that formed the foot of the throne. He waited for Ben and Karin and the last Delta soldier to arrive before looking up at Komodo.

"What you got up there?"

The Delta team leader had climbed onto the seat of the throne. Now he moved to the edge and stared down at them

"Whoever built this throne included a not-so-secret passage. There's a back door behind the back of the throne up here. And it was open."

"Don't go near it," Drake said quickly, thinking of the trap systems they had passed. "For all we know it flicks a switch that sends this throne straight down."

Komodo looked guilty. "Good call. Problem is—I already have. Good news is…" He grinned. "No traps."

Drake extended a hand. "Help me up."

One by one they climbed up onto the seat of the obsidian throne. Drake took a moment to turn around and take in the view over the abyss.

Directly opposite, across the massive chasm, he saw the same stone balcony they had occupied earlier. The balcony where Captain Cook had quit. The balcony where the Blood King had most likely lost any last remaining thread of sanity he had possessed. It seemed like a step away but it was a deceiving mile.

Drake made a face. "This throne," he said quietly. "It was built for—"

Ben's shout interrupted him. "Matt! Bloody hell. You won't believe this."

It was not the shock in his friends voice that sent fear shooting through Drake's nerve endings but the foreboding. The apprehension.

"What is it?"

He turned. He saw what Ben saw.

"Fuck me."

Karin crowded them out. "What is it?" Then she saw it too. "No way."

They were looking at the rear part of the throne, the tall upright that someone might rest against, and the part that formed the rear door.

It was covered by the now familiar whorls— the beyond-ancient symbols that appeared to be some form of writing— and the same symbols that were inscribed upon both the time displacement devices and also on the great archway under Diamond Head that Cook had called the Gates of Hell.

The very same symbols Torsten Dahl had recently discovered in the tomb of the gods, far away in Iceland.

Drake closed his eyes. "How can this be happening? Ever since we first heard about the nine bloody pieces of Odin, I feel like I've been living a dream. Or a nightmare."

"I bet we're not done with the nine pieces yet," Ben said. "This has got to be manipulation. Of the highest order. It's like we've been chosen or something."

"More like cursed." Drake growled. "And quit with the Star Wars crap."

"I was thinking a bit less Skywalker, a bit more Chuck Bartowski," Ben said with a little smile. "Since we're geeks and all that."

Komodo was regarding the hidden door with impatience. "Shall we continue? My men gave their lives to help get us this far. All we can do in return is find an end to this hellhole."

"Komodo," Drake said. "This *is* the end. Has to be."

He pushed past the big team leader into a giant passageway. The space was already larger than the door that led into it and, if it was possible, Drake sensed the passage widening, the walls and the ceiling withdrawing further and further until—

A cold, stiff breeze caressed his face.

He stopped and dropped a glow stick. By the faint light he fired off an amber flare. It flew up, up, up, then down and down without finding purchase. Without finding a ceiling, a ledge or even a floor.

He fired a second flare, this one more to the right. Again the amber infusion vanished without trace. He snapped a few glow sticks and threw them ahead to illuminate their way.

A sheer cliff edge dropped off six feet in front of them.

Drake felt intense vertigo, but forced himself to continue. A few more steps and he faced the void.

"Can't see a thing. Bollocks."

"We *can't* have come all this way to be thwarted by the bloody dark." Karin voiced everyone's thoughts. "Try again, Drake."

He sent a third flare into the void. As it flew this one picked out some faint highlights. There *was* something on the other side of the chasm. An enormous structure.

"What was that?" Ben breathed in awe.

The flare plummeted quickly, a brief spark of life lost forever to the darkness.

"Wait there," the last remaining Delta soldier, a man with the call-sign Merlin said. "How many amber flares do we have left?"

Drake checked his webbing and his pack. Komodo did the same. The number they came up with was about thirty.

"I know what you're thinking," Komodo said. "Fireworks display, right?"

"One time," Merlin, the team's weapons expert, said grimly. "Find out what we're dealing with and then hump it back to a place where we can call in support."

Drake nodded. "Agreed." He set aside a dozen flares for the way back and then readied himself. Komodo and Merlin came up to stand beside him at the edge.

"Ready?"

One by one, in rapid succession, they fired flare after flare high into the air. The amber light blazed brightly at its highest point and threw out a brilliant glow that shattered the dark.

Daylight came to the eternal blackness for the first time in history.

The pyrotechnical display began to have an effect. As flare after flare continued to shoot up and explode before drifting slowly downward, the great structure at the other end of the gigantic cavern became illuminated.

Ben gasped. Karin laughed. "Brilliant."

As they gazed in wonder, the pitch black was set on fire and a stunning construction began to appear. First, a series or arches cut into the rear wall, then a second series beneath that. Then it became apparent that the arches were in fact small rooms—niches.

Below the second row, they saw a third and then a fourth and then rows upon rows as the dazzling lights drifted down the great wall. And in each niche great glinting treasures reflected back the brief glory of the drifting amber inferno.

Ben was stunned. "It's... it's..."

Drake and the Delta team continued to fire flare after flare. They made the massive chamber appear to burst into flames. The magnificent conflagration flashed and raged before their eyes.

At last, Drake fired the final flare. Then he took a moment to appraise the mind-numbing revelation.

Ben was stammering. "It's huge... it's—"

"Another tomb of the gods." Drake finished with more worry in his voice than wonder. "At least three times the size of the one in Iceland. Jesus Christ, Ben, *what the hell is going on?*"

*****

The journey back, though still fraught with danger, took half the time and half the effort. The only major obstacle was the big chasm where they had to rig another zip-wire to travel back across, although the chamber of Lust was always going to be a problem for the guys, as Karin pointed out with a wry glance at Komodo.

Once back through the archway, Cook's Gates of Hell, they hoofed it back through the lava tube and out onto the surface.

Drake broke a long silence. "Wow, that's the best smell in the world, right now. Fresh air at last."

Mano Kinimaka's voice came out of the surrounding dark. "Make that *Hawaiian* fresh air, man, and you'd be nearer the mark."

People and faces drifted out of the semi-dark. A generator was fired up, lighting a hastily-erected set of string lights. A field-table was being erected. Komodo had called in their position as soon as they started up the lava tube. Ben's signal returned and his mobile bleeped on four separate occasions with voicemail. Karin's did the same. The parents had been allowed to call.

"Only four times?" Drake asked with a grin. "They must have forgotten you."

Now Hayden came up to them, a battered, weary-looking Hayden. But she was smiling and she gave Ben a tentative hug. She was followed by Alicia, glaring with killer-eyes behind Drake. And in the shadows, Drake saw Mai, an awful tension stretched across her face.

It was almost time for their reckoning. The Japanese woman, rather than the English woman, seemed the most ill at ease about it.

Drake shrugged the dark cloud of depression away. He topped it all by flinging the trussed and gagged figure of the Blood King onto the rough ground at their feet.

"Dmitry Kovalenko." He growled. "The Bell-end King. The most depraved of his kind. Anyone fancy a few kicks?"

At that moment, the figure of Jonathan Gates materialized from the growing hubbub around the makeshift camp. Drake narrowed his eyes. He knew Kovalenko had personally murdered Gates's wife. Gates had more reason to hurt the Russian than even Drake and Alicia.

"Take a shot." Drake hissed. "Fucker won't need all his arms and legs in prison anyway."

He saw Ben and Karin flinch and turn away. In that moment he caught a glimpse of the man he had become. He saw the bitterness, the vengeful anger, the spiral of hate and resentment that would lead to him becoming something not unlike Kovalenko himself, and knew all these emotions would eat away at him and eventually change him, make him over into a different man. It was an end that neither of them would want...

...Alyson or Kennedy that is.

He turned away too and put an arm around each of the Blakes' shoulders. They were staring eastward, past a set of swaying palm trees toward distant glittering lights and the rolling ocean.

"Such a sight might change a man," Drake said. "Might give him a renewed hope. Given time."

Ben spoke without turning. "I know you want a Dinorock quote right now, but I ain't gonna give you one. Instead, I could quote several relevant lines from *Haunted*. How about that?"

"You're quoting Taylor *Swift* now? What went wrong there?"

"That track is as good as any of your Dinorock. And you know it."

But Drake would never admit it. Instead, he listened into the chatter shooting back and forth behind them. The terror plots had been foiled competently and quickly, but there had still been some loss of life. An inevitable consequence when dealing with fanatics and madmen. The country was in mourning. The president was on his way and already promising another complete overhaul of the U.S. intelligence system, though it was still unclear how anyone could have prevented Kovalenko from hatching a plan twenty years in the making when, during all that time, he had been considered a mere figure of myth.

Much like the gods and their remains they were finding now.

Still, lessons had been learned and the U.S. and other countries were determined to take it all on board.

The question of charges being brought against those people in authority who had acted under coercion and out fear for the wellbeing of their loved ones was going to tie up the judicial system for years.

But the Blood King's captives had been freed and were being reunited with their loved ones. Gates was promising that Kovalenko would be made to retract the blood vendetta, one way or another. Harrison had been reunited with his daughter, albeit briefly, and the news only made Drake sad.

If his own daughter had been born and loved and then kidnapped, would he have done the same as Harrison?

Of course he would. Any father would move heaven and Earth and everything in between to save his child.

Hayden, Gates and Kinimaka drifted away from the hubbub until they stood near Drake and his group. He was pleased to see Komodo and the surviving Delta soldier, Merlin, with them too. Bonds forged in comradeship and action were everlasting.

Hayden was quizzing Gates about some guy called Russell Cayman. It seemed the man had replaced Torsten Dahl as head of the Icelandic operation, his orders coming from the very top... and maybe even from a foggy and distant place *above* that. Cayman was a hard man, it seemed, and ruthless. He usually ran black-ops and, it was rumored, even more secretive and select operations both at home and abroad.

"Cayman is a troubleshooter," Gates was saying. "But more than that. You see, no one seems to know whose troubleshooter he *is*. His clearance is beyond top-level. His access is immediate and unreserved. But, when pushed, nobody knows who the hell he actually works for."

Drake's mobile rang and he tuned out. He checked the screen and was pleased to see the caller was Torsten Dahl.

"Hey, it's the mad Swede! How's it going, mate? Still talking like an arsehole?"

"It would seem so. I've been trying to contact someone for hours and I get you. Fate is not being kind to me."

"You're lucky to get any of us," Drake said. "It's been a rough few days."

"Well, it's about to get rougher." Dahl came back.

"I doubt that—"

"Listen. We found a drawing. A *map* to be more accurate. We managed to decipher most of it before that wanker Cayman classified it a top-level security issue. By the way, did Hayden or Gates find anything out about him?"

Drake blinked with confusion. "Cayman? Who the hell is this Cayman? And what do Hayden and Gates know?"

"Doesn't matter. I don't have a lot of time." For the first time Drake, realized his friend was whispering and in a rush. "Look. The map we found, at the very least, points to the locations of *three* tombs. Did you get that? There are *three* tombs of the gods."

"We just found a second." Drake felt the wind knocked out of him. "It's huge."

"I thought so. The map appears to be accurate then. But Drake, you have to hear this, the *third* tomb is the biggest of all and it's the worst."

"Worst?"

"Filled with the most terrible gods. The real nasty ones. The evil ones. Tomb three was kind of like a prison, where death was forced rather than accepted. And Drake. . ."

"What?"

"If we're right, I think it holds the key to some kind of doomsday weapon."

FORTY-THREE

By the time another darkness descended over Hawaii and the next stages of some ancient mega-plan were being instigated, Drake, Alicia and Mai left it all behind to bring an end to their own crisis once and for all.

By chance, they chose the most dramatic setting of all. Waikiki Beach, with the warm pacific, starkly lit by the full moon, rolling in to one side, and the rows of tourist hotels blazing out to the other.

But tonight, it was a place for dangerous people and harsh revelations. Three forces of nature came together in a meeting that would forever change the course of their lives.

Drake spoke first. "You two have to tell me. Who killed Wells, and why. That's why we're here, so there's no point pussyfooting around anymore."

"It's not the only reason we're here." Alicia eyed Mai with venom. "The sprite here helped kill Hudson by keeping quiet about her little sister. It's time to get me and my man a little old-fashioned vengeance."

Mai shook her head slowly. "That's not true. Your fat, idiot boyf—"

"In the spirit of Wells, then." Alicia hissed. "I want me some Mai-time!"

Alicia stepped forward and punched Mai hard in the face. The small Japanese woman staggered, then looked up and smiled.

"You remembered."

"That you told me the next time I punched you I should hit

you like a man? Yeah, you don't tend to forget something like that."

Alicia unleashed a flurry of blows. Mai retreated, catching each one on her wrists. The sand around them churned, swept into errant patterns by their quick-moving feet. Drake tried to intercede once, but a blow to the right ear made him think twice.

"Just don't friggin' *kill* each other."

"Can't promise anything," Alicia muttered. She dropped and swept Mai's right leg. Mai landed with a grunt, head cushioned by the sand. When Alicia advanced, Mai threw a handful of sand in her face.

"Bitch."

"All's fair—" Mai lunged. The two women came face-to-face. Alicia was used to close combat and hit hard with elbows, fists and palms but Mai caught or dodged every one and returned the blows in kind. Alicia caught hold of Mai's belt and tried to pull her off balance, but all that she achieved was to partially rip open the top of Mai's trousers.

And leave Alicia's defenses wide-open.

Drake blinked at the developments. "Now that's more like it." He stepped back. "Continue."

Mai took full advantage of Alicia's mistake and, against a warrior of Mai's class, there would only be the one. Blows rained down on Alicia and she staggered back, her right arm hanging limp with agony and her sternum burning under multiple strikes. Most warriors would have folded after two or three, but Alicia was made of sterner stuff, and even at the end, she almost rallied.

She threw herself back through the air, kicked out, and stunned Mai with a two-footed blow to the stomach. Alicia landed on her back in the sand, and body-flipped herself straight up.

Only to meet a face plant of the hardest order. The stomach kick would have taken out the Hulk, but it hadn't even phased Mai. Her muscles had absorbed the blow with ease.

Alicia went down, lights almost out. Stars swam before her eyes, and not the ones that twinkled in the night sky. She groaned. "Lucky fucking shot."

But Mai had already turned to Drake.

"*I* killed Wells, Drake. *I did.*"

"I realized that earlier," he said. "You must have had your reason. What was it?"

"You wouldn't have said that if *I'd* killed the old bastard." Alicia groaned from below them. "You'd have called me a psycho-bitch."

Drake ignored her. Mai shook sand from her hair. After a minute, she took a deep breath and stared him deep in the eyes.

"What is it?"

"Two reasons. The first and simplest—he found out about Chika being kidnapped and threatened to tell you."

"But we could have talked about—"

"I know. That's only a small part."

Only a small part, he thought. The kidnapping of Mai's sister was a small part?

Now Alicia struggled to her feet. She too faced Drake, uncharacteristic fear in her eyes.

"I know," Mai began, then indicated Alicia too. "*We* know something far worse. Something terrible—"

"Christ, if you don't spit it out, I'm going to shoot you both in the bloody head."

"First, you must know Wells would never have told you the truth. He was SAS. He was an officer. And he worked for a tiny organization so far up the food chain it governs the *Government.*"

"The truth? About what?" Drake's blood had suddenly run cold.

"That your wife—Alyson—was murdered."

His mouth worked but no sound emerged.

"You got too close to someone. They needed you out of that regiment. And her death made you quit."

"But I was going to leave. I was going to leave the SAS for her!"

"Nobody knew that," Mai said softly. "Not even she knew that."

Drake blinked a sudden wetness from the corner of his eyes. "She was having our baby."

Mai stared, ashen-faced. Alicia turned away.

"I never told anyone before," he said. "Never."

The Hawaiian night groaned around them, the heavy surf whispering the long-forgotten songs of the ancients, the stars and the moon gazing down as impassively as they had always done, keeping secrets and listening to the promises a man might often make.

"And there's something else," Mai said into the dark. "I spent a lot of time with Wells when we were running around Miami. Whilst we were in that hotel, you know, the one that got shot to bits, I heard him talk on the phone at least half a dozen times to a man—"

"What man?" Drake said quickly.

"The man's name was Cayman. Russell Cayman."

THE END

(Matt Drake will return in The Tomb of the Gods *—the final part of the initial 4 part series.)*

This is the third book in an initial 4 part series.

Part 1 – The Bones of Odin, Part 2 – 'The Blood King Conspiracy', Part 3 – 'The Gates of Hell' and Part 4 – 'The Tomb of the Gods' are available now.

I would love to hear from you! All genuine comments welcome to:
davidleadbeater2011@hotmail.co.uk

Or – through Twitter:
@dleadbeater2011